CODE
GREY

CODE GREY

GREY

Clea Simon

W🌐RLDWIDE®

TORONTO • NEW YORK • LONDON
AMSTERDAM • PARIS • SYDNEY • HAMBURG
STOCKHOLM • ATHENS • TOKYO • MILAN
MADRID • WARSAW • BUDAPEST • AUCKLAND

Recycling programs
for this product may
not exist in your area.

Code Grey

A Worldwide Mystery/June 2017

First published by Severn House Publishers Ltd.

ISBN-13: 978-0-373-28410-8

Printed in U.S.A.

For Jon

ONE

LIKE ANY ILL-WITTED Hare trapped in the hunter's snare, she was caught, her limbs clasped tight about her heaving sides not by a subtly laid cord but by the captor himself. The Treacherous Beast had come upon her from behind, laying hold of her body as her Lungs gasped out for liberty as essential as the very Air. No matter her desperate struggle; 'twas too late. Her corporeal self, Traitor to her will, would not answer, as her cries, stifl'd by the pressure upon her face, subsided painfully to one last startled gasp. The taste of Leather, of a glove, upon her face, holding her and binding...

'OH, HELL AND—' Dulcie caught herself before she said more. 'Zounds!'

It wasn't deadly. It was merely uncomfortable. Merely, well, Cambridge in March, and Dulcie had been reading while she walked.

Hopping over to a lamp post, Dulcie reined in her temper and pulled off her boot, emptying it of the half-melted slush that had slid in. Even as she had been reading—the text on her cell phone, something she'd sent herself only a few minutes before—she hadn't been totally unaware of her surroundings. She had stepped off the curve on to pavement, of that she was sure. Except that as her foot descended, the slate-grey solidity below her had melted around it, like something from a Gothic horror tale, resolving itself into that disgusting mix particular to New England at this time of year and slipping, just as inexorably, into her boot. The only good news was that even as she caught herself, newly wet and increasingly cold, and hopped back up on to the slick dry pavement, she hadn't dropped her phone.

'Bother,' Dulcie muttered as she pocketed the distracting device. Only an optimist could call this spring, she thought as she slipped her soaked sock back into the boot's wet interior. No matter what the calendar said, it was hard to consider this anything more than another winter thaw, a tease. An accident of the calendar, her own '*treacherous beast*.' Because on top of everything else, she was alone, heading home to an empty apartment. This week the university was on recess—ten days if you counted the weekend—and while in the past she had enjoyed the break from classes and students and all the rigmarole that went with being a graduate student, this year the quiet was a bit much. Not only had most of her students taken off for warmer climes, but even her friends had deserted her.

Not deserted. That was too harsh. Trista was presenting a paper in Texas. Her blonde and multiply pierced friend had successfully defended her own dissertation the year before, but now she was busy scrambling for what she could do once her postgrad fellowship here ended. And after the flood—a burst pipe—had closed not only the English grad students' office space but also part of the computer labs, Trista's boyfriend Jerry—an applied math doctoral candidate, like Dulcie's own sweetie, Chris—had chosen to accompany her to Austin. Then Chris's mother had practically begged him to come home to New Jersey—something about a failing aunt and family obligations. Dulcie was welcome, too; they had both made that clear. (Chris, in particular, had pleaded.) But if she was going to finish writing her dissertation this year, she really needed to buckle down. Despite the repairs and a flurry of belated maintenance work—most of the buildings in the Yard had antique plumbing—the main libraries had stayed open.

Not that this mattered now. What mattered was that she was standing in Harvard Yard with a wet foot, dark descending, and no prospects for anything but a cold, cheerless walk home.

She took a step. Her boot squelched.

'Argh!' she yelled as the icy wet squirted up between her toes, and just as quickly she put her mittened hand over her mouth. It was reflex, nothing more. Dulcie wasn't sure why she was even worried. She was alone. Utterly alone. During spring break, no one can hear you scream.

CAMBRIDGE HAD IT in for her. As Dulcie crossed the street, the wind picked up. A Nordic blast, more suitable for February than this late March day, it hit Dulcie like a slap. Or, no, more like a scrape, as if careless claws had raked her face. Freeing one hand from its mitten, she raised it to her cheek. It wasn't her imagination. The grit and sand that had been laid down on icy walkways all winter long had been freed by this last dubious thaw as if purposely to pelt her.

'Insult to injury,' Dulcie muttered, wiping her face as the wind continued to build, chasing her through the arched brick gate on to university property. Whipping around Sever Hall, its unlit classroom windows framed by scaffolding, it howled like some trapped beast as it made its way around the other empty university buildings that filled the Yard.

That sound—along with the raw scrape on her cheek—gave Dulcie pause, reminiscent as they were of a particularly displeased feline. 'Please, don't tell me this is a message, Mr Grey.' She turned away from the blast, away from the open Yard with its stark and leafless trees, and toward the pale shelter of a wall, the better to evoke the feline spirit who still occasionally visited her. 'Because if it is, I really think you have better means at your disposal.'

A loud thud was the only response. By the wall, a sign—'Closed for Repairs'—had fallen over, another victim of the gust. And not, as she had half hoped, the result of a giant, playful paw. Unless…

At times, Dulcie believed, the elements were more than mere weather. Sometimes, she thought, the kind spirit she knew as Mr Grey would use the outside world to guide her. Today, however, she couldn't see any rhyme or reason in the pummeling. Even at his worst, the ghost of her late, great pet would never be this ungentle.

No, this was simply March in full leonine fashion. Only, shouldn't it be more lamblike by now? Another blast answered that question, and Dulcie turned again to find herself facing the library's re-cessed back entrance. The blue security light glowed like a beacon by the brick foyer. It was past time for the stacks to close, but perhaps one of the guards she knew would be on duty. She thought of Ruby, with her welcoming smile, or the new guy, Kyle, who had remained freckled all winter long. Maybe one of them would have an extra pair of socks. Or a space heater, where she could dry off. It wasn't like Chris was waiting for her at home.

She didn't need the next arctic blast to convince her. With a squish, Dulcie turned and raced toward the library entrance.

'Oh! Excuse me.' Dulcie stopped short. The brick-lined passage wasn't empty. At her approach, a skinny man had pressed himself flat against the wall. 'I didn't see you.'

'Didn't see. Couldn't comprehend, more likely.' The other occupant scowled as he recovered his com-posure, his face skull-like above his worn tweed overcoat. 'Unable to fathom the unplumbed com-plexities. Unplumbed and disemboweled, excavated to extinction.'

'Jeremy? I'm sorry I startled you.' The scowl-ing man stood a head taller than Dulcie, but she couldn't be frightened of him. Jeremy Mumbleigh—'Mumbles' to many of her classmates—was one of those unfortunates who inhabit university towns. A one-time scholar who had gone off the rails at some point but still hung around his old haunts, the skinny man was more scarecrow than scary, a silver-

haired casualty of the academic battlefield. 'Are you
all right?'

'All right, or all left?' He raised an eyebrow, as if
his question made logical sense. 'Turn right to stay
right. Which way are we turning here, for good or
for ill?'

'Jeremy, it's me, Dulcie.' Unlike some of her classmates, Dulcie felt only pity for the man. In part, that
was because she could see how alike they were. Although Chris and certainly Trista would pooh-pooh
the notion, Dulcie saw the tall man in the threadbare tweed as a cautionary tale. A reminder to keep
her focus, and finally to finish her dissertation. She
also saw how he was shivering, his arms wrapped
around himself as if to add their poor warmth to that
of the worn coat.

'Are you hungry, Jeremy?' Dulcie didn't have
much of a budget, but she could certainly stand a
fellow scholar a bowl of soup. She thought of Lala's
rich split pea, thick with bits of ham, and her own
mouth started watering. Besides, the company would
do them both good. 'Would you want to come to
dinner with me?' She kept her voice soft. The man
was skittish.

'Dinner, winner.' He turned away, and she saw
that he was scratching on the brick. Writing one of
his long nonsense verses, she thought at first, though
in this weather his words would probably be erased
by the wind. But, no, it looked like he was drawing:
she saw ears and—were those whiskers? Yes, it was
a cat. 'Cat's dinner for a winner. The kind-hearted
woman will save the sinner.' Jeremy seemed to be

illustrating his own rambling. 'It's a secret. You can't tell anyone.'

He turned suddenly, with a look of such ferocity that Dulcie stepped back.

'I wouldn't,' she stammered, unsure of what exactly she was agreeing to. Jeremy had never been violent, despite what some of her classmates had whispered. But he had never looked quite so...intent.

'It's a conspiracy, you know.' His voice, low and deep, was as piercing as his gaze. 'And they won't stop until they've gotten it all.'

TWO

'I'M BEING CAREFUL, CHRIS. You know I am.' Dulcie
could hear the peevishness creeping into her voice.
'I promise,' she added, in a softer tone. Chris was
honestly concerned, she knew that. He never liked
her going out after dark, and being several hundred
miles away with his anxious mother wasn't helping.

'I got the latest text alert.' He wasn't going to be
mollified so easily.

'That was about the burglaries.' Dulcie was trying to be reasonable. 'The ones we already know
about,' she added, before Chris could worry more.
'And those were on campus, Chris.'

She heard a grumble and took a deep breath. The
university's text alerts were, in general, a good thing,
warning the campus community about problems or
delays. But the latest series, reminding people about
a string of robberies, didn't seem particularly well
thought out. She'd gotten one while walking home,
the buzzing phone making itself known through all
her layers. When she'd seen the message from Chris,
she'd known what he was calling about. The general
alert had been designed to scare, at least a little. But
the information it conveyed wasn't new.

The problem lay with those pipes. Originally laid
in an ornate maze of steam tunnels that ran between

most of the older university buildings, the repairs they required had necessitated the packing up of several freshman dorms, as well as a dozen university offices, and maintenance crews were busy emptying out ancient basement storage units as they searched for the source of the leaks. Dulcie had never been more relieved that English and American Lit had its own headquarters a few blocks away. Although the offices, a tiny clapboard house, were closed for the break, and Nancy—the motherly secretary who staffed it— was enjoying a well-earned week in Aruba, Dulcie's home away from home was safely away from the ruckus in the Yard. She couldn't say the same for all the offices in the campus's busy center. With all the activity, doors would be left unlocked—and possessions would go missing, even if for utterly innocent reasons.

Still, there was no denying that somebody was taking advantage of the situation. The thieves were targeting empty dorm rooms and offices—places left dark and vacant—and while the university police couldn't ascertain exactly what was being taken until the students returned and employees could re-enter their offices, it was assumed that any valuables left unsecured were at risk. At least, that's what the text warned about. Only there was one problem: anybody who had already left for the break couldn't really do much about security now. The only people around were those like Dulcie, who didn't live on campus.

'I'm not worried about the apartment,' said Chris, sounding quite reasonable. 'Honestly, Dulce.'

Dulcie relaxed. Of course he wasn't. Though they

didn't talk much about it, they both knew that their current cat, Esmé, had more powers than the average house pet.

'I worry about *you*, Dulcie. You saw someone huddled in a doorway, and you went to join him? What if you had accidentally interrupted a burglary?'

'But I didn't.' He wasn't being logical. 'It was Jeremy. You know, Mumbles?'

'Great.' He didn't sound any happier about that.

'Chris,' she said. 'You know he's harmless.'

'I know you think he's harmless.' Despite the miles between them, she could hear the strain in his voice. 'But, really, Dulcie, what do you know about him?'

'I know he was a graduate student here, same as I am. I know he had some kind of breakdown—'

Chris interrupted before she could finish. 'I mean, what do you know of him now, Dulcie? How does he even live? For all you know, he could be the one doing these break-ins. Or maybe, I don't know, he's a look out.'

'Chris...' Dulcie struggled to find the words. 'You don't know him. I do. I mean, I kind of know what he's gone through, you know?'

'No.' Her boyfriend's voice was firm. 'I don't. And neither do you, Dulcie. You see him as a kind of cautionary tale. A worst-case scenario of what can happen if you don't finish your dissertation. I get that, I really do. But Dulcie, you're not like him. You're going to write your thesis and get your degree, and even if you didn't, you'd be OK. Mumbles is...well, he's something else again. For starters, he's really sick. And Dulcie? He's not a metaphor—the romantic hobo or a Depression-era poet on the rails, or something. He's a man, a disturbed man, and it scares me when you're alone with him.'

By the time they got off the phone, Dulcie was exhausted. Sometimes, it seemed, these long-distance conversations were worse than no contact at all. Here she was, curled up on the sofa, an afghan over her lap and warm, fuzzy socks on her feet. Chatting with Chris should have been a cozy end to the evening. Instead, it had left her feeling unsettled and even more alone.

'Why is that, Esmé?' The round tuxedo cat had left the room as her voice had gotten heated and only now returned to regard Dulcie with a quizzical glance. 'Why can't we just have a conversation?'

In response, the feline jumped up on the sofa, landing heavily.

'Watch it, kitty!' Dulcie pulled her feet out of the way as Esmé gave her a cool look, indecipherable by human standards, and began kneading the edge of the blanket.

'It's not like I'm exactly alone here.' Dulcie watched as the little cat worked, her whiskers directed forward as she concentrated. 'It's not as if…' She paused. Maybe that was what was bothering her. It wasn't just that Chris was acting as if Dulcie didn't have any common sense. That was bad, but in truth she knew she tended to get carried away sometimes. Books just seemed so much more real than, well, mundane events. It was that he was doubting their other feline companion—Mr Grey. Her beloved pet had never let her down. Surely, he would watch out

for her now. He would warn her if she were in any
real danger, wouldn't he?

'Mrrup,' Esmé chirped, which Dulcie took as
agreement. But when the feline turned and sat, Dulcie
realized she may simply have been congratulating
herself on a job well done.

'Well, we all have our own projects and concerns,
don't we, Esmé?' Dulcie watched as the little cat settled down, purring. 'And at least you and I are getting our work done.'

Careful not to disturb her pet, Dulcie reached for
her laptop. Before Chris had called back, she'd been
looking over her notes for the latest chapter of what
would, at some point, be her dissertation. This chapter dealt specifically with the new pages she had
found, handwritten pages that appeared to be part
of a forgotten work by the anonymous Gothic novelist who was the focus of the dissertation. Identifying them among the unclaimed papers file of the
esteemed Mildon Rare Books Collection had been
Dulcie's latest coup.

Dulcie had been given a head start, she acknowledged that, in the form of printed pages that read like
part of this same book which had been included in a
gift to the library the previous year. Those pages told
of a seductive yet evil lord, a murder and a mysterious stranger. The documents she was working on now
seemed to contain an earlier part of the story—the heroine was obviously being abducted, perhaps by that
same evil lord. While Dulcie had yet to find a surviving copy of the finished novel, her years of study had
given her the skill to recognize various phrases and

descriptions in the battered and torn sheets and to attribute them to her subject, the anonymous author of a little-known Gothic, *The Ravages of Umbria*.

It was exciting stuff, and Dulcie was eager to see how the story turned out. But the work was slow and painstaking. Through careful reading, Dulcie had pieced these fragments together, deciphering their faded and stained writing, until now she had a good thirty pages that were clearly part of the larger manuscript. They were essential in building the case to consider this novel as part of her subject's canon.

But writing about it, writing in the strangely dense and self-conscious style demanded by academia, was not easy, and at this point in the evening Dulcie was finding it difficult to get her concentration back. She almost wished that Chris hadn't called. Of course she missed her boyfriend. Their tiny apartment was too quiet without his lanky presence, and even Esmé's rambunctious frenzies—those mad dashes the little cat made from room to room at random intervals—seemed less energetic without him around.

To get back into the mood, Dulcie decided, some re-reading was in order. After all, this new novel was a major discovery—*her* discovery. Just because piecing the story part of it together was fun didn't mean it wasn't work. Besides, now that she was safe at home, she could read on a proper-sized screen, and not have to worry about where she stepped.

She gasped for air as the hand withdrew from over her mouth. Gasped and braced for a cry, when another sensation—one more chilling still—caught her breath once more and still'd her heaving bosom. Cold Steel, the touch of its fine edge as indisput-able as the threatn'ng words now whispered in her ear. 'Choose carefully, my Lady, for your cry may be your last and Pity would it be for such a voice as yours to fall Silent from the world.'

'Unhand me.' She struggled to hold her voice both steady and soft. 'Leave me be, and go, for I know of your villainy and will not disregard such a threat.'

'Your Knowledge matters not, my lady.' The deadly pressure eased, though not the grip that tightened 'pon her e'en as he answered, his silken voice a Serpent's hiss into her ear. 'For who would believe one such as you, dishonored and befouled. A Mad woman, as all shall know, who has fled the safe Haven of her husband's hearth to pursue phantoms of the mind.'

Dulcie was so engrossed that when her phone burbled again, she ignored it. The number was familiar: the kitchen phone from the commune where her mother, Lucy, lived. Her mother hadn't liked the idea of her daughter staying alone in the city, despite her own history as a single mother and free spirit. To be fair, Dulcie reasoned as she glanced at the phone, Lucy had never been much for solitude. Even before Dulcie's father had decamped—his last missive was from an ashram in India—Lucy had favored groups, and most of Dulcie's childhood had been spent in the commune—what Lucy called an arts colony—in the woods of the Pacific North-West.

She'd call her mother back later, Dulcie decided,

shrugging off the nibble of guilt. It wasn't like her mother would know her only child had dodged her call, no matter what psychic abilities she claimed to have.

Dulcie only had a few more minutes of peace before the phone started up again. The sound—half chortle, half mew—was one Chris had sampled for her from Esmé's increasingly odd vocabulary. It signaled a text coming in—something from the university. Out of the corner of her eye, Dulcie could see the phone, skittering from its own vibration across the small coffee table. With a determined sigh, she turned back to the screen.

'*Whadda?*' The sound quality was really quite amazing.

'Mrup?' Esmé responded to the sound by jumping on to the table beside it.

'It's nothing, Esmé.' Dulcie reached out blindly to calm her pet, her face still in the laptop.

'Meh!' Her forefinger connected with the wet leather of the little cat's nose.

'Sorry, Esmé.' Dulcie withdrew her offending hand as the phone burbled again.

'Heh!' With a grunt, Esmé leaped from the table, kicking the phone as she launched her stout body.

'*Whadda...*' The burble faded in an ominous way, and Dulcie gave up. Ducking down, she found the phone half under the sofa, and flicked it on. It had taken a lot of abuse, between the predations of the cat and Dulcie's own carelessness, and Dulcie found herself holding her breath as she hit the buttons to wake it.

'Come on…' Dulcie wasn't sure when she'd started talking to inanimate objects. It worried her, some-times, that she was becoming like Lucy, who evoked the concept of a greater spirit whenever anything—from a hand mixer to her own adult child—didn't behave as she wanted. That was an issue for another time, however. For now, her entreaty worked and the little machine lit up.

Alert! the small screen read. *There has been an-other incident on campus. Possible attempted bur-glary has resulted in one injured party…* A real alert, then, not simply another warning. She scrolled down, past the contact numbers for those who had concerns and questions and past the reminders to stay safe. Down below, a longer version of the emergency mes-sage read like a news story, albeit a very terse one.

The incident occurred soon after six near the back entrance of Widener Library. The suspect, a former member of the university community, has been de-scribed as male and in his late fifties… She didn't need to read further. With a gasp of horror, it hit her. The 'incident,' as they were calling it, had happened less than an hour after she had left. The suspect they were describing had to be Jeremy Mumbleigh.

THREE

'TWAS A NIGHT much like that which she remembered, whipp'd by winds that howled like Wolves as she fled the fiend as she would Damnation itself, leaving as she did behind all that she had once held dear and close. The Storm beyond the narrow pane hammered, loud and livid in its fury, as if the desire to return her to those Terror-drenched nights were perforce the sulfurous Fuel that burned so wild and fierce. As a whine and cry like that of a Creature neither vital nor at its peaceful rest pierced the night, she hunched o'er her desk, desperate to get this last Testimony on to the page before her, into its Secret store where safe from prying Eyes it could remain till that Time when Fate and Friendship might vouchsafe its Warrant.

Thoughts of such a Future safe from all Woes and Turmoil shook her then, as the frantic Winds could not, loosing a Tear that dashed upon the Page. One drop and yet she gasped. One such mark could betray her, could unmask all her desperate Hope. She could not risk such a Traitor to survive.

A TRAITOR. THE word was on Dulcie's lips as she awoke, the dream as vivid as the text that had inspired it. Probably because she had fallen asleep reading, a habit that she indulged in when Chris wasn't around. Partly, she acknowledged, because she felt that she had been a bit disloyal. Not to Chris. Even as she was enjoying the brief respite, she knew her life would be much more warm and full once he returned. But to her mother, Lucy. Whose call she had not returned.

She reached for the phone now to see if her mother had left a message.

'Hello, is this on?' the voice mail began.

Dulcie smiled. Her mother might claim to converse with the spirits, but she was at least three decades behind more mundane forms of communication.

'Dulcinea, I hope you are listening.' Then again, maybe her mother wasn't as clueless as she'd thought. 'I have a message for you. It's the mark of the beast, dear. The beast that you are bound to.'

With that the call ended, whether by design or a mechanical mishap of her mother's, Dulcie had no idea. The mark of the beast, well, maybe her mother did have a vision. Dulcie could still see the scratches from her latest play session with Esmé. 'I'm certainly bound to you, aren't I?'

'Mrup!' Despite the early hour—the cloudy sky outside was barely light—the tubby little cat was wide awake. And, if the lashing of her tail were any indication, ready to play.

Reaching under the bed, Dulcie located the well-chewed catnip mouse that was Esmé's current favorite prey and tossed it. As the cat pounced, Dulcie checked the clock. Too early to call the west coast, particularly if her mother had been on one of her vision quests—

Dulcie suspected a peyote potluck—with her friends. Besides, she decided, she had something more important that she needed to do. As quickly as she could— with a few pauses to toss the mouse—Dulcie dressed and readied herself to go out.

Only someone else had another idea. 'What?'

Esmé had dropped the toy at her feet and now stared up at her. 'OK, one more.'

Dulcie reached for the battered mouse, but it soon became apparent that Esmé had lost interest. '*Rather like you have...*' The thought, like the stray swipe of claws across skin, made her wince.

'I have not, Esmé.' She paused. 'Why am I even talking to you?'

She wasn't avoiding work. Not at all. She could complete this one errand and still be at her carrel by nine. And, despite the skeptical look in Esmé's round green eyes, Dulcie knew she was doing the right thing. Pulling on an extra pair of socks—the inside of her boots had not yet dried—she geared up for the walk into the Square.

'I have to go, Esmé.' She reached for her scarf, a present from Chris. 'It's my civic duty.'

'Meh!' The tuxedo cat threw herself at the trailing wool. Maybe the long fringe at the edge was irresistible—a novel alternative to the long-loved mouse. But Dulcie couldn't help wondering if something else was on her pet's mind.

'Esmé, no!' Dulcie pulled back, only to find the cat still attached. 'Are you stuck?'

'Eh!' The cat's cry turned to one of distress as she struggled to disengage her claws.

'OK, come here.' Scooping up her pet and the rest of the dangling muffler, Dulcie carried both over to the sofa. 'You'd think that with retractable claws, you'd be able to get out of this kind of jam. I mean—wait!'

Esmé, perhaps sick of being lectured, had started to struggle. Dulcie could feel the little cat's hind claws through her jeans.

'*Let go!*' The voice, female and insistent, sounded in Dulcie's head, even as her cat gave a more typical mew. '*How dare you!*'

'Hang on.' Dulcie managed to get the wriggling animal between her legs and then used both hands to unhook her claw from the offending scarf.

'*That was unfair!*' The cat jumped down and immediately began to wash her paw, using her teeth to pull out the threads of wool still caught in the claw. '*I never...*' The voice faded away into growl-like grumbling.

'Esmé, if you hadn't pounced in the first place...' Dulcie bit her lip. Feline dignity could only take so much of an insult. 'It was a case of wrong place at the wrong time, kitty,' she concluded, as she carefully wound the muffler around her neck. 'That's all.'

'*No, it wasn't.*' The low grumble continued. Dulcie turned away to hide her smile. '*You wanted what I had, and I won't forget it.*'

With a mental note to store her scarf carefully upon her return, Dulcie pulled on the matching hat and made her way to the door.

ESMÉ MISSES YOU, Dulcie texted as she walked along the sidewalk. Not having Chris there made her realize how much she'd grown used to their daily interactions. Even when he was working nights, he'd rouse for a bit in the morning, long enough for them to touch base.

When no response popped up, she typed more. *She attacked the scarf you gave me.* With a ping, the message went off into cyberspace. *She thinks it belongs to her, and that I was stealing it. Maybe she thinks I'm the local thief?*

Dulcie crossed the street before checking her phone again. There was no answer. It meant nothing. Chris might be having breakfast with his mother. He might still be asleep. But the stillness of the little screen made Dulcie feel that much more alone.

'MS SCHWARTZ! GOOD MORNING.' The hearty welcome that greeted her did a little to banish the empty feeling. Detective Rogovoy might look like an ogre, but his heart was as big as the rest of him. But although Dulcie had asked for the detective specifically upon arriving at the ultra-modern headquarters of the university police, she still jumped at the sound of his voice, full of growl and grumble despite the friendly words it conveyed. 'Why am I not surprised to see you here?'

'I'm answering the call for information,' Dulcie explained. She wasn't sure, but she thought the big man rolled his eyes. 'The university text alert,' she clarified.

'We weren't necessarily...' The big man made a sound like rocks rolling down a mountain and wiped his hand over his mouth. 'Never mind.' He sighed, sounding strangely tired for first thing in the morning. 'You're here. Come on back to my office.'

He turned and she followed, feeling a little like a pebble in the wake of an avalanche. At least, she thought as they made their way down a long interior hall, his staff liked him. Several of them smiled up at him as they passed, and only one—another large gentleman, with a buzz cut like a stiff, grey brush—stared with something like concern.

'So, Ms Schwartz, is your thesis all done? All your students packed off for the break?' Rogovoy settled heavily behind his desk, leaving Dulcie to sit in the scratched-up wooden chair facing him. 'You don't have enough to do?'

'What? No.' She smiled to think that he had so little understanding of the grad student's lot. 'I'm utterly swamped. To be honest, I was hoping that I could simply throw myself into writing during the break. Make some real headway on my dissertation, but—'

'But you saw the latest alert and decided you had to help us solve the crime wave.' He definitely sounded tired. 'Because you had some special insight.'

'Exactly!' Dulcie remembered why she liked the detective. 'Only, it's not an insight exactly. It's an actual bit of information. You see, I was at the library last night.'

'What a surprise.' Rogovoy had slouched over and seemed to be talking into his hand.

'And I know that you have the wrong idea about your so-called suspect—'

'Oh?' Rogovoy sat up. 'And how do you know this?'

'Because I know.' Dulcie paused. She needed to be clear. 'Because I deeply suspect that you've picked up Jeremy Mumbleigh. The man everyone calls Mumbles. He fits the description, and I know he was hanging out in the entrance to Widener last night. But, Detective, I have to tell you, you're wrong if you think the recent break-ins have anything to do with Jeremy. He wouldn't do anything like that. He was a degree candidate at one point.'

The large policeman looked at her, his face twisted like he was in pain.

'Detective, are you all right?'

He dropped his head and shook it, and Dulcie rose from her seat. 'Detective?'

'No, no, I'm fine.' He raised one plate-sized hand to stop her from approaching. 'It's just…your logic…'

'I'm not naive, Detective.' Dulcie had the distinct feeling that the big man was on the verge of laughing at her. 'I do know there is malfeasance in the university community. But he was—*is* a gentle soul. He may have gone off track a bit. But he would never do anything actually wrong. And he certainly would never hurt anyone.'

'Ms Schwartz, what are you talking about?' He was looking at her now, his craggy face serious.

'The alert described another attempted robbery, and said that somebody had been injured. I know that some of the students talk about him, and he can be strange.' The memory of the thin man's latest ramblings came to mind. Something about a secret? 'But he's harmless.'

'And you know this, how?' He was leaning toward her. 'Because if you've been spending time with this guy, I need you to think long and hard about your own personal safety choices, Ms Schwartz.'

'I haven't been spending time with him.' She shook her head. The detective was making it sound like more than it was. 'I do see him around. We all do, and I have never had any indication that he was anything more than a lost soul.' She paused. She was tempted to tell Rogovoy more. To explain that if the former student had been a threat to her in any way, she would have heard about it—not from some alert, but from Mr Grey. She didn't get the chance.

'Look, Ms Schwartz, it's not so simple. What happened—it's probably going to be in the paper anyway—is that we had a distress call. Some passer-by reported sounds of a scuffle, so we put out an alert. One of our top guys was in the area, and he found someone—maybe your guy, maybe not. He had fallen into one of the excavations. He put up quite a fight when the uniforms went to fish him out.'

'But that doesn't mean—' She didn't get a chance to finish.

'No, we do not know the extent of the suspect's involvement yet,' said Rogovoy, carefully enunciating every word. 'Look, Ms Schwartz, I know you have a kind heart, and that's a good thing. But you can't take in every stray who comes your way.'

She tried once more to protest, but that big hand went up again.

'No, don't say it,' he said. 'You and your lost causes and your hunches… Sometimes you've got to listen to reason.

'We've got a whole task force dealing with these

robberies, Ms Schwartz, with Lieutenant Wardley from property theft heading it up, so you know the bigwigs are taking it seriously.' The burly detective shook his head. 'My take is it's all this damned construction. For every rotten pipe the maintenance crew unearth, they're finding a dozen more that need to go. They're doing patch-up work on the steam tunnels now, trying to shore up half the buildings in the Yard while they figure out which joists are holding up what floor and what pipes go where. Everything's topsy-turvy, what with the excavations and all. That's fertile ground for crimes of opportunity, and we have reason to believe the person we pulled out of the hole is a person of interest. This city is tough on the homeless. I know that. But something happened, and whatever I think of Wardley, he's got a reputation for handling this sort of thing.'

'But if this Wardley is in uniform…' Dulcie stopped. 'Maybe I should be the one to talk to him. Jeremy gets spooked easily.'

Rogovoy was shaking his head. 'Not going to happen. I'm not in that loop, but what I hear is that we might not even be getting a statement from him.'

'But why?' None of this was making sense.

Rogovoy sat there for a moment, his mouth set like a crack in a boulder. Dulcie waited, unsure of what to add. Finally, with a heave of his shoulders, he continued. 'Look, Ms Schwartz. I'll be frank. Odds are, the guy we took in is going to face some charges. But he was the one who was injured, Ms Schwartz. He passed out soon after our guys got him out of the hole, I hear. And, frankly, he's not in good shape.'

FOUR

'DULCIE, CALM DOWN.' Chris didn't seem to understand the gravity of the situation. 'Please, honey, I'm not following you.'

Detective Rogovoy had been ushering Dulcie out of his office when the phone rang. And while she wanted to argue—to keep the big detective talking and extract at least a bit more information from him—she had picked up Chris's call automatically. Now she was out on the sidewalk, breathless from trying to get a few more words in, and trying her best to explain.

'It's Jeremy, Chris.' She was yelling, she knew that. It was so frustrating not to have him understand. 'You know, Mumbles? The cops picked him up. He's in the hospital.'

'Wait, Dulcie,' Chris broke in. 'You don't even know if it is Mumbles they've arrested.'

'Not arrested. Not yet, anyway.' Dulcie tried to remember if the burly detective had mentioned any specific charges. 'But it's Jeremy. I'm sure of it.'

'I'm sorry, Dulcie, but what was he doing that—'

'He wasn't doing anything!' A woman in a fur hat turned and stared. Dulcie shot her a look and kept talking. 'That's the infuriating part, Chris. Detective Rogovoy wouldn't tell me exactly what was going on, but he did say that Jeremy may face charges of some sort, which is simply impossible.'

'Impossible?' Chris even sounded like an echo. 'Dulcie you don't know—'

'That's just what Rogovoy said, too.' Dulcie's exasperation was sinking into a dull despair. 'But I do know, Chris. I do.'

'Dulcie?' Her boyfriend's voice had grown softer. 'I know you like him, but really, honey, it's not like you're close to the man.'

'Chris, I've known Jeremy for years. He's gentle. I know he's not really all there. But there's still a nice guy under all the craziness. I can tell. Only the police aren't going to see it. He's always been nervous around the police.'

'Dulcie…' He paused, and Dulcie braced herself. Why was it so hard for people to believe in someone else? Granted, Jeremy was odd, but that didn't make him a criminal.

As if he could read her mind, Chris started talking again. 'Maybe whatever it is wasn't his fault, Dulcie. Maybe he got caught up in something.'

'Yes!' Dulcie's voice was rising again, but this time with excitement. 'That's it exactly. He must have been in the wrong place, at the wrong time.'

'The weather has been so lousy, even with the thaw…' Chris seemed to be building her case for her.

'And he was sheltering in the entranceway of the library when I saw him. He was shivering and the wind was foul. He was only there because he wanted to get warm.'

'Well, there you go.' Chris sounded like he believed her. Better yet, he sounded like he trusted her judgment. 'That explains everything.'

'So, you think the police are wrong?'

'It's obvious.' Chris always said that when he was working out the logic of a problem. Luckily, Dulcie knew by now, this would be followed by an explanation in layman's terms of what was so clear to him. 'Mumbles meant no harm,' Chris began, to Dulcie's satisfaction. 'But he's homeless and it's cold out. He must have been breaking into buildings to find a place to stay.'

'But, Chris—' She kept walking, careful to avoid the puddles that were still rimed with ice.

Her boyfriend wasn't listening. 'Dulcie, think about it. What do we know about these break-ins? The cops haven't been able to determine if anything is being taken, right? So maybe the point of it all has been simply the forced entry, without any theft. Hey, you could say that what he's been doing makes sense. Why should the university leave all these buildings empty when there are guys like Mumbles out in the cold?'

'Chris, I don't know.' He was wearing her down. Besides, she'd reached the Yard. As Chris reiterated his argument, point by point, she passed Memorial Hall, which housed the graduate students' offices. As she walked by, she looked longingly up at the huge brick edifice. In a week, her tiny office down in the great hall's basement would be up and running again. Stuart Truckworth, the head of facilities and maintenance, had personally promised the department that none of the student offices had been flooded, and that none of their contents would in any way be compromised. Still, with the ongoing work, the big doors were locked shut, orange hazard signs posted at the entrance and on the stairs. She was effectively homeless, she realized. Well, except for the fact that she had a cozy apartment only about a mile away, with food and a cat to keep her warm. And if she didn't…?

'Maybe you're right, Chris.' She thought of how thin Jeremy had been. How cold he had appeared, hunched in that thin, old tweed. 'Maybe he did something—just to survive. Maybe it wasn't even him.'

'There you go, Dulcie.' Chris sounded happy. Dulcie hoped it was because he had won her over. 'Now, what are you going to be working on today?'

As she turned her back on her empty offices, Dulcie tried to tell him. It was hard to concentrate on work with everything else that had happened that morning. But by the time she got to the library—to the grand front entrance with its vast portico—she was talking excitedly about her current chapter.

'I don't have all my notes,' she was saying as she climbed the marble stairs. 'I didn't think to write up the citations, but I know exactly where in my office they are. And so I'm writing with a couple of TKs as place holders. You know, for "to come"?' He grunted assent. Chris's discipline—applied mathematics—might be more rigid than hers, but they'd been together long enough for him to understand the gist of her process.

'Anyway, I'm pretty sure I can get through this chapter by the time you come back. I mean, there's

nothing going on to distract me.' She thought she
heard a cough and stopped. 'Chris, are you OK?'

'I'm fine, Dulce, really. Go on.'

'Anyway, if I keep up this pace, I really will have
my dissertation done by spring. By real spring, I
mean.'

'Well, I really hope you can keep your focus then,
Dulcie.' There was a note of something—amuse-
ment?—in his voice. She decided to ignore it. 'And
Dulcie? I miss you.'

'I miss you too, Chris.' His timing was perfect.
She had reached the big glass doors, beyond which
cell conversations were forbidden, and so with a kiss
and a promise of another call later, she hung up and
powered down to get ready to work.

*'A CLOSE EXAMINATION of the antecedents of this work
reveal numerous markers, indications of authorship in both the source material and in the textural
analysis.'*

She stopped and shook her head. Two hours in
her carrel, three levels below that grand marble entrance, and even her own writing was beginning to
sound foreign to her. After five years, the language
of academia was almost a second tongue to Dulcie.
Only sometimes, she thought as she sat back in the
molded plastic seat and rubbed her eyes, she wished
she could use her first language. What was wrong
with her chosen profession that she couldn't simply
say what she meant?

*'I've found lots of indications that my author
wrote this book, too.'* She smiled as she imagined

typing something so prosaic into her laptop. '*She refers to the same stories. She uses a lot of the same phrases. It's all there. All you have to do is follow the clues.*'

No, that would never do. She could almost imagine the way Martin Thorpe, her adviser, would blanch, his eyebrows arching up toward his receding hairline. Dulcie had grown used to Thorpe. He hadn't been her first choice for a thesis adviser, and they had certainly had disagreements over the years. But he wasn't a bad soul. Only timid. And since his career was inextricably linked to hers, he had every reason to want her to succeed. If only he wasn't quite so hidebound. Why couldn't a scholar write in plain English? After all, she *had* found lots of indications. And she did consider them clues. Clues that the author of the great, forgotten Gothic novel, *The Ravages of Umbria*, had written another book, one that Dulcie was piecing together now.

Clues. Closing her eyes to rest them, Dulcie let her thoughts wander as well. Between Chris's phone call and Detective Rogovoy's morning grumpiness, she had let herself be shown out way too fast this morning. She had gone into the police station with the intention of giving them information. She'd seen herself as a resource, a responsible member of the university community. But now that she had time to think about it, she realized that she had her own questions that she'd wanted answered. First and foremost—assuming that it was Jeremy the police had picked up—what did they assume the poor man had done?

Maybe she should reach out to that task force—
the one Rogovoy had mentioned. If they had any
evidence, surely as a member of the university community she had a right to hear it. It was pretty obvious they didn't have answers, only clues—and clues,
Dulcie well knew, were as easy to misread as people.

Jeremy Mumbleigh was a wreck. She couldn't
deny that. But that didn't mean he was a criminal.
Not even an unintentional one, as Chris had implied.
After all, when she had seen him, he'd been sheltering in a perfectly legal doorway. He hadn't even
been trespassing.

Maybe he had wandered by a break-in as it was
taking place. Maybe he had heard a noise and gone to
investigate, and that was when he had fallen. Maybe,
she thought, and the idea made her sit up straight,
Jeremy Mumbleigh had tried to stop a crime and
been thrown into the hole. After all, the university
was Jeremy's home. Maybe he'd wanted to defend it.

She knew what Chris would say. She could almost
hear the words. He would smile and credit her active
imagination. 'You always do want to think the best
of everyone,' he would say. But he was a computer
person. He lived in a world of black and white, or
ones and zeros. He didn't understand how someone
could get caught up in something. Especially someone essentially vulnerable, like Jeremy.

'It's a secret.' She heard his voice like a whisper
in the air. 'You can't tell anyone.'

FIVE

IT WASN'T SIMPLY CURIOSITY, Dulcie reassured herself.
It was common courtesy. One visited people when
they were hospitalized. It was what one did.

Lucy, Dulcie's mother, may have thrown over her
Philadelphia Main Line upbringing for a bohemian
lifestyle—there was certainly little trace of it in
Dulcie's counterculture childhood deep in the woods
of the Pacific North West—but some things did remain. Lucy might have evoked the goddess when
teaching her daughter manners. It didn't matter—the
basic rules were the same, whether because actions
returned thrice-fold on the do-er or because Emily
Post said so.

With that in mind, Dulcie tucked away her laptop
and notes and left her carrel behind. Despite Detective Rogovoy's evasiveness—and Chris's skepticism—Dulcie felt sure that the person involved was
Jeremy—and if he had been both hurt and unfairly
maligned it was up to her to do what she could to
right the situation. The only question, really, was
whether to stop by Lala's first. A bowl of split pea
soup could be so nourishing, and certainly better
than whatever the infirmary dished up. But, no.
Dulcie caught herself. She had no idea whether
Jeremy would be ready for such hearty fare, and

she really should put his welfare first. A visit, and maybe a bit of conversation to clarify the events of the previous evening. Then she would treat herself.

Quite warmed by her sense of decency, Dulcie barely felt the cold that had once again descended, freezing the previous day's puddles into sheets of ice. The midday sun reflected off the glazed brick, making Dulcie squint.

'Watch it!' A large backpack, riding on an equally large person, nearly knocked Dulcie off the sidewalk. She staggered back as the pack bearer scowled.

'But I didn't...' She didn't get a chance to finish. He had already moved along, that big pack bobbing above the crowd, and as she turned to continue on her way, she felt herself slipping, her boots not getting any traction on the icy brick.

'Whoa!' She let out an involuntary whoop as her feet slid out from under her.

'*Be careful.*' The voice was as comforting as the strong, firm hands that caught her, righting her to her feet. But when she turned to thank her rescuer, she was unable to figure out who had helped her.

'Thank you!' She called at the backs of the crowd, waving madly.

'*You must pay attention!*' The voice, like a whisper in her ear, almost caused her to whirl around again—even as her waving threatened to once again send her flying. '*Dulcie, please.*'

'Mr Grey?' Dulcie caught herself. It wasn't only the ice: her beloved cat never seemed to be visible when she could hear him. Turning to look for him might only make his voice disappear. 'Was that you?'

A low purr, almost like a chuckle, rumbled some-where close.

'Well, someone helped me out there.' Dulcie smiled. Maybe Lucy was right. Maybe the universe was fundamentally benevolent. 'And it's nice to hear your voice again.'

'*Dulcie, you're not listening...*' The voice was be-ginning to fade in the lunchtime hubbub. '*There was a warning...*'

'I will be more careful, Mr Grey.' Dulcie could barely resist the urge to turn around. To search for the source of that voice. That comfort. 'I promise.'

'You promise what?' A tall woman with dyed red hair was eyeing her curiously.

'Nothing,' said Dulcie, turning slowly away. She would be more careful. She would. But for now, Mr Grey was gone.

'I'M SORRY. ARE you family?' The soft-spoken orderly looked like he'd been up all night. Still, Dulcie was warmed to see him be so attentive.

'No, I'm a friend.' She had asked to see Jeremy Mumbleigh as soon as she'd gotten to the health ser-vices and been told that, yes, the infirmary did have a patient by that name. But although she'd been di-rected to the third floor of the Holyoke Center com-plex, she'd been stopped at the nurse's station there.

'Oh.' The orderly looked down at a computer screen, perhaps looking up a bed number or a room. 'Bother,' he said. 'I was hoping to fill in some infor-mation about the patient's family.'

'Oh.' That gave Dulcie pause. She had never

thought about Jeremy's background. The university was his family.

'You wouldn't happen to know where he lives, for instance. Would you?' The orderly looked up at her. 'Or how to reach his next of kin?'

'No, I'm sorry.' Dulcie thought about it. 'Can't you ask him?' Jeremy might be excitable, but with some gentle coaxing, he could usually be brought back into some kind of conversational mode.

'Never mind.' The orderly was once again focused on the screen. As Dulcie stood there, he started typing. 'We do get a fair number of homeless people in the winter.'

'But he's not homeless…' Dulcie protested. 'He must have had some ID on him. You knew who he was.'

A shake of the head. 'He had a university library card, ten years out of date, and a meal plan card for Cranston House. I don't think they even have those any more. Anyway, from those we got his name, but that's it. Nothing with a current place of abode. And given his overall condition, in the lack of any further information, we're labeling him as indigent.'

'But he's a member of the university community.' Dulcie was insulted for him.

'It's not a bad thing.' The orderly looked up again, his eyes tired and sad. 'This will get him into the social services system. Maybe they can set him up with a place. Maybe get him some treatment.'

'He doesn't need…' Dulcie caught herself. Jeremy wasn't functioning. The fact that she could talk to him, that she wasn't scared of him, wasn't enough. 'What kind of treatment?'

'I think it's clear that he's delusional.' The orderly's voice was gentle. 'When he came to, he was muttering something about a secret.'

'A secret?' Dulcie thought back. 'Yeah, that's one of his things. It doesn't mean anything though.'

'That's not what the cops think.' The orderly's mouth closed tight, as if he'd given something away.

'They can't really believe that...' He was shaking his head, so Dulcie decided to play her trump card. 'I was speaking with Detective Rogovoy about this earlier. He knows that Jeremy is harmless.' This wasn't that much of a stretch. She had told the burly detective about Jeremy.

'Maybe that detective didn't hear the latest then.' The look of fatigue had become one of resignation. 'We had a hell of a time getting him to give up his coat, and it wasn't until we did that we saw what he was hiding.'

Dulcie waited, unsure of what was to come.

'He had a book he was holding. Wouldn't let go of it for the world.'

'I don't understand.'

'I'm not sure I do, either.' The orderly was staring at his screen again. 'But one of the EMTs saw the library stamp on it. You know, the old kind? I guess it—ah—was some kind of valuable book, one that's been missing a while. There's been all kinds of fuss about it. The cops wanted it, and one of the university librarians even came down to health services to check it out.'

'But why would Jeremy hide a book under his
coat? He's a scholar, or he was.' Dulcie caught herself, her own words providing a sad sort of motive.
'He values books, I know he does.' She rallied to his
defense. 'But he wouldn't steal. Not from the library.'

The orderly shrugged. 'Maybe he thought it was
his. Maybe he liked the look of it. All I know is
that the police were interested, but that was nothing
compared to how this librarian was reacting. Little guy? Big glasses? He was almost hyperventilat-
ing from excitement. Wanted to talk to Mumbleigh
right away.'

'Did he?' Dulcie had a good idea who the librarian in question was—and if he was that excited, then
the book really was of particular value.

'Didn't get to.' A phone rang, and he picked it up.
'Excuse me.'

'That's not fair.' Dulcie waited. From the description—the glasses almost bigger than the man—the
librarian had to be Thomas Griddlehaus, the director of the Mildon Rare Book Collection. But surely
Jeremy had an explanation. Maybe he had found the
book. Clearly he thought he was protecting it—from
the elements if not from some actual wrongdoers.
Most likely, it had all been some kind of horrid mistake: an inexperienced clerk had allowed the frail
scholar to check out a work without proper clearance,
accepting that expired card. At any rate, Jeremy deserved a chance to defend himself. To explain himself to Griddlehaus, if not to the police.

'Sorry about that.' The orderly had hung up. 'But
so you see, if you can't help us with information

about the patient, I'm afraid there isn't anything else I can do for you.'

'Yes, there is.' Dulcie felt her temper rising. Jeremy, her friend, needed a protector. 'You can let me see Jeremy Mumbleigh right away. I have no doubt he can clear this up—and can clear his name. He only needs to be with somebody who understands him. Somebody who doesn't terrify him, and he'll explain the book, explain how he got it. Everything.'

She was already thinking of the lunch she'd stand him to—or bring in, if he still wasn't up to sitting at Lala's. In fact, she was so fixated on that warm soup that she almost missed the deep sigh that emanated from the orderly in front of her.

'What?' she said, when his lack of response finally registered. 'Doesn't he have any rights?'

'I wish it were that simple,' said the orderly, a sad smile softening his tired face. 'I wish you could talk us all through this. You see, Mr Mumbleigh's injuries seem to have addled him a bit, maybe more than he has been, and that means he can't give permission. And so unless you are a family member or his legal caregiver, I'm afraid I can't let you see him.'

SIX

'HULLO?'

For the first time that Dulcie could remember, she had no appetite for lunch.

Hungry instead for an explanation, she had rushed back to the library—not to her carrel, but to the underground haven known as the Mildon Rare Book Collection. Not only was this library-within-a-library the source of some of her greatest discoveries, its director, Thomas Griddlehaus, was someone she counted as a friend. The description given by the orderly hadn't been that specific. But considering its general parameters—little man, big glasses— she was pretty sure the official summoned had been Griddlehaus. Surely, Dulcie had thought, Griddlehaus would be able to explain why Jeremy Mumbleigh had been in possession of a rare text. As an added bonus, he'd undoubtedly be able to tell her about the book itself.

Eager to get some answers, Dulcie trotted up to the special elevator—the one that descended to the underground sanctuary—and found herself silently urging it on as it whirred its way down. Motion-sensitive hall lights came on as she exited, making her way to the special collection and her librarian friend. But when she arrived at the hall's end, she found nobody there.

'Mr Griddlehaus?' The entry to the special collection was open—a low counter on which lay a ledger—but its keeper was nowhere in sight. 'Hello? Are you here?'

He had to be, Dulcie figured. In his absence, the metal fire doors, installed to protect the collection's priceless papers, would have been pulled down. Unless something was very, very wrong...

She took a breath and looked around. The library was so quiet. Too quiet, she couldn't help but think. But just as she was about to retreat and seek help, she heard a voice.

'Hello!' The cry came from the back and sounded a little strained. But the voice was familiar, and followed quickly by a muffled cry. 'Bother!'

Unsure what to expect, Dulcie signed herself in on the old-fashioned ledger—one of the few low-tech touches that remained in the gleaming modernist preserve—and ducked around the counter in search of her friend.

'Mr Griddlehaus, are you all right?' She found him in one of several back rooms, where drawers of uncataloged papers lined the wall. He looked up, glasses reflecting the light, from one opened drawer. 'Do you need help?'

'Ah, Ms Schwartz.' He removed an archival-quality box. 'Would you please come here?'

Dulcie hesitated. No matter how long she had been coming to the Mildon, protocol still held sway. Clients—researchers and other graduate students like herself—waited in the reading room, sitting at the long, white table while staff—basically Griddlehaus—fetched their requested material. In five years of graduate studies, Dulcie had never actually set foot inside the drawer room.

'Ms Schwartz?' Griddlehaus's voice was as soft as ever, but that note of stress that Dulcie had heard at first was ratcheting up ever so slightly. Partly, she could now see, because even as he held one of the long, green boxes in one hand, his other balanced a second.

'Sorry.' Hurrying in, she took the box gingerly, holding it with her fingertips, as if the box itself, rather than its contents, were fragile. 'Shall I?' She nodded toward the public area.

'Yes, please.' Griddlehaus turned back to the opened drawer, while Dulcie removed her charge to the white table.

'I'm glad you're still open,' she called back as she reached for the white gloves required for the handling of documents. She had questions for the librarian, but those could wait until he joined her. 'What with all the work going on.'

'It has been truly inconvenient,' she heard him reply. 'Just this morning, I had to circumnavigate Dudley before I could even approach the entrance.'

'Tell me about it,' Dulcie responded as she stared at the box. Normally, she would be sitting here as the Mildon director presented the box, opened it, and withdrew the documents for her to study. Then again, normally she would not have entered the drawer room. She pulled on the gloves.

'And the noise? I swear that even down here, I can hear someone drilling.'

'I believe you.' Surely, it could do no harm.

She opened the box to reveal one of the Mildon's many treasures. The special collection held documents of all kinds, on everything from papyrus to onion skin. This one was paper, a mere scrap, centered in the protective embrace of a clear polypropylene folder, but years of study had trained her to recognize its age and fragility—roughly two hundred years old, she estimated. A thick page, more board than paper. Or, no—she leaned in—a manuscript page that had become attached to another, perhaps an earlier attempt to stabilize the friable paper. Carefully, using both hands so as not to bend the artifact, she lifted it, protective sheath and all, out of the box and laid it carefully on the tabletop to examine it.

'Ms Schwartz?' The librarian's voice broke her concentration.

'Yes?' Only one line of the handwriting was legible: '*Then surely she did Flee*,' it read. Angled and graceful, even where the iron gall ink had worn through the paper, the remaining lines of cursive were not immediately readable—she would have to spend several hours examining it to do that—but there was something on the other side. A strange bit of glitter...

'Ms Schwartz!' She looked up. Griddlehaus was standing behind her, his eyes wide behind those glasses.

'I'm sorry.' She stood, backing away from the table. 'I know I shouldn't have. It was just...'

'No, no, I understand.' He came over and looked down at the page. 'How curious…'

'What is it, Mr Griddlehaus?' Dulcie couldn't help but feel that he was looking at the same thing she had noticed: a slight sparkle on the page in the form of a curving line.

'That mark—' He didn't get a chance to finish, because just then a siren started up, a loud wail that made them both jump back.

'What?' Dulcie looked around, startled.

'It's not us.' Griddlehaus had run over to the front of the library, where a small control panel still showed a steady green.

'Excuse me.' They both turned to see a tall, thin man in khakis by the library entrance: Stuart Truckworth. 'I'm afraid we have to evacuate.'

'But why?' Griddlehaus motioned toward the sensor.

'Is there a fire?' Dulcie was suddenly aware of how deep beneath the exit they were.

'No, nothing like that.' The facilities manager looked harried rather than scared, she was glad to see. Still, he stretched out his long hands and motioned to them. 'But I do need you to come with me. There's been a water main break. Another one.'

'One moment, please.' Griddlehaus turned back toward the table and froze, staring at the document lying there. Although the Mildon's power seemed undisturbed, the hallway lights appeared to have gone out, and the emergency strobe was casting strange shadows across the open entranceway. In sync with the flashing light, the alarm was still wailing at a volume that made it hard to think.

'I'll get it.' Dulcie saw her colleague's dilemma and stepped forward, showing her hands. 'I've got the gloves on.'

'Please, hurry,' said Truckworth, his hand on Griddlehaus's back, as Dulcie carefully replaced the document in the box.

'Hang on.' Dulcie slipped around Truckworth to bring the box back to the drawer room. She couldn't take the time to re-file it, even if she knew where it was. But anything was better than leaving the box out, exposed—at least to a breach in protocol.

'Thank you,' said Griddlehaus, as the facilities manager fussed. 'Now, let me just lock up.'

'Please!' Truckworth trundled Dulcie over to the emergency stairwell, even as she pulled the gloves off, and held the door until Griddlehaus joined her.

'I'll let you know as soon as we're all clear,' the facilities manager yelled as the siren blared, ducking back into the shadowed hall.

THE NOISE EASED as Dulcie and Griddlehaus made their way upstairs, and by the time they surfaced at the main level the alarm was either inaudible or had been turned off.

'Dulcie!' She turned to see a heavy-set woman waving. Her friend Ruby, from the circulation desk. 'They smoked you out?'

'I guess.' Dulcie made her way over, Griddlehaus in tow. 'Do you know what's happening?'

She shook her head. 'More of the usual, I'm guessing.'

'Well!' Beside her, Griddlehaus huffed. 'If you'll excuse me, ladies, I'm going to inquire as to what's going on.'

'That man.' Ruby was talking in her library voice. Unfortunately, that voice was as loud as her tropical-print shirt. Ruby's sole colleague on the desk kept his head down. Her oversized voice was the price for her nearly psychic cataloging skills, but the security guard who had been snoozing against the wall jumped. 'Doesn't he ever take a break? Don't you?'

'Not this spring.' Dulcie looked around at the empty room. 'It seems like you're on vacation scheduling.'

'It's not spring break, it's all the construction work.' Ruby rolled her eyes. 'Hang on.'

Dulcie waited while her friend maneuvered her large girth around her sole colleague and through the desk's small gate. It didn't seem to matter to Ruby that the cavernous room was mostly empty. She still gestured Dulcie over to the far wall before continuing her explanation.

'It's a mess,' she said, her voice as low as it got. 'It's crazy.'

'The repair work?' Dulcie asked, a note of anxiety creeping into her voice. 'The flooding under Mem Hall didn't go any farther, did it?'

'Oh, I don't know about that.' Ruby waved away Dulcie's cry of dismay. 'I don't even know if they've gotten that far.'

'What do you mean?'

'They're tearing up everything.' Ruby leaned in. 'Everything! I hear that there won't be running water in the employees' lounge for two weeks. And the mess!'

'The pipes were worse than they thought?' Despite Ruby's cavalier dismissal, Dulcie couldn't help worrying about the office she shared with her colleague Lloyd. It was in the upper level of the grad student office, but that only meant it was in the first basement. Half underground, if there were more flooding—or even more drastic construction work—her cozy nest might be, well…it didn't bear thinking about. Besides, Ruby was still talking.

'I guess,' her friend said with a shrug. 'Or Truckworth needs work for his crew. From what I've seen of the plans, they're digging up everything. It's going to be positively archaeological.'

'Like the dig in the Yard?' The previous autumn, more routine maintenance work had uncovered shards of Native American pottery. The site had been given over to Archeology 101, which was working with the local Wampanoags to preserve the artifacts. The site had been covered for winter, but the dig was ongoing. Dulcie didn't know what had happened to the maintenance work. She did know it was one of the Yard's newest tourist attractions, when weather permitted.

'What? No.' Ruby was looking at her strangely. 'Dulcie, are you all right?'

'Yes, I'm sorry.' Dulcie smiled up at her friend, trying to mask her nerves. 'I'm just a little distracted. You were saying?'

'It's nothing.' Ruby's round face turned gentle. 'Here I am, going on…and you're the one who's locked out.'

'I am,' Dulcie confessed. 'I didn't think the Mildon would ever be closed. But I guess there was a rupture in a water main?'

'That's what I'm talking about,' Ruby cut in. 'It's because they're taking down those antique interior walls without stopping to think what this old wreck is hiding.'

'Old wreck?' Dulcie waved her off as it hit her: not only had she been stopped from examining the document, but she had never gotten around to asking Griddlehaus about the book that had been found in Jeremy's possession, her original reason for seeking out the timid scholar. 'Bother. Did you see where Griddlehaus went?'

'No, he took off.' Ruby craned her head around. 'If I see him, I'll tell him you're looking for him.'

'Thanks, Ruby.' The smile was genuine this time. 'And—I am sorry about all the mess.'

'This place has been here a few hundred years,' her friend said. 'I figure it'll stand a few hundred more.'

Dulcie only nodded. The library wasn't that old. It had only recently celebrated its centenary. But it had been built to enlarge on—and replace—an older college library. Ruby must have been referring to the university. Or maybe the settlement. Those pottery shards had made it abundantly clear that the Yard was a social center long before anybody had heard of pizza or all-nighters.

'Mr Griddlehaus?' It had taken Dulcie another twenty minutes, but she had found him, hunkered down in the reading room. Like circulation, the vast room was nearly empty, the green-shaded lamps over its central wood table glowing like a sign of spring. And at the very end of the table, balding pate reflecting that soft light, was the little librarian, bent over what looked like a large-format book.

She had walked up as quietly as she could, not wanting to disturb him, and then waited, watching as he ran his finger down one page. He was so intent on it that she began to regret her silent approach. Surely, no one likes to be snuck up on.

'Excuse me?' She spoke as softly as she could, but still he jumped, spinning around so quickly he almost lost his glasses.

'Ms Schwartz!' He reached up to adjust those glasses, their large, square frames too big for his face. 'I'm so sorry. I hadn't thought that you would be waiting around and what happened—the alarm...'

'It's OK, Mr Griddlehaus.' She pulled out the chair next to his and sat. 'It shook me up as well, and I knew you were going to inquire.' A horrible thought hit her. 'You weren't—the collection—it's...'

'It's safe.' He reached out to pat her hand, then quickly withdrew again. 'I located Mr Truckworth and he assured me that the flood is nowhere near the Mildon. It has played havoc with the electrical grid, I gather, although our circuitry seemed to be in fine shape. However, according to the powers that be, without the elevator and without the proper lighting and alarms in the hallway, the collection is considered unsafe. We are banned until further notice.' He sighed. 'Sometimes, I wonder if this is all even necessary.'

Dulcie nodded, responding as much to the skepticism in his voice as his words. 'Ruby was telling me something about the extra work they're doing. Something about the foundation?'

He nodded, and the light shone off his lenses. 'You'd think they would have properly excavated, but never mind. I don't want you to worry. The Mildon is safe as—well, safe as the upperclass houses. Well, as safe as they are now, at any rate.'

'That's good to know.' It was, and despite Griddlehaus's strange phrasing, Dulcie felt her anxiety level ratchet down a notch. 'But I was actually hoping to talk to you about another matter.' She paused, unsure how to continue. 'I gather you know Jeremy Mumbleigh?'

'Of course.' Griddlehaus blinked up at her. 'I've known Jeremy for years.'

'You have?' This was unexpected.

He nodded, those glasses flashing again. 'I remember when Jeremy first came to the university for his studies. He was, well, he was not unlike you, Ms Schwartz. So earnest, so committed.'

He paused, lost in thought, and Dulcie felt her spirits sink. It was true, then. Only a dissertation stood between her and being called Mumbles.

'Oh, I wouldn't want you to think…' Griddlehaus reached out again, his hand, soft and pink on her wrist. 'I didn't mean…'

Dulcie held up her own hand to stop him. Clearly,

her concern had shown on her face. 'It's fine, Mr Griddlehaus. *I* am going to finish *my* dissertation.'

'If only that was all it was,' Griddlehaus said with a sigh. But before Dulcie could probe further, he went on. 'You were asking for a reason, no doubt?'

'Yes.' She gathered her thoughts. 'I was told that you identified a book that Jeremy had on him when he was taken to health services last night.'

'A book?' Griddlehaus's eyebrows shot up as enlightenment dawned. 'So that's who found it! Well, that explains it.'

'Excuse me?'

'Everybody in the library system knows Jeremy, Ms Schwartz.' Even though they were alone, the librarian leaned toward Dulcie, his voice low. 'Some of us old-timers have even been known to let him use that outdated card he still carries. Nothing so valuable, of course, but he clearly loves books, and he manages to take good care of them, somehow.' Griddlehaus paused, momentarily lost in thought. 'Anyway, this was clearly a mix up—but it did prove useful.'

Dulcie shook her head, utterly confused.

'The book.' Griddlehaus looked at her as if his point were obvious. 'It was a first American edition—well, part of the first edition. The 1833 *He Could Not Tell Her* was printed in two volumes, you know.'

'Of course,' said Dulcie. 'But—I'm confused. You sound as if Jeremy did you a favor, but you're one of the reasons he's been arrested.'

'I am?' Griddlehaus blinked in shock, looking more than usual like a white mouse. 'But I thought…

all I did was identify the volume. The university police officer asked for my advice. I immediately recognized the binding. It had been partially restored,
you see. Half of the binding had been replaced here
in the university.' Seeing the expression on Dulcie's
face, he redirected his thoughts. 'My assumption
was that someone on the staff had been able to locate it, either through diligence or sheer good luck.
That perhaps it had been misfiled, somehow. Perhaps
during some previous renovation.'

'You didn't know that Jeremy has been accused
of stealing it?' Dulcie asked in disbelief. 'The police
seem to think he might be involved with the break-
ins on campus.'

Griddlehaus only shook his head, a stunned look
on his pale face. 'But that makes no sense. It's not
like someone simply grabbed it and took off with it.
As you know, Ms Schwartz, it's a minor work, although an important part of our collection. But it's
been missing since 1989.'

SEVEN

'BUT WHY...' DULCIE PAUSED, unable to sort out the questions that flooded her mind. 'Why do they think Jeremy stole it, even though it's been missing for so long?' That one, at least, got out.

Thomas Griddlehaus shrugged. 'It is university property,' he said. 'And it did disappear from the collection around the time of the stacks heist. I'm sure you've heard of that.'

Dulcie shook her head.

'Before your time,' said the librarian. 'But I would've thought... At any rate, that's why we have our current security protocol. And why, I am sure, the university is being so careful about the current construction work. Work was being done on the library that summer, and a portion of one of the more recently acquired collections went missing and was presumed stolen. Most of the works were recovered eventually, but not all. Between you and I, there was talk about how perhaps there was never a theft on a grand scale, and that instead, in all the hubbub, many works were merely misplaced. They weren't the most showy books in that particular collection, and frankly many of them were not highly valued by the powers that be. The book found on Jeremy's person was one of those.'

'Then maybe it wasn't stolen at all.' Dulcie knew she was grabbing at straws. 'Maybe it had been mis-filed and Jeremy found it.'

'It is true that he would have recognized it,' said Griddlehaus, looking thoughtful. 'He is—was—quite the scholar in his day.'

'You don't think he's had it for all these years, do you?' Dulcie couldn't help but wonder.

'I don't know.' Griddlehaus looked as mystified as she was. 'Where would he have kept it?'

'So you think he's homeless, too?' All those times she had seen him in doorways, shivering, came back to her now.

'I don't know what to think, Ms Schwartz,' he replied, the reading-room light reflecting off those big glasses. 'Do you?'

THE CONVERSATION HAD gone downhill from there. Griddlehaus had been unable to tell her when the Mildon would reopen; his only answer—'not long, not long at all'—seemed to be born more from wishful thinking than from any hard evidence. Her friend had also been unable to answer her questions about Jeremy. Not only did he not know where the injured scholar spent his nights, he also didn't know if the poor man had any family—or any contact at all with the past, beyond the university.

'And now,' he'd said finally, blinking up at her through those thick lenses, 'there is a matter I was involved in researching…'

'Of course.' Dulcie nearly jumped back. 'I'll let you be.'

'MAYBE IT'S JUST as well if he gets hooked up with social services,' Dulcie said to herself as she made her way down the street. Although few of her questions had been answered, her dormant appetite had re-emerged. Jeremy might not be able to enjoy Lala's yet, but she could.

'Welcome!' Lala herself was at the counter when Dulcie walked in. As always, she took a moment to acclimate herself. The tiny storefront was fragrant with spices and grilled meats, and Dulcie's stomach grumbled in appreciation. 'Just you?'

'Just me.' Dulcie heard the note of sadness in her voice. So did Lala, and the big proprietress looked over her shoulder as she led Dulcie to a small table, the question clear in her eyes.

'Chris is visiting his mom,' Dulcie explained. 'And Trista, well, all of them are gone. In fact, I was wondering…' She stopped. How welcome would a threadbare street person be in a restaurant, even one as welcoming as Lala's?

Lala pulled out a chair and sat, clearly waiting for Dulcie to continue.

'You ever think about something too late?' Dulcie sat opposite her. Something about the big woman was comforting. 'Something that maybe you should have done for someone?'

'It is rarely too late.' Lala's voice was soft and deep.

'Maybe not.' Dulcie thought back. 'I was wishing that I had followed through and taken someone here to eat. But maybe…well, I'm not sure he would have been welcome.'

Lala's eyebrows went up, and before she could protest, Dulcie rushed to explain.

'Not because of you. I mean, he's—well, he's kind of odd. And he's clean. At least, I think he is. But he may be homeless.'

'You mean Jeremy?' With her accent, the 'J' sounded soft as a caress.

Dulcie sat back in surprise. 'You know him?'

'Of course.' Lala sounded surprised. 'He is as much a part of the Square as you or I, or Out of Town News.'

'I guess.' Dulcie looked at her friend with new respect. 'I was thinking…he's so skinny.'

'Appetite like a bird. No.' Lala held up a hand as if to stop herself. 'A bird eats more. Now, for a cold day, soup.' Having prescribed for Dulcie, she stood up.

'Wait, Lala?' Dulcie hadn't realized what a font of information the big restaurateur would be. 'Do you know if Jeremy has any family? Or where he lives—or anything?'

She shook her head. 'I don't know where you live. Or you me.' She turned to walk toward the kitchen. 'This is the city,' she called over her shoulder.

A slim young waiter showed up less than a minute later, bearing not only a wide saucer of Lala's famous split pea soup but also several slices of herb-crusted flat bread.

Dulcie dipped her spoon into the soup and for a little while thought of nothing else. It had been a while since she'd indulged. When Chris was home—Dulcie couldn't help but think of their Cambridgeport apartment by that term rather than her boyfriend's

natal New Jersey—they had been working on cooking more together, and even packing lunches for the
days when they were stuck on campus. This had
been Chris's idea: he'd applied his math skills to their
budget, and even Dulcie had been able to understand
the resulting numbers. Now that Chris was no longer working the more profitable overnight shifts, if
they wanted to take any kind of vacation this summer—out west to visit Lucy or maybe even a brief
sojourn at the Cape—they had to start cutting back
somewhere.

By the time she'd moved on to the bread, though,
other thoughts began to intrude. Who was Jeremy
Mumbleigh, really, and how had he come into possession of a rare book? Dulcie did not want to believe
that the skinny, scared man was a thief. She couldn't
believe that he'd been carrying around the missing
volume for more than twenty-five years. There had
to be another explanation. But the first step toward
finding it—and to helping him clear his name—was
to uncover a bit more about the man himself.

But how? As she dragged her bread through the
last puddle of thick green soup, she found herself
wondering about trails and traces. And about how
she could find out more about Jeremy Mumbleigh.

The university offices were closed for the break,
even those that weren't having their basements excavated. Besides, any authorities with any information
were unlikely to share it with Dulcie: her experience at the health services had driven that home. She
wasn't a family member, and she had no legal reason to delve into Jeremy's past. As she walked, she

thought about what Lala had said. Was it true that in a city nobody really got to know anybody else? She thought of Chris and their absent friends—but they had all met through the university, and that was more like a village than the surrounding city.

Jeremy was part of the university too, she told herself, her thoughts circling back. And yet all she knew about him—

She stopped. His library card. He had been a member of the community. A small, well-knit community. And while his heyday was probably long before the rise of the Internet, there had to be some trace of him in one of the databases. A paper or a class schedule or...

Pushing her bowl aside, Dulcie pulled her laptop from the oversized denim messenger bag she always carried and set it up on the table. As she waited for her various search functions to wake, she licked the last of the breadcrumbs from her fingers and started typing: JEREMY MUMBLEIGH. It would do for starters.

She got the phone book. There was the Jeremy Mumbleigh who owned a dry cleaners in Topeka. Another whose wedding photo showed a very different individual. The one intriguing lead—*Jeremy Mumbleigh Convicted*—proved to be from seventy years before, too early by any stretch of the imagination.

'You are done?' Dulcie looked up to see Lala glaring, her heavy arms crossed over her chest.

'I—I'm sorry, Lala.' Dulcie reached for the last

piece of bread, swiping it over the remnants of the soup. 'I just had an idea about Jeremy.'

'Huh.' Lala didn't sound convinced, and as she reached for the laptop, Dulcie had to fight the urge to grab it back. It wasn't much of a machine, but Chris kept it running in tip-top condition. If the chef smacked it to the ground in a fit of pique, she'd be hard pressed to replace it.

Dulcie held her breath as Lala lifted the laptop like a pizza, on one flat palm. With the other, to Dulcie's surprise, she began typing. 'Your search is too broad,' she said, without looking up. 'Here.'

Dulcie reached up for the machine and lowered it back to the table. Lala had accessed what looked like the university news offices. *Mumbleigh Wins Dorchester Prize*, read one entry. *Scholar Identifies Mystery Gift as Legacy of Early American Collector.*

She clicked through to find a picture of a tall young man, bearded, standing rather awkwardly over the short round figure of the late Dean Goodman. It was Jeremy, all right, even down to the awkward slouch—the result, Dulcie guessed, of always being the tallest person in the room.

'Now, dessert?' Lala was beaming. 'I have honey cake.'

'That would be lovely, Lala.' Dulcie smiled right back, relief and gratitude warming her even more than the soup had done. 'Thank you.'

LATER, BACK IN her carrel, Dulcie wished for more of that honey cake and, even more deeply, for more of Lala's formidable research skills. That article and

the three that had followed had given her a much
better sense of who Jeremy Mumbleigh had been. A
rising star in her own field, though he never looked
any more comfortable in front of the camera, he had
been instrumental in analyzing the work of several
early nineteenth-century authors. He had won the
Dorchester—the largest of several prizes the university devoted to library research—for his work with
an anonymous donation that had come in years before and had mystified the library staff.

Dulcie smiled to think of it. Griddlehaus, she was
sure, would not have been thrown by the worn travel-
ing cases and their confusing contents. She pictured
him as she had left him, bent over a reference work
with furious intent.

Jeremy must have had similar zeal. Thanks to
him, Dulcie read, the collection, a bequest whose
paperwork had somehow been lost, had belatedly
been credited to one Josiah Stavendish, a distant
American cousin of the eighteenth Earl of that name.
As befitted a wealthy American with close ties to
European nobility, he had collected several important pieces, of which the two-volume *He Could Not
Tell Her*, a minor American Gothic, had been only
one of the lesser prizes. The most valued, the piece
that had made the collection headline news, was an
early, privately bound copy of the Islington Bible,
which Stavendish had reputedly won from a South
African collector in a high-stakes poker game. The
book was a treasure in its own right—one of the few
surviving copies of this particular translation, which
had been done illegally and smuggled into England

during the Reformation. But what had garnered all the attention was its jewel-encrusted cover, bestowed upon the faded and hand-copied manuscript in the flurry of new wealth following the Glorious Revolution of 1688.

Dulcie knew the Islington Bible, of course. Everyone who studied in the department did. To scholars, like Griddlehaus and herself, the Islington's fancy cover was beside the point—the gilding on the lily. What were really of interest were the colloquialisms inside—what the proscribed translation revealed about the language and the mindset of the time. Those words might as well have been scrawled in blood for all their rarity, and their frailty—light and the years had already nearly done the text in. But to the tourists who queued up to gape at it during the two days a year that it was on display, those cabochon-cut emeralds and rubies were the treasure.

True to form, the next three stories she clicked to were all about the Islington Bible. Close-ups of the jeweled cover and the creation about its special display case, along with the plans for public viewing, were given in detail. A jeweler's appraisal of those large stones had resulted in a bit of disappointment: for all their size, it seemed they were flawed. 'Too showy,' Dulcie muttered to herself.

Except for its crowd appeal, that gawdy cover— Dulcie could picture its reds and greens and the heavy, worked gold—was nothing. It was certainly no better than the majority of the collection, books that the next article had described as 'period pot boilers,' or, in other words, junk. Popular fiction that—

according to the release—had little or no scholarly value.

The university, Dulcie read on, had initially been hesitant to deaccession even the less worthwhile pieces. While the donor had been unknown, the terms under which the collection had been donated were up in the air, and breaking the terms of a bequest could mean the loss of the valued pieces, as well as the dross. Jeremy's work tracing various inscriptions and tying them in with publication dates and distribution of the more mass-marketed publications had helped the university locate the family that had originally made the gift. And that meant, she read, that he had eased the university's path toward winnowing out the collection.

And that's when the story began to get odd.

Libraries, Dulcie knew, got rid of material all the time. Works were replaced by updated editions. Academic trends changed and collections followed suit. Less popular material was sifted out, and duplicates sold or gifted to institutions that lacked copies. Sometimes, and the thought made her grimace, books were even destroyed. It happened.

Dulcie clicked on to a later article. Once the donor had been identified, she read, the university had appealed to Stavendish's heirs. Side by side portraits showed Stavendish, formally posed, and two fashionably attired young women, his descendants, smiling by the university's main gate. They had given their permission to cull the gift, the article explained; their main concern being the public access to that showy Bible. And thus, it had seemed that the fate of the less prized parts of this particular collection were sinking fast.

Only Jeremy Mumbleigh had fought back.

Dorchester Winner Returns Prize read the next headline. This piece—written as a straightforward news story—detailed how, in protest to the library's stated intentions of breaking up the bequest, the graduate student had given back both the award plaque and the accompanying sum, a hefty ten grand. The writer had then speculated on Mumbleigh's future, noting that—in the convoluted math of higher learning—that sum had already been subtracted from the winner's grants for the following year.

A final piece had quoted the beleaguered scholar, who had both appealed to the university's better instincts and railed against its 'tyranny.' There were no further articles about the controversy—or about the library's plans. Nor were there any later mentions of the one-time wunderkind. Dulcie clicked through to the main university search engine and then back to the earlier stories—to no avail. Jeremy Mumbleigh might as well have fallen off the face of the earth.

EIGHT

For a few seconds, Dulcie sat motionless, stymied by the dead end. Then, with a sigh that could probably be heard throughout the abandoned lower level where she sat, she faced up to the inevitable. This must have been when Jeremy Mumbleigh got off track. Any allies he had made in the university were probably put off by his stubborn stance, and by the rather un-kind—and, in retrospect, rash—things he had said about the library's treatment of the bequest and the university in general. Even if he had been right about trends changing—and Dulcie knew enough about how history had disregarded her favorite genre, the Gothic novel, to be grateful for such a champion—his attitude would not have helped his case. Without friends and without funding, he had probably been forced to withdraw.

Somewhere in there, Dulcie suspected, the poor man had had a breakdown. Maybe, she thought, the battle had started it, kicking off some deep-seated insecurities or feelings of paranoia. More likely, she admitted silently, the fervor of his fight—calling out everyone from the university president to the head of the librarian's union—had been an early symptom. A sign of an unraveling mind trying desperately to hold everything together.

The frustrating part was that she might never know. The official university press had no more about the star scholar, and anything in the health services would, of course, be confidential. What bothered Dulcie even more was the lack of any biographical information. Would it have been so difficult to identify Jeremy by a home state or a secondary school?

Apparently so, she realized, after she had gone back over the previous articles and failed, once again, to find any such mention. It was time to admit she had hit a dead end.

Dulcie closed her laptop and looked around. Somewhere, not far away, she knew work was on-going. The water main break that had closed the Mildon must be on or near this level—the deepest in the building. But here in the stacks, there was no noise. Outside, the afternoon had to be drawing on, but the light here remained if not bright, then even. Unchanging, especially now, when no casual visitors passed by to spark the motion-sensitive fluo-rescents that hung over each aisle. Down here the spring thaw didn't matter, nor did the icy wind that had frosted the city. Even the sound of that wind, a howling lonely sound, was muted down here, re-placed by the hum of machinery, as ventilation and electrical systems went about their business, oblivi-ous to Dulcie and her concerns. And the books—they were the constant. Protected from the elements, they would last as long as, well, as long as such things could last. And since Dulcie had seen papyrus preserved and parchment restored to its original legibility, she knew that could be nearly forever.

Of course! Dulcie sat up with a start. Her research of Jeremy Mumbleigh might have come to an end, but there was always another avenue to explore. Hadn't her years of studies taught her that? Chuckling to herself, she reopened her laptop. The scholar might have dropped from the public eye. But the collection he had fought so hard to protect—that had to be traceable.

A few keystrokes brought Dulcie back to the original article—the one that explained how Jeremy had linked the collection to Josiah Stavendish. His grandson, Ashley Stavendish—Dulcie opened up another window to refresh her memory—had been quite a big deal in the early part of the twentieth century. A literary critic who styled himself a scholar, he had gone from critiquing contemporary works—sometimes with devastating wit—to writing about works of the past for such journals as *McLure's*, *Collier's* and the fledgling *Time* magazine. He had even published some of his own fiction, Dulcie recalled as she skimmed a footnote, although there had been some scandal about one of his stories, and that part of his career had been quickly eclipsed.

The confusion, Dulcie read on, had come about because the donation had not come from Josiah Stavendish nor from the descendents pictured. Instead, the gift—in the form of two worn and stained steamer trunks—had been left to the university by a third woman who styled herself Stavendish's great-great-grand-niece, though whether she had any actual physical relationship with either the collector or the critic was an open question. What Mumbleigh had discovered, by studying the books in those trunks, was that the collection had originally been compiled by the wealthy collector, but had been passed down to the critic, and come finally to the woman who had made the bequest.

At least some of it had—and therein lay the rub. Now that Dulcie was looking for stories on the Stavendish bequest, rather than on the scholar who identified it, she found herself going down a rabbit hole of arcane articles. First off was the question of whether the contents of those trunks could even be called one collection. Even before the donor had been identified, the contents were derided as 'incoherent,' which, in scholarly terms didn't mean that the books were unreadable so much as that as a collection they didn't adhere to one theme or style.

'They should see my library,' Dulcie muttered to herself, skimming one archivist's disparaging essay. Anyone who knew her would understand *Cat Care for Dummies* next to *The Wind in the Willows*, right up against two different editions of the incomplete *The Ravages of Umbria*, each with varying and—to Dulcie—wrong-headed essays whining about the 'un-literary excesses' of the unknown author.

One of the arguments, and Dulcie had to admit that she could see the sense in it, was that the donation contained more than one person's collection. That although someone had inherited a fine bunch of books, as well as some lesser works from Ashley, over the years the distant niece's own, less patrician

purchases had gotten mixed in. After her death, the
entire load had been packed up and donated by her
daughter—the great-great-grand-niece. That lack of
cohesion had been behind the ultimate decision to
unload some of the collection.

'Purging a fine library of commercial detritus,'
one librarian had been quoted as saying. 'Looking
a gift horse in the mouth,' was how Dulcie saw it.

Maybe there was an element of sour grapes. The
university, Dulcie was surprised to see, had not even
been the first choice. A small private library outside
Philadelphia had been offered the collection. But
burdened by the sky-rocketing costs of the mid-
seventies energy crisis, they had turned it down, saying that they could not afford proper care. So by the
time it came here, she figured, it was already viewed
as more a burden than a benefit. Add in that the
collection had been associated most recently with
women—and the living donor young and rather
pretty—and Dulcie suspected the university powers that be had devalued the gift still further. Still,
it seemed an ungrateful way to respond. A feeling
she had obviously shared with Jeremy.

'I wonder if any of those librarians are still
around?' Dulcie asked her screen. If any were—and
if any of them had experienced a change of heart—
perhaps one of them would act as an advocate for
the poor scholar. But while her machine hummed
and purred, it didn't cough up any names. And before she could think of another direction, a soft ping
caught her attention.

Hey sweetie. It was Chris on email. *Figured you*

were in the library when you didn't answer your phone.

She smiled. He knew her habits so well. He'd probably have some ideas about how to pursue this.

I am looking into what happened with a collection, she typed. *The Stavendish*, she added.

The screen remained blank for so long, she wondered if he had gone. Or, no, she decided, he must be typing a long, involved answer. She knew she could count on him.

The reply, when it finally arrived, was a bit shorter than she had expected. *New direction for the chapter?*

No, she responded and then hesitated. Chris was no stranger to Dulcie's struggles. He had sided with her as she expanded the original idea for her dissertation and supported her in her fight for more time as she uncovered new material about her thesis subject. Recently, however, he had begun to wonder out loud if perhaps her thesis adviser was right. If, perhaps, she had a mental block against finishing her dissertation—perhaps even against leaving the university. He had sounded quite understanding when she had told him her decision to stay behind this week, saying that he thought it would be good for her to really focus. To make some progress. To admit now that she was spending her time researching something utterly unrelated to her dissertation might sound, well, like she was frittering away her time.

Not exactly, she amended her response. *But it pertains.*

These things were always easier to explain in person. Even tonight, when they spoke on the phone, would be better.

Better get back to it, she added, before he could question her further. *Love you*. And with that she closed the program.

Besides, she told herself, by the time she spoke to Chris again, she really could have some work done. Opening her notes, she once again congratulated herself on her foresight. Knowing how easy it was to lose references, she had inserted links to the appropriate files into her outline. All she really had to do was open a topic, look over her notes, and put them in order on the page.

This one, for example, would be a good place to start. *Contrast high v. low lit*, she had written. The link was to an article of the time, disparaging the '*lending library smut destined for Shop Girls and their Ilk*.' It was a great quote, and Dulcie pondered for a moment how to best set it off. Critics didn't change, she noted, and then wrote that down.

As they have through time… Well, that was regrettable. She'd fix it later. *As they have through time immemorial, critics have derided popular fiction.* There, that was better. Suddenly, inspiration struck. *Nearly a century later, the then-popular critic Ashley Stavendish would write similar words, although his own private library would prove to be just as rich in such potboilers and popular novels.*

Was that going too far? She'd have to check to see if the provenance of any of those disputed books had been proven. A few clicks and she was back in the articles about the collection. No, as far as she could tell, nothing had been decided. Well, she could ask Griddlehaus. He'd at least have a lead for her to follow. Unless…

Throwing her belongings back in her bag, she raced for the elevator. How foolish she had been. How silly to have overlooked a resource unlike any other. She was tapping her foot as she waited for the elevator, thinking up questions as she cleared the front desk and stepped out of the library's back exit. There she hesitated. Already the light was fading, the shadows lengthening. It was later than she thought, maybe too late to visit.

She dug out her phone. As it powered up, she thought of Jeremy out in this weather and wondered how he'd made it through the winter. He had to have a home somewhere, an apartment or a friend who had kept him warm and dry. And now, well, the health services wouldn't just let him go.

'Hello, health services? I'm wondering if I may speak with a patient.' Visitors might be limited to immediate family. Phone calls, certainly, wouldn't be. 'Jeremy Mumbleigh—he's on the third floor.'

There was a pause and Dulcie waited to be connected. Jeremy wouldn't be at his best on the phone. She knew that. But if he would give permission for her to visit, then…

'Hello?' The voice was familiar, but it wasn't the one she expected. 'Detective Gus Rogovoy here. How may I help you?'

'Detective Rogovoy!' Dulcie found herself unaccountably pleased. Clearly, the large detective had reached the same conclusion that she had. 'I'm so glad you're there. I knew you'd realize that Jeremy was a resource, not a suspect. But if you could put him on the phone for a minute—'

'Ms Schwartz?' The detective didn't sound surprised to hear from her. He did, however, sound tired.

'Yes,' she replied. 'I was looking into that book—'

'Dulcie.' It wasn't just the use of her first name. Something in his tone had changed, and Dulcie stopped, waiting. 'Dulcie—Ms Schwartz—stop now. Please.'

'What…' She was suddenly afraid. 'What is it?'

'Your friend. It looks like we may not be pressing charges.'

Dulcie snorted, a half laugh of relief. 'Well, I'm glad of that, Detective. I knew you'd see the light about Jeremy.'

'No, Ms Schwartz, that's not what I meant.'

She ignored the chill that was beginning to creep up her back and kept talking. 'You can't still think that he's a thief. I'm sure there was some confusion about that book. Maybe—'

'Ms Schwartz.' Louder this time. More insistent.

'Maybe he found it, or he was worried that with all the construction work, it would be damaged—'

'Dulcie!' His bark stopped her cold. 'Please, that's not what I meant. I was trying… Dulcie,' he said, his voice soft again. 'I'm afraid your friend is more seriously injured than we had originally believed. This is now an assault case. Jeremy Mumbleigh is in a coma.'

NINE

'WAIT, NO.' WHAT she had heard made no sense. 'You said he fell. That he got hurt…'

'We did.' Rogovoy's voice was back to its regular growl. 'We thought at first that he just ignored the caution tape, that he took a header into the hole—into some kind of sub-basement, over by the library. But now it's looking different, like the injuries aren't consistent with a fall. We think he had some company.'

'Jeremy? But who?' Dulcie racked her brain. 'Who would want to hurt Jeremy?'

'Could have been a mugging. Could have been another homeless person, fighting for something he had on him, or, hell, for a place to sleep. We see a lot of this, Ms Schwartz. I'm sorry that this is a guy you—'

'Wait.' The edge of an idea was tickling at Dulcie's mind. 'Which library sub-basement?'

'No way, Ms Schwartz. I gather you heard about the book we found, but I'm not having you turn this into something about literature or something.' Rogovoy's words had an edge she couldn't explain. 'This was about a homeless guy who ran into someone bad, and something happened. And, yes, we checked. None of the local shelters knew him.'

'He wouldn't have gone to a shelter.' Dulcie thought about the man she knew. He might have been poor and hungry, but she was pretty sure he considered himself a scholar, not a pauper. 'He would have seen that as beneath him.'

'That's one way of looking at it.' Rogovoy's comment was almost obscured.

'What do you mean?'

'Look, the shelters do their best. Especially in the winter, they do a ton of outreach. But not everyone wants to go to one. I mean, they have rules.'

'You mean, like lights out at a certain hour?' Jeremy would hate it if he couldn't read late into the night.

'Like no getting high, Ms Schwartz.'

'Get high? But Jeremy didn't do drugs.'

Another rumbling sigh.

'Do you have a toxicology report?' Dulcie had learned a thing or two about investigations. 'You don't, do you?'

'Ms Schwartz, I told you about Mumbleigh as a courtesy. Because you seem to consider him a friend. I probably shouldn't even have done that. Now, please, leave it to us. We see this kind of thing way too often. He had stolen property—that book you eluded to. Maybe he wanted to sell it, to score. Maybe he tried to and ran into someone who didn't want to pay. Maybe someone else had the same idea. Violence against street people is just not that rare. I'm sorry, Ms Schwartz. You're a good kid, and you think the best of everyone. That's nice. But this is a big city, and there are a lot of characters in it. Not everyone is who you think he is, Ms Schwartz. Most of us aren't at all.'

With that he signed off, leaving Dulcie at a loss.

As she stowed her phone, she looked around. She was still standing in the back of the library, in the sheltered passageway where she had encountered Jeremy not twenty-four hours before. She had chatted with the threadbare scholar here, and while he had made no more sense than usual, neither had he made any less. Now he was in a coma, another victim of the city.

She felt the tears begin to well up, and leaned back against the brick wall, letting the memories flood through her. Jeremy, his face gaunt as he rattled on about dialectics. Jeremy, earlier in the semester, lecturing a passing gaggle of freshmen on the proper care of hardcover bindings. Jeremy, most recently, muttering about a secret...

Dulcie sat up, eyes wide open. The Jeremy Mumbleigh she knew was always well groomed, not only clean but clean-shaven. If he wasn't a regular at any of the shelters around town, then he had to have a home of some sort. And knowing him as she did, it was a place where he could keep books safe.

As she started the cold walk to her own home, Dulcie had an idea. Her old room-mate Suze had been working as a legal-aid lawyer while she studied for the bar. She would have a better idea of where a poor scholar might live than Detective Rogovoy. And she wouldn't scoff at the idea of a decent man, down on his luck.

TEN

'HONEY, I'M HOME!' Dulcie called out as she entered the apartment. Esmé was nowhere to be seen, but Dulcie continued talking, desperate to cheer herself up. 'What? No welcome? Does somebody not want dinner?'

'Meh.' The tuxedo cat appeared at that final word and brushed against Dulcie's leg, before Dulcie scooped her up for a hug.

'Sorry, kitty,' she said as the little cat squirmed. 'But you're the only one here to greet me, and I've had a rough day.' Esmé, like Mr Grey, seemed perfectly capable of understanding her—and communicating when she wanted—but right now, all Dulcie wanted was the warm, soft animal contact, a fact the little feline seemed to recognize as she relaxed and began to purr. 'The police have the wrong idea about Jeremy,' she murmured into her pet's lush black fur. 'They think he's just another homeless guy, an easy victim. I've got an idea of how to help him, but...' She paused, the words hard to form. 'I didn't get any of my work done.'

It was easier to confess this to the cat than it would be to Chris. Still, Esmé must have disapproved, because just then she twisted her way out of Dulcie's grasp and scampered off to the kitchen.

'I know, I should be working, Esmé.' Dulcie hung up her coat and then made her own way into the kitchen. 'But the police are being so frustrating, and yes, I should feed you, too.'

'*Wrong idea?*' The face that looked up at Dulcie looked quizzical, partly because of the off-center white blaze on the velvety nose. Partly, however, there had been a question in the wisp of a thought that had whispered in Dulcie's ear.

'Yeah, I think so.' Dulcie felt compelled to acknowledge her own uncertainty as she reached into the cabinet for the cat's dish and a can of Fancy Feast. 'They think that this was just some random attack. That Jeremy was just another homeless guy who got mugged or got into a fight.' She didn't even want to voice the possibility Rogovoy had suggested—that the poor scholar had been looking for a safe place to get high.

'Also, they're saying he stole a book.' She emptied the soft mash into the dish and found herself staring at it. 'But Griddlehaus says that the book has been missing for years. So I don't know why they even say he stole it. It might be that he *found* the book. After all,' she paused, as the ideas formed in her head, 'he would have recognized it. It was part of the bequest that he identified—part of the bequest that was his undoing.'

She stopped to consider. It was possible, she had to admit, that Jeremy would have mixed feelings about the collection. He hadn't wanted the university to break it up. He had lost his fellowship because of it—and maybe his peace of mind. That could have

left him feeling a little resentful. Or maybe that he
had a certain claim on it. Maybe he saw the volume
as his by right—or as some sort of compensation.

She would talk to Suze about that, too. In the
clinic, her friend had to deal with lots of clients who
had various mental illnesses. She might have some
insight into how a man who had been wronged and
then been cast out might think. Approaching the
problem from the other side, Dulcie realized, might
also pay off—and in that case Griddlehaus might
also have some ideas. Dulcie had become so caught
up in the drama of Jeremy's life that she had failed
to find out how his quest had ended. He had lost his
battle, but had the university then gone on to break
up the collection or had it relented? Had parts of
the bequest been sold off or—she shuddered at the
thought—pulped?

Perhaps there had been feedback from other
sources. Once Jeremy had identified the donor, it
seemed likely that there would be family members or
other heirs who might have a vested interest in what
happened. Maybe one of them had complained—or
retrieved the unwanted part of the collection. Had
they been informed that this particular volume—a
bit of nineteenth-century fluff—had gone missing
all those years before? Had they been informed that
it had been recovered?

Dulcie imagined how the university would present it: a thief, caught red-handed, a valuable volume
hidden beneath his coat. A deranged homeless man,
an inevitable victim of his violent milieu.

'But maybe that wasn't what happened,' she said,

watching the cat eat. 'Jeremy had championed the collection once before. Maybe he did so again.'

Reaching for her own bowl, Dulcie poured out some cereal while playing with another possibility, one she would only dare try out on the cat. 'Esmé, what if Jeremy wasn't a bad guy at all?'

The cat paused in her own dinner to look up at her person.

'Because what do we know?' Dulcie didn't seem to notice the clear-eyed gaze as she poured the milk and took her own seat at the breakfast table. 'Maybe Jeremy didn't steal the book—maybe he had nothing to do with the break-ins on campus. Maybe he found that book, down where they were excavating by the library.'

Dulcie mulled this over as she began to eat, spooning up the cereal without tasting it. 'Jeremy would have recognized the book, I bet. He would at least have seen that it was a valuable volume—one that shouldn't have been left someplace that could flood or where the rain could get in. In which case, Jeremy wasn't a failed robber, a thief who was injured while trying to make off with a valuable prize. Doesn't it make much more sense that he once again endangered his life trying to save a book?

'Esmé.' Dulcie put down her spoon to stare straight into those round green eyes. 'If I'm right, then I think it is entirely possible that Jeremy Mumbleigh is a hero.'

ELEVEN

'DULCIE, I DON'T think you should be involved in this.' Suze sounded stern. Dulcie knew her friend worked long hours at the legal clinic across town, but still...'Let it be.'

'I can't, Suze.' Dulcie tucked her feet under her. After that rather unsatisfying bowl of Cheerios, she had heated some leftover noodles for dessert, and the combination had left her feeling both sleepy and full by the time she called her former room-mate. Now she struggled to get comfortable. 'He's in health services—in a coma—and the cops aren't doing anything about it.'

'Wait, I thought you said they were investigating?' Dulcie could hear the sounds of Suze preparing her own dinner, the clank of cutlery making her regret her own slapdash meal and—almost—her decision to call. 'That they're considering this an assault?'

'Well, yeah.' Dulcie backtracked, thinking hard. She had been hoping for answers, not questions. 'But they think it was just some homeless thing. Plus, they think he stole the book they found on him.'

'And, it was library property, right?' The sound of running water. Dulcie envisioned pasta. 'And he had no explanation.'

'He was unconscious. And when he wasn't, he

wasn't making much sense.' It sounded bad, even to her. 'You remember Jeremy—Mumbles, right?'

'I'm sorry, Dulcie, I don't.' Suze had spent most of her last few years at university in the law school library. 'But Dulcie? I think maybe you should stay out of this and let the system work. You've got a big heart, but this one might just be beyond you.' Voices in the background: Suze's boyfriend had come home. 'I've got to run, Dulce. But give me the quick update. How's your dissertation going?'

By the time Chris called, Dulcie was too disheartened to put on a brave face.

'I don't want to talk about my dissertation, Chris,' she said, lying on the sofa. 'Poor Jeremy is in a coma. They think he was attacked—that it might have been some homeless thing.'

'Oh, Dulcie.' Chris's concern helped, and she started to sit up. 'I knew you shouldn't be hanging around him.'

'Chris, that's not the point...' The conversation didn't get better. Although it ended with Chris offering to come back early—or to buy a ticket for her on the first bus down tomorrow—everything her boyfriend said seemed to make her feel worse. If he wasn't stressing Jeremy's mental health—or lack thereof—he was reminding her of how she had relied on Detective Rogovoy in the past.

'He's not, you know, some ogre,' Chris said, his rational approach only making her feel worse. 'And he does know what he's doing.'

'He doesn't know the history, Chris.' Dulcie had managed to explain something about the Stavendish bequest, and about Jeremy's campaign to save the books. Only her boyfriend had seen that as evidence of the man's decline, rather than vice versa. 'And you don't know what those books are worth.'

'Dulcie, can you hear yourself?' Chris's voice was soft. 'I'm sorry I left you there alone. You're under so much pressure. Do you think you can get some sleep? I'm worried about you.'

'You don't have to worry about me.' Dulcie tried to rally, if for no other reason than to reassure her boyfriend. 'I've got Esmé and Mr Grey to keep me company. Besides, I'm going to get this dissertation written. I am.'

'I know you are, Dulcie.' Dulcie could hear Chris's mother calling his name. 'Look, hug Esmé for me, will you?'

'Of course I will,' she said. But the little feline had made herself scarce. Dulcie had rarely felt more alone.

TWELVE

THESE WORDS COULD prove her downfall. Such a stern Fate held her Pen hostage for a breath, as she paused to consider such an outcome. These selfsame lines that she had once dash'd across the paper and now labored o'er by candlelight to posit such a Theory, such a Life, did now prove as slipp'ry as the Knife, wet with Blood, that had held her Hostage. From her own hands, these lines could prove Traitor, were they to be revealed...

'DON'T YOU HAVE a paper to write or something?' It was the hour. It had to be. Dulcie had woken from her dream with a sense of dread and an idea—and had decided that action was better than more sleep. That had gotten her out of bed and prompted her to call on Detective Rogovoy bright and early. Only the gruff detective, as she was finding, was not in the brightest of moods this morning. At least, not yet.

The only logical deduction, Dulcie had decided, was that she hadn't properly explained herself to the grumpy detective. 'I do, and I will,' she said, to answer his rather abrupt question. 'But I'd like to see the book that was found with Jeremy Mumbleigh.' She repeated what she'd said as soon as she reached him. 'I may be able to explain a little about its provenance.'

She couldn't hear his response, partly because he had ducked down, covering his face with one over-sized hand. When he looked back up at her, however, he was smiling slightly, his eyes warm and kind.

'It's provenance?'

'Yes, it's history. Where it comes from.' She couldn't believe he was unaware of the term. 'I have reason to believe that this particular book may have a long history with Jeremy Mumbleigh, or maybe vice versa.' She paused to figure this one out. 'Anyway, I think the reason he had it has to do with when he was a grad student.'

'Oh?' One eyebrow arched up, and Dulcie launched into her theory, only stopping when she noticed that those big shoulders were bumping up and down as the detective chuckled.

'Ms Schwartz, what would I do without you?' As Dulcie finished she realized Rogovoy was openly smiling, his eyes nearly hidden inside the folds of his face. 'My life would be so dull.'

'You're teasing me.' Dulcie couldn't help but feel a bit put out. 'But I believe it might be relevant. A man has been attacked. Gravely injured. So if I could just—'

Rogovoy raised a big hand, stopping her before she could continue. 'I'm sorry, Ms Schwartz. I should have told you earlier, only you were so intent on explaining it all to me.'

'What?' Dulcie heard the sharp note in her tone, but it couldn't be helped. 'Are you going to say you no longer have it?'

'No, I wouldn't dare.' The big man had the audac-

ity to chuckle again. 'But it is evidence and until all
the paperwork is filed—' She had started to protest,
but he kept talking over her. 'Until all the paperwork is
filed, I'm not going to mess around with it. Lieutenant
Wardley is heading the task force, and recovering stolen property is his bailiwick. I'm sorry, Ms Schwartz.
You'll be able to see it soon enough.'

'Evidence.' She shook her head sadly. 'So you still
think Jeremy stole it?'

'It was found on him.' Rogovoy sounded just as
sad. 'And whatever you may think—however it got
there—it is university property.'

It wasn't as if Dulcie didn't have any recourse. As a
university scholar, she knew she had options. It was
that she simply couldn't think of how to access them,
just then. And so she had let the big detective escort
her out of his office, and had even let him put that
large, flat palm on her back as he guided her through
the overheated modern building and into the glassed-
in foyer that could have served as an airlock for some
kind of time machine. It wasn't until she stepped out
through the second of the glass doors and back into
what passed for spring in New England that she realized she was missing an essential piece of information. A piece of information that could be more
important than Rogovoy knew. She had to find out
where, exactly, Jeremy and the book had been found.

She turned to re-enter. She could still see the
hulking detective, who had paused to chat with a
colleague inside the reception area—another big
man, the one with the buzz cut.

She reached for the handle, and as she did she caught her reflection in the glass. She was short, she knew that—in the mirror Dulcie barely came up to Rogovoy's armpit, even though he was nearly a room away. Her red curls would have given her another inch of height, probably, had they not been squashed down by her knit hat, and in her winter parka she looked a bit wider than usual. All in all, not an authoritative figure. Not a person who could demand information, not once she had been told to let it go. Had been, in effect, dismissed.

She let her hand fall from the door as she backed on to the sidewalk. The wind, which had been almost non-existent as she'd walked into the Square twenty minutes earlier, was picking up, and she pulled her collar up in a vain attempt to keep it out.

'*Because it can sneak in...*' The voice was so soft, she thought at first it was her own thought spoken aloud. Only she hadn't been thinking about the wind exactly. '*Because you don't notice it, until it has made itself heard...*'

'Mr Grey?' Still holding her collar shut, Dulcie found herself standing straighter. 'Are you saying you could slip in—or I could?'

A low rumble. The sound of a far-off motor scooter, or perhaps a purr. '*Now, Dulcie, we are not mice, to slip off into holes. But just because we are not lions either...*'

'I get it, Mr Grey,' said Dulcie, a new spirit in her voice. And she did.

'I'm looking for Mr Griddlehaus?' Twenty minutes later, Dulcie was back in the library, seeking her friend. A sign by the elevator informed her that Mildon was still closed. 'Is he around?'

'Try the lab,' said the bored first year who was manning the desk. 'You know where that is, right?'

'Of course.' While the details of paper restoration were not her forte, Dulcie had an antiquarian's appreciation of the work that was done in the university's conservation lab, across the campus. In the ultramodern building, adjacent to the Science Center, some of the top experts in the world labored, piecing together and repairing works on paper, parchment, and even older media once thought utterly beyond help.

It made perfect sense that Griddlehaus, still exiled from his usual domain, would go to ground there. Dulcie tried not to think of a mouse—her interaction with Mr Grey made her feel it was a bit disrespectful—but as she made her way across the Yard, she couldn't help but mull over the similarity. Besides, maybe that was what Mr Grey had meant about sneaking in. Not only should the slight librarian be able to fill her in on what had happened with the Stavendish collection, he would probably be able to locate the hole where Jeremy had been injured as well.

Excited by the thought, she ran the last few yards across the open plaza, letting the wind propel her to the door.

'Dulcie Schwartz.' She identified herself to the grey-haired woman who answered her knock. She seemed surprised to have a visitor, but her smile was warm when Dulcie introduced herself. 'I'm looking for Thomas Griddlehaus?'

'Margaret Constantine,' the older woman said, holding the heavy door open. 'Please, come in.'

'Ms Schwartz!' The bespectacled librarian blinked up at her once she found him. 'I see you've met our top conservator. Have you come to see our latest?'

'Well, actually...' Dulcie paused. She didn't want to be rude. Plus, she was intrigued. 'I would love to see what you're working on.'

'Please, come this way.' The woman in the spotless lab coat gestured for her to join them by the light table where she sat on a high stool. Taking the magnifying lens that the conservator offered, Dulcie peered down. The gentle light illuminated what looked for all the world like a chewed-up piece of tree bark, roughly hewn and still attached to a chunk of wood.

'This is our prize,' said the conservator, her voice as soft as the pearl grey of her bun.

'Ms Constantine is bringing it back,' Griddlehaus added, his voice reverential.

'Wonderful,' Dulcie responded dutifully. Closer up, she could make out that the tree bark was most likely leather, the cover of what seemed to be a pile of pulp. 'What is it?'

Griddlehaus looked more startled than usual. '*He Could Not Tell Her*, of course,' he said. 'I assumed this was what you came for.'

'No, I—' She caught herself. 'Wait, is this the volume that was found on Jeremy Mumbleigh?' She looked down at the torn leather again, battered almost beyond recognition. If he had been responsible for this, he wasn't the man she had thought he was. 'I thought that was still in evidence?'

'As far as I know, it is.' Griddlehaus reached out as if to touch the cover, stopping himself before his bare skin made contact. 'But, of course, it had to be stabilized first. Now, if we could only find the second volume. I don't know why it wasn't sent for re-binding when this volume was first worked on, or why a complete re-binding wasn't done.'

Dulcie's face must have shown her confusion. The conservator took the magnifying glass back and began to explain.

'I'm afraid we've been lax in our care,' she said, as she pointed out where the binding had nearly rotted away. 'As you can see, there's significant worm damage to the upper edge here, and I'm afraid a little moisture was also introduced at some point.'

'I'm sorry.' Dulcie was. To see a book in this state, nearly unreadable, was horrible. 'This weather can't have been good for it, either.'

'Ideally, this volume will never have to suffer the New England climate again.' Griddlehaus chuckled. 'It's never going outside again. At least, not in our lifetime.'

Dulcie looked up, confused. 'But isn't it going back to the library?'

'We transport most materials through the tunnels,' Margaret, the conservator, explained. 'And this one may not go back to the library. At least, not immediately. The police are insisting that they want it once we're done with it. I gather it has some forensic value to this Lieutenant Wardley? We are hoping to convince them otherwise, of course. We don't know how

they plan to store the piece, and we do want to mini-
mize further damage.'

'Of course,' said Dulcie. She knew about the subterranean tunnels that connected most of the Yard.
She simply hadn't thought about their practical appli-
cation. 'Is the rest of the collection in similar shape?'

'Some pieces are.' Griddlehaus was shaking his
head. 'This is far from the worst, I'm afraid, though
I fear its treatment may have been a sign of how little
it was valued. Unforgivable, really.'

'Mr Griddlehaus.' She paused, wondering how
to phrase her questions. 'Whatever happened to the
rest of the Stavendish bequest? You know, the books
that the library wanted to deaccession?'

'Ah, yes.' He nodded, but his small, round face
took on a thoughtful look. 'You know, Dulcie, I'm
not sure it *was* resolved. After all the brouhaha and
the fighting, I think that everyone just wanted to forget about it for a while. Why?'

'Well, I was wondering about where Jeremy was
found,' Dulcie explained. 'If, perhaps, he stumbled
upon something, with the repair work and all.'

Griddlehaus shook his head, clearly not compre-
hending.

'I just don't think…' Dulcie bit her lip. 'He isn't—
he wasn't the type to steal. Not a book,' she said.
'And so I was wondering if he found it, lost or mis-
laid, when he fell. Perhaps the excavation opened
up some place that people had forgotten about. Do
you know?'

Her friend was still shaking his head, his pale face
sad. 'I'm sorry, Ms Schwartz. I know you want to

think well of Mr Mumbleigh and, well, I know that we haven't been the best caretakers—this poor sample makes that clear—but I'm afraid that's not likely.'

'But why?' Dulcie waited.

'When the officers asked me to identify the book, they had it still wrapped in Mr Mumbleigh's overcoat, which was sopping wet and covered in mud. I was told he'd been pulled out of a part of a sub-basement storage room where the pipes had burst—and where they'd been leaking for months, perhaps years—part of that same leak that drove us out yesterday, I believe. The entire substructure had given way. The surrounding excavation could have fallen in, really. It was quite dangerous.'

Dulcie waited. Clearly there was more.

'But the damage to this volume is only to the binding, Ms Schwartz. The inside, as you can see, is in quite good shape. Very fine, I would say, if I were to put it on the market. Perhaps better. No worm damage. Very little foxing. It couldn't have been kept in that storage space. I can't begin to guess where this volume has spent the last twenty-five years, and I know it needs work—professional work. But the repair work Ms Constantine is doing now is relatively minor compared to that necessary to some of the works we see. I can tell you that whoever has had it all these years has kept it as befitting a true treasure.'

THIRTEEN

'HOW STRANGE,' DULCIE said to herself, not for the first time that day. 'How utterly odd. And, really, how sad.'

Her visit with Griddlehaus had been interesting, but ultimately she had left the conservation lab with more questions than answers. Jeremy Mumbleigh was as much of a mystery as the book he had shielded, and now, more than ever, she regretted not spending more time speaking to him. Even before that last interaction, in the library entranceway, there had been the afternoon she had run into him behind Canaday, the freshman dorm that was now being excavated. Or had it been Weld? She was walking by Canaday as she tried to remember. Both were red brick, which he did like to scratch at, engraving the soft surface with his meandering verse, and both had provided a chance for conversation as well, their walls offering a bit of shelter from the winter winds. Yes, she remembered chatting with the scruffy scholar over by that wall. Even then, she had noticed how thin his wrists were, how gaunt his face.

All the missed opportunities—not only for conversation, but for simple kindness. If only she had reached out to him, even once…

''Scuse me,' a gruff voice called. 'Miss?'

She looked up. A large man wearing a hard hat was waving. Unsure, she smiled and waved back.

'Miss? You can't be here.' A look of alarm blanched his face. 'Miss!'

Dulcie stopped, wondering what could be wrong. He was pointing, and she looked—to see a large gaping hole about a foot ahead of her.

'Oh!' She stopped short, then looked up at the man on the other side of what was really quite a considerable pit. 'Thank you.'

He muttered something she couldn't catch as she made her way around the hole. Whatever it was, she suspected it wasn't complimentary, and emboldened by her regrets about Jeremy, she decided to speak out.

'This is a hazard, you know.' Circumnavigating the pit, she made her way up to the construction worker. 'This should be roped off, or marked in some way.'

'Yeah, we know.' He was big—bigger than Detective Rogovoy—and Dulcie suspected that he had been surprised by her approach. His face, which was as white and full as the moon, was turned away.

'Sir? Are you going to do anything about it?' Dulcie pressed her advantage. He might be large, but she was determined. 'Are you?'

'May I help you?' She turned toward the new voice: a lanky man in a parka and khakis.

'Yes, I wanted to know why this hasn't been…' Dulcie stopped as the pieces came together in her head. 'You're Stuart Truckworth, aren't you? The head of facilities and maintenance?'

He nodded. 'Yes, and you are in a dangerous area. If you'll please—'

Dulcie didn't let him finish. 'This is where the accident happened, isn't it? Where someone was arrested?'

'I don't know anything about that, Miss.' The face, pale and drawn, was difficult to read. 'What I do know is that this area isn't safe. It's a hard hat area only.'

'Then it should be marked.' Dulcie was quite ready to act affronted, especially if it got her some answers. 'And I can see that this excavation runs from the freshman dorm up toward the library.'

'You can see that, but you can't see the sign?' There was no sign of any smile, so Dulcie had to assume he was serious.

'What? No.' He was pointing, and she turned around. Sure enough, about twenty feet behind her, a series of orange traffic cones crossed the main walkway, which was blocked by what was apparently the back of a large sign, attached to a sawhorse. 'Oh, that. Well, shouldn't you have tape up, or something?'

'It was torn down, Miss. There was an incident.' The moon-faced construction worker had stepped up. He put his arm out, as if to escort her—or to block her from walking farther. 'We only just got the OK to go back to work, so if you please…' He nodded to Truckworth. 'Sorry, boss.'

'So this is the place!' Dulcie ducked around his arm. 'I need to get a sense of it.' Two steps, and she stopped. Now she could see why the big construc-

tion worker had had a look of panic on his face. She
had been very close to the edge. And she could see
why a fall would be a very bad thing.

Where she was walking had been an old paved
path, its asphalt cracked and crumbling after a winter of frost heaves and pot holes. Avoiding those,
she had stepped off the path on to a dusty crust that
looked more like coffee grounds than something
where grass would ever grow, but as she looked
over the edge of the hole once more, she could see
the bare white roots of some shrub or distant tree,
like the remnants of a torn cloth. And she was grateful for even that support. As she leaned forward, a
few small clods broke from those reaching roots.
Dulcie watched them fall—at least twenty feet, she
guessed—to what appeared to be a concrete block
below. As they did, something down there moved.
A larger clod of earth, perhaps, or…

'Please, Miss.' A hand on her arm startled her.
It was the round-faced construction worker, and he
was holding her firmly. 'Take a step back now, Miss.'

'Wait.' She put her hand on his, not that she could
have pried his fingers loose. 'What is that?' From
her vantage point, it looked like the top of a box. Or
a crypt. 'Was someone buried here?'

'No, ma'am.' He was pulling on her arm, urging
her back. 'Just part of the infrastructure.'

'It doesn't look like pipes.' Dulcie wasn't ordi-
narily afraid of heights, but this drop had startled
her. Now that she was trying to figure it out, however, she found herself leaning over. What had been

moving down there? Had it been an animal? Could
it have been…

'It's the old tunnels, ma'am. The storage area is all
connected to the tunnels.' He was edging in front of
her, moving her back. 'You heard we had flooding.
Well, this is how the water traveled.'

'The tunnels?' She looked up at him, curious. 'I
don't understand,' she said, as she turned to keep
herself from stumbling. 'I thought the tunnels were
in good shape.' That conservator—Margaret Constantine—had referred to them as a safer alternative
to outdoor travel.

'Who told you that?' He shook his head. 'These
haven't been used since they updated the HVAC systems, maybe thirty years ago.'

Of course. Dulcie remembered. What she was
looking down on weren't the communication tunnels,
used to cart books away from the weather, but the
steam tunnels, the ancient and somewhat primitive
heating system that had long ago been abandoned
for more efficient means. What she hadn't known
was that those particular passages still existed, when
clearly they were vulnerable to water and wear.

Looking down into the excavation, Dulcie realized the scope of the problem. 'The entire Yard must
be riddled with tunnels,' she said out loud. Really,
it was a wonder that every building didn't collapse.
'How typical,' she clucked to herself. 'Rather than
remove them, the university probably simply closed
a door and forgot about them.'

She walked away, the sound of a jackhammer
roaring up behind her, and another question rose

in her mind. If Jeremy hadn't fallen, as she'd first thought, what had he been doing down there? No matter what Rogovoy might say, the threadbare scholar had had enough sense not to seek shelter in a flooded old tunnel.

BLOCKED FROM HER usual path, Dulcie found herself walking around the long way. At least it gave her time to think. Someone had to, she reasoned, because clearly the police had not.

She could see why, at first, everyone had thought Jeremy had been the victim of a horrible accident. Like her, he might have strayed from the path, taking the familiar short cut around the big stone building. Unlike her, he had not been stopped. That alone could have explained the fall down to the concrete flooring below, and the injuries that had laid him low. But to think that he'd been attacked…been thrown down into…

Into what? Dulcie couldn't tell if the hole she had nearly stepped in had been part of the original repair plans, or if it was simply a sinkhole that had opened up as a result of the work and the vagaries of the weather. She did know that it didn't offer what anyone would call shelter. Although she still couldn't explain how he had come by that book, Dulcie knew one thing: Jeremy Mumbleigh hadn't been injured fighting over this particular excavation.

'MS SCHWARTZ?' SHE was standing at the front desk of the library, her ID in her hand, when the question broke into her reverie. The lanky, red-haired guard

looking at her had scrunched his pale eyebrows together in concern. 'Are you all right, Ms Schwartz?'

'Yes, thanks, Kyle. And, please, call me Dulcie.'
She looked up at the new guard, wishing she knew
his last name. She'd been thinking of Jeremy—and
of that hole—even as she had made her way into
the library. 'I was just thinking about all the work
they're doing.'

'You and everybody else,' he grumbled. 'You
don't know what a pain it's been.'

'I believe it.' She smiled in sympathy. 'I gather
the old steam tunnels are totally falling apart.' She
pocketed her ID. It was time to get to work, to really focus on what she came in for, but if the skinny
guard had some insight…

'It's not just the steam tunnels,' said Kyle, his
voice growing tetchy. 'The place is going to be a
mess for months.'

'I'm sorry.' She sympathized, waiting to hear
more.

He seemed to want to talk. 'They're happy enough
to keep the book tunnels open. To send me down
there when someone needs something. But do they
ever stop to think about what's going on down
there? Or how vulnerable they make everything?'
He seemed to be talking to himself as much as to
her. 'There was supposed to be a plan. Something
about using the tunnels in case of an emergency—
they had people down there, measuring and everything. I don't know. If there's a bomb, I wouldn't
want to be underneath a couple of tons of brick and
stone, would you?'

'There'd be all the books, too,' said Dulcie. To her, the image was vaguely comforting. Kyle looked so discomfited by the idea, however, that she changed the subject. 'Do you know when the Mildon is supposed to reopen?'

He didn't seem any happier as he shook his head. 'Honestly? They don't tell me anything. But from what I hear, every room in the substrata is being evaluated. And if it's not water damage, then it's rats.'

Now it was her turn to shudder. Rats. The idea of rodents—of unauthorized visitors of any kind—in Griddlehaus's preserve was incomprehensible. The Mildon had a state-of-the-art air-filtration system. A fire prevention plan that involved the replacement of the usual atmosphere with fire suppressants, and an impermeable gate that could stop a tank from getting in. Surely, such a pristine environment was not connected to those outdated tunnels.

As she made her way down to her carrel, Dulcie couldn't help but wonder. Most likely, she decided, Kyle was wrong about the library's vulnerability— the noise and the mess had been wearing on them all. He was, after all, only a guard and a disgruntled one at that, not one of the elite cadre of clerks and scholars who actually ran the library. If anything, he might be misguided—the Mildon might be adjacent to some vents or plumbing fixtures, but it had its own security and ventilation systems. Its alarms hadn't gone off when the water main had broken, and its lights had stayed on.

The rats, however. They were a different problem, and Dulcie consoled herself with the thought

of her spectral guardian. Mr Grey might no longer
be a feline in the flesh, but he would protect her
against rats, wouldn't he? At the very least, he would
warn her.

With that, Dulcie put aside thoughts of vermin and
opened her laptop. She wasn't giving up on Jeremy—
far from it. But until she came up with a new line of
inquiry, she should get some of her own work done.
With a twinge of guilt, she let herself click on to one
of her favorite documents—a detailed analysis of a
fragment that had never, as far as she knew, been
studied before. This might not be life-saving work,
but it was thrilling. Payback for the hours she had
spent, identifying the torn fragments and painstakingly piecing them together, word by word, from
burned and damaged papers.

It helped that the scene she had re-created was
exciting. In it, the heroine finds a body—the body
of a man who may have been her lover or something less benign. He is lying, dead, in the library
of a stately house, his head crushed by a piece of
statuary. Brushing aside thoughts of Jeremy—his
head had not been crushed, he was still alive, even
if not yet conscious—she made herself focus. First,
there was the ambivalent relationship of the heroine
to the victim. Was he her hero? Her tormentor? Had
she been the one to attack? Although Dulcie identified with the heroine of the novel—it seemed clear
to her that the heroine was a stand-in for the anonymous author—she could not rule out the possibility
that she had been the one to *cave in that fine phy-
sique...dashing out his Life with all the encumbent*

Fears and Glories.' No more could she dismiss the idea that the author had been playing on the usage of 'dashing,' which had acquired its current usage around 1697.

Whether the protagonist was also a murderer was, of course, not particularly relevant to her dissertation. If anything, the idea of an anti-hero—an anti-heroine, to be specific—would make the work even more notable. A female picaresque in the tradition of Moll Flanders. Still, Dulcie had felt validated when she had uncovered a reference to a secret door in the library. For starters, it firmly placed the work in the canon of her author, not only for its Gothic overtones but for its resemblance to an English 'priest hole,' a fixture of noble houses that had remained adherents to the 'true faith' during the period of religious upheaval brought about by Henry VIII. American authors were more likely to reference the old world's monolithic traditions, its hierarchies and birth lines, than to incorporate a reference to one of the great splits in the upper classes.

On a more personal level, Dulcie had been gratified to see the possible resolution of what she had begun to think of as a locked-room mystery. If the hidden door led to some outside passage, then it became more likely that the protagonist wasn't the killer. Though if the door simply led to a bolt hole, then the possibility that she would soon encounter the murderer made for an exciting alternative. Although, at the insistence of both her thesis adviser and her better instincts, Dulcie had almost entirely given up her work searching for additional fragments

of the book, she had promised herself that as soon
as her dissertation was submitted, she would allow
herself at least a few more weeks in the Mildon.
Surely among the scraps and fragments, she could
find a bit more of the story that had so captured her
imagination.

An examination of the text, she began to type, *offers several clues about its author's identity. There is, for example, the 'Beam of Light so narrow as to first escape her Notice,' that reveals the edge of a concealed door or hiding place...*

Forty minutes later, she had her thoughts mapped
out. She also had a cramp in her foot from the way
she'd been sitting, and a crick in her neck as well.
While she had spent a good portion of her graduate
career down here in the library, Dulcie usually wrote
in her office or at home. Now, stretching until her
joints popped, she remembered why. These molded
plastic chairs weren't made for long-term work, at
least not for a body like hers.

She stood and stretched again and looked around.
The library hummed like a living creature, but despite her earlier fears there were no other vital beings in sight. Not even, she noted with a touch of
melancholy, any sign of anything that might not be
qualified as alive.

'Mr Grey?' Maybe it was the idea of the beam
of light, or a secret passage. Maybe she was simply
lonely. 'What do you think of all of this—of what
happened with Jeremy?'

It wasn't just the air-filtration system. Dulcie definitely heard a rise and fall in the rumble, the natural rhythm of a purr.

'*Remembering...*' The susurrus of the sounds around her seemed to form a word. '*Memory...*' No, she definitely heard that—and the familiar voice filled her with warmth. '*So many ways we can slip into the past,*' the voice said. '*So many ways we still may sidle inside a life...*'

'You aren't talking about yourself, are you, Mr Grey?' Dulcie had to smile. As if she could forget the long-haired cat who had—no, who still—meant so much to her. 'You must be talking about Jeremy, right?'

'*And just as easily, slip away...*' The voice faded as, somewhere, deep inside the building, a machine changed gears. The low rumble clicked over; another tone began. And Dulcie was once again indisputably alone.

FOURTEEN

DRIVEN BY LONELINESS as much as hunger, Dulcie surfaced about an hour later—and found that the world as she knew it had changed.

Gone was the reverential quiet of the massive library's main lobby. Gone the peaceful order of academia. In its place was a hum of activity that would have been too much even during final exams. And the men and women who were tramping over the polished marble floors? Most of them were wearing uniforms.

'What happened?' Dulcie asked when she found her friend Ruby. 'Did somebody get hurt?'

After her own near mishap, Dulcie imagined the worst. The floor had given way, she assumed. The periodicals room no longer existed, replaced instead by a gaping, water-filled hole.

The truth, when Ruby managed to pull her aside to whisper, in awed tones, was worse.

'There was a break-in.' Ruby's voice, even hushed, was louder than most people's and Dulcie noticed the sharp look two uniformed police shot their way.

Ruby did, too, and dragged her friend over toward the counter where her old-fashioned date stamp lay. There she leaned over Dulcie, her eyes wide, her voice a breathy rasp. 'We were breached!'

'In broad daylight?' Dulcie glanced over to the main entrance. Sure enough, the weak spring sunshine was still streaming in, illuminating the puddles on the building's stone steps.

Ruby nodded. 'They came in through the—you know.' She was pointing down at the floor.

'Through the plumbing?' Dulcie remembered her fears of rats and found her imagination running wild. Not rats—demons—digging up through some infernal depths.

'They came through the tunnels.' Dulcie turned. Kyle had come up behind her. His freckled face was even paler than usual, and he was sweating. 'They must have been burrowing through the walls for days, the police said. And about an hour ago, they broke through.'

'What…' Dulcie was hesitant to even ask. The library housed such treasures. There were the ancient Phoenician papyri. A Shakespeare quarto. Works of such scholarly value that they could never be replaced. 'What did they take?'

Ruby shook her head. From the horror on her face, it was clear she was having similar thoughts. 'If a private collector…' She didn't have to finish. Once a priceless piece disappeared into the vault or private gallery of a Russian oil tycoon or some South American robber baron, it was likely to be lost, for all intents and purposes. Even with the university's resources, she knew, only about two-thirds of stolen works were ever recovered. Global scholarship would be the poorer.

'Whoever did this must have been working on

commission.' Dulcie's mind was racing. 'Someone wanted something—the Shakespeare. Or the Beowulf...'

'Maybe they didn't get anything,' said Ruby. 'Judy—one of our new clerks—heard a noise. A loud pop, she said. With all the problems with the pipes, she was worried. She went to make sure we weren't having another flood, and that's when she saw the lights—a flashlight, she said, or maybe two. And she had enough of her wits about her to pull the alarm.'

Dulcie shook her head, puzzled. She'd been involved in her work, but not that involved.

'The alarm's silent.' Kyle explained. The incident seemed to have energized him. 'It goes straight to the university police. It's a safety thing.'

Ruby nodded in agreement. 'They sure got here fast. I guess they've been on high alert.'

'Ladies,' a uniformed officer interrupted. 'Sir, would you come this way?'

'Sure.' Dulcie was curious. 'Are you going to tell us what's happening?'

The cop raised his eyebrows, which were quite impressive, and Dulcie couldn't help wondering if he did it for effect. 'We'd like to ask you some questions, if that's convenient.'

'Oh, of course.' Dulcie tried to hide her disappointment as she let herself be herded over to a table by the administrative offices. There, the big cop—the one with the hair like a stiff, grey brush—took down her name and university ID number. She'd hoped that Detective Rogovoy would be the person taking her information. Then she'd remembered the task force.

Still, she thought, this might be useful. At the very least, it would prove that Jeremy Mumbleigh could not have been involved in the break-ins.

'So, Ms Schwartz?' The big man's voice wasn't quite as gruff as Rogovoy's, but it had a similar weight. A cop voice, Dulcie figured. 'Can you tell me when you came to the library today?'

'Can and will.' She smiled a little and reminded herself that language was always changing. This officer most likely had other skills, though she doubted Detective Rogovoy would make such an error. 'I've been down in my carrel for approximately an hour—'

'You have a carrel here?' He stopped writing to stare at her. His eyes, she couldn't help thinking, were rather small under bushy brows.

'Yes, I'm a grad student. This is where I do much of my research.'

'On which floor, please?' He pulled over a map of the library, as if to check Dulcie's answer.

'Level three.' As Dulcie pointed it out on the map, she began to wonder about the man's intelligence. 'Where it's marked "research stations".'

'Did anyone see you working down there?' He started scribbling again, shielding the page with one hand as he wrote.

'No, it's been deserted.' Dulcie tried to see what he was writing. 'It's spring break.'

'But you're here.' He looked up, those small eyes dark and piercing.

'Yes, I'm working.' Dulcie had had enough. This man might be the head of the task force, but he clearly didn't understand scholarship. 'I'm here just about every day, and a lot of people here—Ruby Jaleo, Thomas Griddlehaus, the new guy Kyle— know me. This is as much my work place as…as… well as the Garden Street headquarters are yours.'

It was a weak ending, but it was the best she could do. Unless: 'Just ask Detective Rogovoy about me.' She looked around in vain. 'He knows me. He knows that I'm working on my dissertation.'

'I'm sure he does, but there's no need.' His tone had softened now. The pressure of the job. 'I have to find out where everyone was in order for us to fig- ure out what exactly happened.'

'What do you mean, what happened?' Dulcie turned back toward the big cop. This was her chance to get some information. 'Can't you ask them?'

The eyebrows came down, a deep furrow between them.

'You didn't catch the burglars.' Dulcie heard her own voice go soft with disbelief. 'They got away. Well, the alarm…' She stopped. The alarm had been silent. 'They must have known. Maybe they saw the woman who tripped the alarm?' Her mind was work- ing fast. 'Or maybe they broke through in the wrong place?'

'Look, I just need your info, and then I can let you go.' The big cop went back to his form, and Dulcie found herself answering the remaining questions by rote. Address. Contact info. Only after she got up and went to retrieve her bag did Dulcie realize what must have happened.

'Ruby, are they talking to everyone?' Dulcie

found the librarian in another corner, where apparently various holdalls were being checked.

Her friend nodded as an officer went through her oversized purse. 'Yeah. Even the people who were on break.' Her voice dropped to her version of a whisper. 'The cops think it was an inside job.'

'They do?' Dulcie had to work to keep her voice down. 'Why?'

'I'm not sure,' Ruby answered, shaking her head. 'I gather Kyle heard something through his connections.'

That was intriguing—and Dulcie was about to follow up when a voice called out, loudly enough that both Dulcie and Ruby looked up. An officer was in the lobby gesturing, and two other officers were running. The three disappeared up the stairs, and Dulcie realized that this was where the cry had originated.

'What is it?' Dulcie started to rise. 'Do you think someone's hurt?'

Ruby restrained her, one hand on her arm. 'Let them do their job, Dulcie. It might be dangerous.'

She was right, Dulcie knew that, and still she craned her neck to see. Maybe one of the burglars had been hiding. Maybe he had taken someone hostage. An image flashed before her eyes—Griddlehaus, small and vulnerable, with a knife at his neck. Once again, she started to stand, and this time her friend could not hold her down.

'I'm going to see what's happening,' she said as she walked toward the lobby. 'Maybe I can help.'

Before she could reach the staircase, an arm appeared, stopping her progress. 'I'm sorry, Miss,' said a tall man in an ill-fitting suit. 'You'll have to wait here.'

'Detective Cintra?' Dulcie looked up at a face as wrinkled as that jacket. 'I'm Dulcie Schwartz. We met through Detective Rogovoy.'

'Ah, yes. I remember you, Ms Schwartz.' The tall detective nodded, his mouth wrinkling up in what Dulcie assumed was his version of a smile. 'I'm afraid you still can't go upstairs.'

'But...' Dulcie was about to press her case when she saw Theodore Linden, one of the senior staffers, being escorted down the wide, marble stairs. A young woman in uniform seemed to be supporting the stout man. He leaned on her with one arm, while the other was raised to his forehead.

'Mr Linden!' Dulcie called, alarmed. 'Are you all right?'

The librarian looked at her, his wide round face even paler than usual.

'Please.' Dulcie pressed against Detective Cintra's restraining arm. 'He's hurt.'

'He's just had a shock.' The tall man put out his other hand to hold Dulcie still. 'And you should go back and sit down. Please,' he added as an afterthought.

Dulcie watched as the rotund librarian was escorted into a small side office, the place where they usually took ID photos, and a door closed. Only then did she reluctantly turn around to resume her place with Ruby.

'They took Mr Linden into the ID room,' she said, her voice flat. 'I think he was hurt.'

'He's probably stunned,' said Ruby, her own voice sunk to a whisper. Dulcie looked up at her. 'We just heard.'

Dulcie shook her head. Clearly she had missed something during her attempt to attack the stairs. 'What happened?'

'It's the Islington Bible,' said Ruby, her whisper now barely audible. 'It's gone.'

FIFTEEN

DESPITE HER OWN earlier plans to take a break, Dulcie
felt a bit adrift once the police let her go. The sun
felt too bright as she found herself blinking beneath
a leafless tree by the library steps. Almost as if she
were a subterranean creature. A mole or some other
small animal, driven to the surface by the disruption. Almost like...

'Mr Griddlehaus!' Dulcie called and started waving
as she saw the librarian scurrying away. 'Over here!'

He looked up, the daylight flashing in his large
glasses. Only after a moment did he acknowledge her,
and with a nod began to walk her way. 'Ms Schwartz,'
he said, once he was close enough, 'I see they allowed you to take off as well.'

'Well, yes.' She considered him closely. Out here,
in the open, he seemed smaller and more vulnerable.
'Was there a chance they wouldn't?'

He shrugged, his shoulders going up almost to his
earpieces. 'The officers have asked some of the staff
to stay behind. I was questioned extensively about
the Mildon, about what's in the collection, and who
has access.'

'But they can't think that you...' Dulcie was ap-
palled.

'No, I don't think so.' The librarian didn't seem

to share Dulcie's outrage and instead appeared to be considering the question. 'Not once they realized we were not directly connected to the rest of the library, and that our security gate has been locked since yesterday.'

'They haven't even let you back in yet?' The concept of Griddlehaus banned from his domain was one Dulcie had trouble imagining.

'No.' He shook his head. 'I did—ahem—confront Mr Truckworth about the possibility. He assured me that the Mildon had not been breached, at least.'

'Well, of course not.' Even as Dulcie exclaimed, the implications hit her. 'So they really do think it was an inside job.' The idea of anybody in the university aiding criminals shouldn't be that foreign, Dulcie knew. And yet, it was.

Griddlehaus was shaking his head slowly, as if thinking over the possibilities. 'It does not seem feasible, Ms Schwartz,' he said finally. 'But it wouldn't be without precedent.'

'Excuse me?' Dulcie hadn't thought the little man could shock her. 'This has happened before?'

In response, Griddlehaus sighed and seemed to deflate a little. Whether it was the morning's furor or his continued displacement from the Mildon, something was weighing on the librarian. Possibly, Dulcie realized as her own belly rumbled, something as simple as hunger.

'Mr Griddlehaus.' Dulcie started speaking before her sense of her own impertinence could stop her. 'Would you like to get some lunch?'

The eyes that blinked up at her looked even wider

than usual. Behind the glasses, she thought, the librarian was shocked by her effrontery. She started to stutter—to grope for the words to apologize. To explain.

But before she could form any, he began to speak again.

'What a lovely idea,' he said, to her amazement. 'Do you know a little place called Lala's?'

TWENTY MINUTES LATER, they were seated near the back. Both had opted for the three-bean burger, though Griddlehaus had expressed concern at Dulcie's request for extra hot sauce.

'Oh, my,' he had said, fiddling with the napkin dispenser. 'Not even when I was an undergraduate…'

Dulcie had smiled, her sense of decorum—and of her friend—restored. It was only after the waiter left them that she felt free to follow up on her companion's bombshell.

'Would you mind elaborating, Mr Griddlehaus, on what you said before?'

'Oh.' He blinked at her. 'It was during my own student days—'

'No, not the hot sauce,' Dulcie interrupted, with a smile. 'I meant, that this kind of thing has happened before?'

'Well, I can't say with any certainty.' He paused while the server put down their drinks: a mug of hot tea for Griddlehaus and a Diet Coke for Dulcie. 'Nor should I be talking about it.'

'Why not?' Dulcie leaned forward, ignoring her drink.

The bespectacled librarian didn't respond, and instead turned to the departing waiter and called, half rising from his seat. 'Excuse me? Would you have some honey?'

Dulcie waited, but even as her companion settled down, he seemed unduly engrossed with his tea, dipping the bag as if to make it steep more quickly and then stirring as if unhappy with the result.

'Mr Griddlehaus?' Dulcie wasn't even sure he had heard her. The waiter returned with a squeeze bottle of honey and her companion focused on that, measuring out two teaspoons and stirring until they had been completely dissolved.

Dulcie waited as he took a sip and then, with a resigned air, removed the tea bag to the saucer and looked up at her once again, his oversized glasses magnifying the sadness in his eyes.

'I should never have said anything.' He shook his head slowly. The waiter returned, carrying their burgers. Dulcie almost wished he had been slower. But when Griddlehaus only toyed with the edge of his plate, she knew he was going to talk. To keep herself from pushing too hard—and because she was hungry and the burger smelled delicious—she lifted hers with both hands and took a big bite.

'To explain, perhaps, I should give you a little history.' His voice was lower even than usual, but back here Dulcie could hear him quite clearly. 'I was not always planning on going into library science, you know. Even conservation was only a sideline for me. A passing interest, I believed at the time.'

She nodded to encourage him and took another bite.

'I imagine you cannot see it in me now,' he continued. 'But back, oh, it must have been close to thirty years ago now, I was committed to a life in academia. On the research and writing side of academia,' he corrected himself.

Now that he'd started talking, Dulcie noticed, he was sounding a bit more like himself. He even lifted his burger and took a small, neat bite. Dulcie, wanting to make her burger last, dragged one of the crispy fries through the hot sauce and ate it while she waited for him to go on.

'I do have my doctorate, of course.' Griddlehaus seemed to be reviving as he ate, his voice growing louder and more confident. 'After several years in Classics, I had decided that there was only so much room for another scholar of Akkadian and had gone a bit wild.' He smiled, although Dulcie wasn't sure if it was the memory of youthful indiscretion or Lala's excellent cooking that prompted the change of expression. 'At any rate, I was about to begin a post-doctorate program that would have allowed me to apply my area of expertise to the metaphysical poets. A more lightweight usage, I agree, but I saw it as a transitional role. Something to help me bridge my formal education with some of my more, well, colloquial interests.'

'I didn't know,' said Dulcie. Perhaps it was just as well. If she had known the librarian considered the Metaphysicals 'lightweight,' she might never have dared share so much about her own enthusiasms.

'I don't want you to think I still hold that prejudice.' He must have seen something in her face. 'I was, well, perhaps the university was a little different back then. Before, you know…'

Dulcie nodded. Neither had to mention what had happened in the eighties, when new theories of education and one particularly enthusiastic dean had resulted in a radical restructuring of the university curriculum.

'Whatever happened to Dean Allworthy, anyway?' The question slipped out before Dulcie could stop herself. The last thing she wanted was to interrupt what was already a very slow-flowing story.

Griddlehaus simply shook his head. 'At any rate, I was here for the summer and with my slight alteration in focus, I had not picked up any sections, and so I was seeking part-time employment.' She nodded. The drill hadn't changed that much in the ensuing decades. Grad students taught; that was how they paid their bills. 'I saw a notice about catalog help. This was when we were just beginning to digitalize everything. Of course, at the time, nobody knew what would happen.' He paused. 'Nobody could have.'

'Of course not.' Griddlehaus didn't have to explain further. He didn't get the chance.

'Dulcie, there you are!' A familiar voice caused Dulcie to pivot in her seat. Ruby was making her way between the tables with more enthusiasm than grace. In her wake, Kyle was grabbing a napkin holder that the large woman had knocked over and restoring it to a startled family. 'I should have known.'

Without waiting to be invited, Ruby plopped down in the chair next to Dulcie's, leaving Kyle to squeeze his skinny frame into the seat by Griddlehaus.

'Hi Ruby, Kyle.' Dulcie turned toward Griddlehaus to make introductions, when she realized that, of course, the three already knew each other. 'Were you looking for me?'

'I figured you'd want to hear the latest,' said Ruby, as she flagged down the waiter.

'I heard about the Islington.' Dulcie waited while the two placed their order. 'Is there anything else? Did they catch somebody?'

'Almost as good.' Ruby reached into the bread basket. 'Hope you don't mind. Interrogation makes me hungry.'

'Wait, they couldn't think that you…' Dulcie looked from her friend to Kyle and back again.

'Ruby's exaggerating,' said the red-headed guard as he took a piece of bread. 'As usual.'

'Easy for you to say,' Ruby managed around a mouthful.

'I believe I am missing something here,' Griddlehaus, who had been sitting silently, interjected. 'Do the authorities have a suspect already?'

Ruby, mouth full, shook her head.

'They can't still think that Mumbles—that Jeremy Mumbleigh—was involved,' said Dulcie. 'Can they?'

'I don't know about that,' said Kyle. 'I mean, I do know that they still think he was involved somehow.'

'But he's in the infirmary,' Dulcie protested, as the waiter brought out their plates.

'Maybe he's the mastermind,' said Ruby as she picked up her own burger with both hands. 'Maybe he's organizing everything from the secure vantage point of a hospital bed.'

'Ruby.' Dulcie was disappointed. The man was

seriously injured. 'I don't know if he's regained consciousness. You can't think that he really...'

'No.' With one sauce-splattered hand, she waved
Dulcie's objection down, and then reached for a napkin. 'I don't. Not really. But it could be. I mean, he
knows the university library system well enough.'

Dulcie looked at her friend, but Ruby had followed up her curious statement by taking a big bite.

'Of course,' Griddlehaus responded instead. 'Jeremy—Mr Mumbles—was quite familiar with the
stacks, as well as with all the access tunnels.' He
looked at Dulcie. 'He worked with me that summer,
you know.'

'But, no...' Dulcie wanted to follow up, to ask the
director of the Mildon what he knew about Jeremy,
but she had more pressing questions. 'Ruby, what did
you mean when you said it was an inside job? Have
they found some clues?'

'Gotta be.' She wiped her mouth. 'Whoever broke
in knew about tunnels that haven't been used for,
what, like twenty years. They came through a sec-
tion of wall that was so old that there weren't even
any alarms on it.'

'No alarms?' Dulcie was confused. 'But the Islington Bible—surely that was alarmed.'

Nobody answered, and Dulcie watched as the
three exchanged glances.

'Wait,' she asked. 'It wasn't?'

'The alarm system on the Islington's case had
been disconnected,' said Ruby, leaning over the
table. 'It was tied in with the fire alarm system, and
that had to be disconnected because of the plumb-

ing work. It was temporary and nobody was supposed to know.'

'I don't believe you.' Dulcie sat back and looked at
her friend hard. 'If nobody was supposed to know…'
She paused. 'You two are having me on, aren't you?'

'No!' Ruby managed to get the syllable out despite having taken another hefty bite. Even as she
chewed she shook her head for emphasis. 'Nuh-uh.'

Kyle, meanwhile, was looking down at his plate.

'I believe our other dining companion may be
our source,' said Griddlehaus quietly. 'And if he is,
then, Ms Schwartz, I suspect his information is quite
reliable.'

The table fell silent, as all eyes turned to Kyle.

'I don't understand,' said Dulcie, when it became
clear that the young guard was not going to volunteer
anything. 'Kyle, were you the one who interrupted
the break-in? I'd thought I heard that a woman—'

'No, it wasn't me.' He addressed the plate, which
still contained most of a burger. 'I mean, I wasn't the
one who heard them. But, well, I did hear *something*.
About the alarm, that is. And about how whoever
broke in had to have access to the original plans,
both from the original architects and from all the
renovations from the last fifty years. And that the
police were going to be interviewing everyone who
has worked at the library who is still in the library.'

'Were you eavesdropping?' Dulcie wasn't sure
how to read the young guard. At times sullen and
taciturn, he could suddenly turn talkative.

But, no, he was shaking his head.

'Tell her.' Ruby was staring at him. Hard.

'You don't know my name, do you?' His expression was inscrutable. 'I mean, my last name?'

'No, sorry,' said Dulcie, feeling a little sheepish.

With a bigger sigh than her response seemed to merit, he explained. 'My folks split up when I was little, and my mom moved away and remarried. But when I couldn't find a job in Cleveland, she kind of pushed me to look up my dad. I don't know. Maybe she thought he owed her—I guess he was kind of a jerk. And it was good at first. I think he was lonely. I think he was glad I came back to Cambridge, even if he didn't want me working here.'

'Wait.' Dulcie wasn't following. 'Who's your father?'

Another sigh. 'My full name is Kyle Truckworth. Stuart Truckworth is my dad.'

'The head of facilities…' Dulcie thought back to the harried older man she'd run into outside the library. 'He didn't want you to work as a guard?'

'Hardly.' Kyle looked down, but Dulcie could still see the color rising in his face. 'I mean I didn't either at first. I wanted to work with him. I'm pretty good with my hands. I'd been talking with him about something in maintenance, and we were getting close again, I thought. But there weren't any openings for the kind of thing I was qualified for, so when this job was posted I went for it and he kind of flipped. I thought he'd be happy that I was showing some initiative, that I'd gone out and gotten it for myself.' Kyle shrugged. 'I guess he only wanted me around if he could keep an eye on me.'

Just then, a buzzing interrupted the table. Ruby and Kyle reached for their phones. Griddlehaus merely looked at them, blinking.

'This has got to be the alert about the library break-in,' said Dulcie, popping a last fry.

'Not very timely, is it?' Ruby was busy punching in her code.

'Oh, wait, I've got something else.' Kyle was using his finger to scroll down, clearly skimming a message of some length. 'Huh, interesting.'

'What is it?' Dulcie, her curiosity piqued, wiped off her hands and reached for her own device.

'News, I assume?' Griddlehaus looked from one of his companions to another.

'Wait I'm not seeing anything,' said Ruby. 'I mean, this is just the alert.'

'I've got—hang on, they got it back,' said Kyle. 'The Islington Bible, they got it back.'

'They made an arrest?'

'No.' Kyle was reading. 'They found it. It's been damaged. The cover was removed. Torn off, this says. They found the insides, about thirty feet down the tunnel.'

'Well, that's a blessing.' Griddlehaus's brow was knit. 'I would assume that such thieves were more interested in the cover than the text and therefore unwittingly discarded the part of the Bible that was actually of greater value.'

Dulcie, who had finally gotten her phone opened, nodded in agreement. 'Yeah, they must have gone for the jewels.'

'No, wait.' Kyle was still reading, flicking the page to read more. 'They have also found the cover. With all the gold and jewels intact.'

SIXTEEN

'GOOD THING THEY were interrupted.' Ruby was the first to speak. 'Lord knows, we have enough negative publicity to deal with right now without a million-dollar heist.'

'Publicity?' Dulcie looked at her friend, who was draining the last of her soda.

'The work in the Yard.' Ruby reached for another napkin. 'The tour guides are all complaining. They come into the library and whine to me like I have some say over it.'

'It is a relief, though, isn't it?' Kyle looked from one to the other. 'I mean, bad enough that someone broke into the library.'

Dulcie was about to agree when she noticed how glum her remaining friend still seemed. 'Mr Griddle-haus?'

'I understand that the university will count this as a win, both in terms of material costs and our public relations. However, we cannot forget that a book was vandalized. If you don't mind, I'd like to get back. I'm sure the Bible is being taken to the conservators, but I have an interest.'

'Of course.' Dulcie looked around for the waiter. 'I'll join you.' Griddlehaus blinked up at her. 'It's

not like they're going to let me back down to my
carrel any time soon.'

TEN MINUTES LATER, Dulcie and Griddlehaus were
once more crossing the cold and wind-blown Yard.
Ruby had already declared her intention of taking
the rest of the day off, and Kyle had shrugged off
Dulcie's invitation to join them at the conservators
with a casual excuse.

'I'm going to see if I can find out anything else,'
he had said. 'If I do, I'll let you know.'

Now as the pair walked in companionable silence,
Dulcie found herself wondering about the young
guard—and about how even a troubled family connection afforded special access.

'So you knew that Kyle was the facilities manager's
son?' She leaned over to talk to her friend, the wind
pulling her words away.

'I did.' Griddlehaus was hunched over. 'I used to
know his father rather well, too, although we have
drifted.' He glanced over at her. 'In fact, we met that
summer that I started to tell you about. He was another graduate student.'

'Stuart Truckworth?' Dulcie heard the surprise in
her own voice. Despite the university's reputation,
she hadn't thought that an advanced degree was necessary for what was essentially plumbing and carpen-
try. Nor, she realized, had she correctly calculated
the librarian's age. 'But he's so much older than you.'

Griddlehaus smiled and shook his head. 'He has
to deal with much more bureaucracy than I do, Ms
Schwartz. That will wear on a man. However, we are

of an age. He was studying literature, same as you, Ms Schwartz. And keen on an academic career as well, until that summer.'

'Oh my! What happened?' As soon as the words were out, Dulcie regretted them. Her tone, she knew, was one of horror—as if her companion had just told her that the grey squirrel that had darted up the bare oak in front of them had once been a French tutor.

'Same thing that happened to me, I gather.' They had arrived at the lab, and Griddlehaus reached for the door. 'We both were working what seemed to be a summer job,' he said as he held the door for Dulcie. 'And before we knew it, our supposedly temporary jobs had taken over our lives.'

'I'm sorry,' she interrupted. 'But before, back at Lala's, you were saying there was a similar breach—an "inside job" of some sort?'

'Yes, well, I'm not sure I should be speaking of it, really.' He turned toward her with an apologetic half-smile. 'It was kept confidential at the time, for reasons that will become clear. Is that your phone?'

Dulcie looked down. Yes, her messenger bag was mewing, one of Esmé's more urgent sounds. 'I'm sorry,' she said. 'I turned it on when we left the library out of habit.'

'Please, don't apologize.' He pointed to the buzzer. 'Simply ring when you're free.' He disappeared inside.

'Lucy.' Dulcie would have let the call go straight to voice mail, were it not for Griddlehaus's courtly gesture. Maybe, she thought, that was a message in its own right. 'I'm sorry I didn't return your call.'

'Not to worry, Dulcinea. I know you can hear me.'

Dulcie smiled to herself. Her mother may have a bad case of empty-nest syndrome, but her psychic self-confidence would never let her feel too bad. 'What I'm worried about is your companion.'

'Mr Griddlehaus?' She had been surprised. Immediately, she wished the words back in. 'That's—I was walking with a librarian friend.'

'No, no, not him.' Lucy sounded peeved. 'The other one—the young one.'

'Chris? He's at his mother's this week. I told you.' Dulcie caught herself. The wind was picking up, and she very much wanted to be inside. That was no reason to snap at her mother, though. 'I did get your message.' She tried to remember the exact wording. 'About bonding with the beast?'

'Very good, Dulcie, but it's not about you.'

'Oh?' Dulcie's feet were going numb. Was it possible that her boot was still damp?

'Not entirely.' Her mother's voice was fading, a not uncommon occurrence where Lucy was concerned, although the commune's phone system might have been to blame. 'You're not the only one with a spirit animal, a companion. There's a message.'

'Yes?' There usually was, and Dulcie looked forward to winding this conversation up.

'Can you trust him, Dulcie?'

'Do you mean Chris?' Dulcie paused. 'Or do you mean my—ah—spirit animal?' Her mother knew a little about Mr Grey, but Dulcie wasn't sure if she wanted her to know more. 'Lucy?'

It didn't matter. The line was dead.

If the caller had been anyone else, Dulcie would

have dialed back. Her mother, however, often ended her calls on such a sudden note. Even if the disconnection had been the result of an accident—the pressing of a wrong button or the lapse of service—Lucy would likely pretend it had been intentional. As Dulcie knew from a lifetime's experience, Lucy never turned down the opportunity for drama.

And she, meanwhile, was missing out. And so she buzzed the conservation lab. As she waited to be let in, she wondered about her librarian friend and his own strange journey of discovery.

'Thanks, Mr Griddlehaus.' The diminutive librarian welcomed her in to the warm lab. 'I was wondering. Do you think maybe I might find I'm better suited to something else?'

'Excuse me?' He blinked. 'I had thought you were interested in the Islington.'

'Oh, I am.' Dulcie filed her fears and followed him over to where the grey-haired conservator—Margaret—was still at work. Only now, the volume before her on the light table was the Islington Bible.

'Hello again.' She pushed up the magnifying headset she had been wearing and stood. 'I'm so glad you're back.'

'Thank you.' Dulcie felt warmed by the welcome. Academia was where she belonged—and this was research at its most raw and primal. She looked over at the famous artifact, now denuded of its gawdy cover. 'I gather you've moved on from *He Could Not Tell Her*?'

Margaret looked down at the frayed and curling pages on the table with what Dulcie interpreted as a bit of regret. 'For now,' she said. 'The police still have not released the cover. I gather they believe they can lift some prints off it.' She said the words carefully, as if amused by the lingo. 'Luckily they brought the interior over to us fairly promptly. I hate to think what could have happened had they tried to do their various tests on paper of this age.'

'I was so relieved to hear that,' Griddlehaus murmured at her side. More clearly, he asked, 'What is the extent of the damage?'

'Not so bad,' said Margaret. 'Not as bad as it could have been.'

'Huh.' Across the room, a bald man looked up from his own work station. 'The book had been thrown to the ground. It was found *splayed out*, like…like a corpse.'

'The Islington did need to be stabilized,' Margaret clarified. 'Whereas the 1833 *Could Not* was really not in bad shape. Besides,' she added, 'Gerald is our master of disbinding. It only makes sense that he's taken over that project.'

Dulcie looked at her, waiting for an explanation.

'The original repair work was not complete,' said the conservator.

She sighed, and Dulcie saw that she was struggling for words.

'Perhaps I should have protested more at the time,' she said at last. 'We were pressed, and there was a strong feeling that *He Could Not Tell Her* was not worth the resources. Sadly, there's no question of stabilizing what's left of the original binding now. I'm afraid it can't be saved at this point. Would you like to see?'

'Yes, please.' Dulcie knew they had come to see

the Islington, but she couldn't help feeling more involved with the book that had been found on Jeremy, especially after hearing more of its sad history.

'You know, we have a connection,' said the conservator as she wiped her hands on her long white apron and stepped around the table. 'You and I. Mr Griddlehaus here has filled me in.'

Dulcie turned from the woman to her friend, the question in her eyes.

'Ms Constantine worked on those pages you've been reading,' Griddlehaus explained. 'The manuscript fragments.'

'Worked on them?' Dulcie thought back to the pages. Worn and crumbling, the writing on their fragile surface faded to the point of illegibility or lacing through the paper like some kind of insect trail.

'You didn't think they came to the Mildon in that condition, did you?' Griddlehaus asked, his voice lilting with amusement. 'Ms Constantine spent hours stabilizing each page, and often piecing together smaller fragments.'

'Of course.' Dulcie thought of one she'd labored over recently. Brown and spotted, water damage most likely, it had come to her assembled like a jigsaw inside its protective polypropylene casing. 'Thank you.'

'My pleasure.' The older woman nodded. 'And more than that, my job. But it is a treat to meet the scholar who is making sense of all those stray scraps. Thomas tells me you believe they are all part of one novel?'

Dulcie nodded. 'I think so, a rather exciting one. In fact, I've just gotten to a part where there's a hidden passage in a library.'

The conservator and Griddlehaus smiled at each other. 'How lovely,' the conservator said, after a moment's pause. 'I remember a time when libraries were mysterious places. I guess they still are, after a fashion. But that's not what you're here for, I gather.'

She turned and led the pair over to a table in the corner. There, the bald man who had chimed in about the Islington was using a magnifying glass to examine the stitches in the binding of the other book, the lamp overhead illuminating not only the damaged volume but also his bald pate and the array of small tools laid out as if for surgery. A press—like a giant frame—encased the body of the novel, holding it open to reveal the inside of the injured cover and the water-spotted facing page. Dulcie had seen presses like this before: one of the rare book dealers in the Square also did repairs. But that shop had smelled of glue and book mold. This bright and airy space made that storefront look like a closet. And peeking around the edge of the press Dulcie could make out the ornate print of a title page.

'Is that *He Could Not Tell Her*?'

'Most of it,' said the man, without looking up. He grimaced as he stared down at the stitching and reached for what looked like a dental pick. 'The heart of it, I dare say.'

'Gerald here has been dying to get at the binding,' Margaret explained, keeping her voice soft. 'To finish what I should have, all those years ago.'

'I'm doing what I can,' said the bald man, replacing the pick on the table. 'We shall see.'

He had removed the paper lining now, and was

carefully peeling it back from the leather with what looked like an ordinary set of tweezers. Dulcie, meanwhile, kept staring at the book. It looked so naked like this. So vulnerable.

'Is that what you usually do?' asked Dulcie.

'When I can,' said Gerald as he set down the tweezers and, after some consideration, took up a scalpel. 'Now we are finally getting down to basics.' His eyes still on the book, he sliced through a thread with one careful motion. 'There!'

'What is he doing?' Dulcie addressed the grey-haired conservator in a whisper as Gerald once again took up the tweezers and proceeded to tease out a fragment of thread. 'Is he cutting the binding?'

'Once Gerald takes the cover apart, we will be able to do a full assessment,' said Margaret, her voice hushed. 'See what can be salvaged.'

'That's Mr Conway's specialty,' said Griddlehaus in a stage whisper. 'Give him a binding, and he can break it down to all its constituent parts.'

'The hope,' Margaret continued, 'is that we—well, Gerald—may be able to restore what remains of the original boards and the spine, and then we can re-back it. If not we replace them with acid-free board.' She shrugged. 'I doubt we'll have that option with the Islington, though. I suspect the university will want that gaudy coat of many colors put back on, at least for show.'

'You'd rather leave it off?' Dulcie looked at the older woman with admiration. This was a dedicated scholar.

'Wouldn't you rather have the real object, as close to what it was meant to be as it can be?' She smiled at Dulcie. 'Like those pages of yours?'

'Of course.' A thought occurred to Dulcie. 'Wait, the pages in the collection. Were they bound together originally? Did you—did this lab—take them apart?'

'Some of them,' she said. 'Yes.'

'But I'm trying to put them together.' Dulcie's voice rose in frustration, and Griddlehaus looked up in alarm. 'If I knew they had been bound together— that they had come to the university in book form—'

'I'm sorry.' Margaret's face showed her concern. 'It wasn't like that. We didn't disassemble a complete book—or even a manuscript.' She looked at Griddlehaus. 'You didn't tell her?'

'I saw no need.' He almost stuttered over the words. 'It didn't seem relevant. More of a distraction, really.'

'What?' Dulcie looked from her friend to the conservator and back again. 'Why wasn't it relevant? I mean, if there are records of how they were ordered—even of which pages were bound together, it would help enormously.'

'They weren't put together as a book,' Griddlehaus said, his voice suddenly sad. 'Someone had used them as filler. As scrap, Dulcie.'

'As filler?' She looked back at the conservator.

'To make the backing boards of another work.' The conservator smiled, as if that could soften the blow. 'It was a form of recycling. But that may be why so many of them were still in good shape—or could be, once again, once we had done our job. In fact—'

'Aha!' A triumphant cry interrupted her narration, and the three of them crowded back around the table.

'What have you found?' Dulcie peered over the bald conservator's shoulder. Gerald was carefully

placing a pane of what looked like glass over a scrap
the size of a safety pin.

'Dutch,' he said, pushing back the magnifier. 'Unless I miss my guess. Gold blocked, for the English trade. Forget your fancy jewels, Miss.' For the
first time he addressed Dulcie directly. 'This is what
makes a book a treasure. Would you like to see?'

He moved back, letting her through, and waited
while she adjusted the magnifier. Sure enough,
up close she could make out the remnant of the
foil—gold letters showing how popular the minor
Gothic used to be. But as Dulcie stared, her eyes
taking in the care that had been lavished on this
now-disregarded book, she felt a nudge—a small
push—that moved her hand ever so slightly to the
right.

'Sorry.' She bent to readjust the glass, but as she
did she caught a flicker—a flash—right by the inside of the exposed binding. There a bit of shimmer,
the twist of a decorative design, was stamped out not
in gold but in silver. 'Wait, what's that?' She asked
without looking up. 'It's not a letter, is it?'

'What?' Gerald leaned over, pulling a larger magnifying lens over the surface.

'No, I suspect it's decorative.' He peered down and
adjusted the lens, then stepped back to allow Dulcie a
better look. 'Perhaps a printer's mark. Why?'

Dulcie squinted down at the squiggle. The way it
curved, the two short lines that crossed it at an angle,
confirmed her initial suspicion. 'Maybe it's me,' she
said at last. 'But it looks like the profile of a cat.'

SEVENTEEN

'THAT'S HIGHLY UNLIKELY,' Gerald responded. 'Please, let me.'

Dulcie didn't feel like she could object. This wasn't her field of expertise. But as she started to back away, she felt a strange reluctance, as if the shiny fragment had some kind of magnetic draw.

'One second,' she said, holding up her hand. Ignoring Gerald, she focused once more on the image before her. What she was doing was rude—unacceptable—and so she was not really surprised to feel the conservator's hand on her shoulder. 'Please.' She shrugged it off.

Maybe it was that motion. Maybe it was the play of the light, catching a crack in the aged and damaged surface, Dulcie couldn't be sure. But even as she pulled away, she thought she saw a movement. The feline face winked.

'It's a cat,' she said again. 'It's definitely a cat.' She stepped back as Gerald took her place, frowning over the fragment.

'How did you… How did I miss that?' He reached for another implement, rather like a blunt-edged tweezer, to pull ever so slightly at the piece's edge. 'How wonderful.'

'Isn't it?' Dulcie felt unaccountably cheered. 'So tiny and yet so precise.'

'May I?' Dulcie had almost forgotten Margaret. The grey-haired conservator's request had the force of a command, and Gerald immediately stepped back. He was watching her face, Dulcie realized, as she focused on the fragment. 'You realize what this means, I assume?'

She hadn't looked up, but both Gerald and Griddlehaus nodded. 'Uh, yes,' Gerald finally responded, his throat suddenly froggy.

'Fascinating.' Margaret seemed to be speaking to herself, and so Dulcie turned to her friend.

'Mr Griddlehaus, I'm confused,' she said. 'What does a cat signify?'

He blinked, and for a moment Dulcie wondered if he had forgotten she was there. 'A cat? Well, if that can indeed be verified it may be a printer's mark. *The* printer's mark, I should say. It's called the Felix.'

'If this is a "Felix" book,' Margaret added, her eyes still glued to the fragment, 'then the university is going to have to re-evaluate its place in the collection.'

'Not to mention library security,' added Griddlehaus, with a significant nod to Dulcie.

'MR GRIDDLEHAUS, WHAT'S going on?' Two minutes later and Dulcie and Griddlehaus were back out in the cold. After the conservator's revelation, the bespectacled librarian had made a rather hasty farewell, and now she found herself hurrying to keep pace, despite their similar stature. 'What does that mean, a "Felix" book?'

He barely paused before responding. 'You heard about the Bethesda find, back in January, didn't you, Ms Schwartz?'

'No, I don't think so.' She thought back. 'I must have been involved with finals.'

'Of course.' He didn't slow his pace. 'Although it did make quite a stir. A private collection put a Felix psalter up for auction. That stamp was located when the psalter went for re-binding, as well. I confess, I was hoping the university would bid but the pricing...' He looked over at her now. 'Two point three million, I believe.'

Despite her better instincts, Dulcie was impressed. 'I didn't know,' she said, her breathlessness only partly occasioned by the pace.

'Well, you wouldn't have.' He turned to look at her without pausing. 'Religious books are not your area of expertise. But I am sure it had many collectors re-examining the inside covers and fly leaves of their dearest volumes, hoping for a similar find.'

Dulcie mulled that over. How odd that the value of a book should depend on something on its cover. Out loud, she posed the more pressing question. 'What does it signify, though?'

'During the Reformation,' he said as they made their way across the Yard, 'religious books were often smuggled around Europe—mostly from the Protestant parts of Germany into the areas controlled by Spain. Then with the Tudor back and forth, books made their way into England, too. But having a banned book was dangerous. Under Mary, the wrong text could get you burned. And so printers—and booksellers, too—worked out a system. Cats were an obvious shorthand. A code, if you will. Working, as they did, against the predations of rodents, the cat has long been called the "printer's friend" and so the cat became a symbol for safety—specifically, that a book was safe. A printer displaying the mark of a cat—the Felix—would indicate that his shop had such books or was open to passing them along. In time, it was used to mark the books themselves, signifying that the bearer was safe to confide in or required safe passage.'

'Wait,' Dulcie broke in. 'Was it the work of one printer?'

'Originally,' said Griddlehaus. 'That's how it got its name, but the term came to refer to any such mark made by the printer or the binder. The Felix was so simple, it was easy to reproduce. A curve and a few straight lines reproduced in silver—or even grey— it could be hidden inside a design, but once found would be immediately recognizable, like a sign or a code. At times, we believe, the mark also indicated a hidden text, which may explain why it was concealed inside the cover like that. Except, well, it all falls apart.'

Dulcie shook her head, breathless and confused, as Griddlehaus turned suddenly to avoid an area marked off with yellow hazard tape.

'We're talking European books,' said Griddlehaus, as if it were obvious, leading her down an unpaved side path. 'Not American, and substantially earlier works, too. If we had found a "Felix" on the Islington Bible, I would have understood it.'

'But it wasn't…' Dulcie felt like she was missing something. 'The page with the cat on it was being used as filler, right? Maybe someone didn't appreciate its rarity, didn't understand…' It wouldn't be the first time, she thought.

Griddlehaus was shaking his head. 'No, it's possible. But we're talking about a mark that hadn't been used for two hundred years by 1833. There must have been a revival of its use, though for what purpose, I'm not sure.'

'Can you find out?'

'Why, yes.' He stopped short and turned toward her. 'That's what I am intending to do.'

He started walking again, Dulcie following behind, her mind filling with questions. As much as she felt she knew Griddlehaus, she couldn't help but think of Lucy's enigmatic warning. As even Lala had hinted, so many of her relationships were superficial.

'Mr Griddlehaus, where are we going?'

'Why, back to the library.' He was actually speeding up.

'Won't it still be cordoned off?' Dulcie asked. 'I mean, it's a crime scene.'

'The main floor, I'm sure.' They'd reached the wide steps that led to the majestic portico. 'That doesn't mean we can't find some place quiet in which to do our own work.'

Keeping her curiosity at bay, Dulcie followed the little clerk around to the back of the building. Sure enough, although two uniformed police were sitting in a cruiser by the rear entrance, neither stopped them as they came in. The guard, an older man Dulcie knew by sight, seemed somewhat flustered, but he watched them pass by.

'You can't—well, you know,' he said. 'The main floor and the stacks are closed.'

'Of course,' replied Griddlehaus, reaching behind him and pulling a small, nondescript key out of a nook in the wall. And before Dulcie could ask what that key was for, he led her off to the right where a closed door, with the word 'Restricted' painted on it, offered an unpromising sight. Black and dusty, it showed no sign of having been used recently—perhaps in years—and Dulcie wondered what kind of storage facility—mops, brooms, printer cartridges—it contained. As she started to ask, however, he had unlocked the door, giving it a slight shove with his shoulder.

'After you, please,' he said, standing back from the passage.

With a glance at her companion, Dulcie stepped through the darkened doorway, as the motion-sensitive lights flickered and went on.

'Oh, my,' she said, looking around. This was no storage closet. Instead, Dulcie found herself in a well-lit reading room, complete with leather chairs and a long wooden table that could function as a desk. Around the edges of the room, wooden shelves—so much nicer looking than the standard metal stacks—held a variety of volumes, and arching floor lamps added a warmer glow to the overheard fluorescents. Except for the lack of windows, it was as cozy a space as any in the main library.

'What is this place?' She stood and looked around as Griddlehaus removed his coat.

'May I?' He held out a hand for hers, and as she unbuttoned, he explained. 'This is, now, one of the staff reading rooms. Formerly, it was an alternative entrance to the stacks. If you take a peek over by that floor lamp—yes, past the Aristotle—you may still be able to make out the outline of the old entrance.'

Dulcie gave him her coat and went to look. Sure enough, the wall was indented. A pedestal holding the bust of the philosopher made good use of the irregularity, which also held a low bookcase. Now that she was aware of it, Dulcie could see how the entire room was shaped like an anteroom or some kind of foyer.

'Was this part of the duct work?' She looked around, marveling. 'I mean, for the air-conditioning?'

'Oh, this quite predates that particular remodeling,' he said with a chuckle. 'My former colleague has always been rather budget conscious, you see. A hangover from his student days, I would assume.'

She looked around at the paneling and the floor-to-ceiling shelves. This room was a little jewel box. 'Mr Griddlehaus, speaking of the old days, you were telling me of an earlier incident...' She paused, curious but unwilling to push.

'I should never have brought it up.' He turned to her with a sigh. 'You see, for years after, there was hope. Hope that all of the objects would be recovered.'

She waited, the question on her face.

'I don't know all the details,' he continued. 'But you already know the outline. One theory was that the books were never stolen at all. Simply misfiled— or misplaced, somewhere in library storage during the renovations. But there was also a theory that some very cunning thieves broke in, perhaps through the tunnels, what with all the construction work that was being done.'

'Jeremy's book.' The realization hit Dulcie. 'I mean, the book he was found with—*He Could Not Tell Her.*'

Griddlehaus nodded. 'As I've said, many of the books were recovered, some of them still on university property, which lends credence to the possibility of misfiling, but it also led to speculation that the theft had been at least facilitated by somebody with access to otherwise restricted areas, hence my earlier reference to a so-called "inside job". In fact, there was some talk that the Felix psalter that sold in January—well, the seller was able to provide a provenance—but there was some talk about other items in the same lot. Nothing came of it, of course, or we would have heard.'

'How awful.' Dulcie was aghast.

'Not that unusual, I'm afraid.' Griddlehaus leaned in. 'We are not encouraged to talk about this, Ms Schwartz, but objects do go missing with some frequency. The bulk of them are found, of course. But not all.'

'So that must be why there's a task force?'

'Lieutenant Wardley, of course.' Griddlehaus cut her off. 'He made his name with the so-called tunnel robbery. Well, within the university, of course. I don't believe anyone was ever prosecuted, but his ability to keep the theft confidential was considered key to the retrieval of most of what was taken. Not that he seems to value books much.'

'I guess he doesn't have to for his job. As long as he understands how criminals think.' Dulcie looked around. 'This place is a wonder.'

Griddlehaus suddenly turned away and began taking papers from his leather holdall. 'I hope it will suffice,' he said. 'I assumed that since your office was closed and we have been banned, however temporarily, from the stacks, such a refuge would be welcomed.'

'It is.' Dulcie smiled. 'Thank you. I was just—I didn't know this room existed.'

'Not many do.' He looked up, revealing his flush of pleasure. 'This is one of the spaces we claimed for ourselves back, oh, not long after I came to work here.'

'That's right.' Dulcie put her bag down but left it closed. Instead, she pulled up a chair opposite her friend, across the table. 'You were telling me about that summer, only you never got to finish.'

'Ah, that summer.' Behind the large lenses, Griddlehaus's eyes took on a dreamy look. 'Yes, I originally saw the position as a temporary one. A way to fund what I believed would be my primary research.'

'That was the summer you met Stuart Truckworth?' Dulcie could imagine Thomas Griddlehaus as a young student. The clerk was still slight and his face had an open eagerness to it, despite his thinning hair and the oversized glasses that revealed the rings around his eyes. She was having a harder time with the facilities boss. He seemed like such a manager, with his khakis and gruff manner, the worry lines creasing his high forehead. She knew it was unfair, but Dulcie couldn't help but see Truckworth as the kind of man who had been born middle-aged.

'Why, yes,' said Griddlehaus. 'I gather he was in rather desperate straits, and there was so much that needed to be done.' He paused. 'I'm not sure if you know what was going on then, but the conversion to digital was primarily one of data entry. I had developed rather good typing skills from my own work and I had a decent working knowledge of the Dewey decimal system, and so that was where I was assigned.

'It wasn't the most thrilling work, I will confess,' he said, his voice lowered a bit. 'The work was more mindless than I had anticipated, merely copying what we had in the card catalog on to floppy discs. Of course, now we would simply scan a document.' He waved his hand as if conjuring the magic. 'And I do like to think I presented a more reliable alternative.'

'Was Jeremy Mumbleigh part of all of this?' Dulcie wasn't clear on the timing, and so she wasn't entirely surprised when Griddlehaus shook his head.

'No,' he said. 'He was firmly ensconced in his studies at that point. He'd made his mark the previous academic year, establishing the provenance of the Stavendish bequest, and the Dorchester Prize meant he didn't have to scramble for work. I don't believe he even taught that spring or summer.'

'Wow.' Dulcie tried to imagine it. Time to study and do your own research.

'He was very happy.' Griddlehaus sounded like he was caught up in his memories. 'Quite gregarious. In a serious way, of course.'

'Jeremy?' Dulcie thought of the shy man. 'Gregarious?'

'Yes,' Griddlehaus confirmed. 'And really quite generous. He often had us over for pizza and beer. We'd sit up talking much of the night about books and provenance. He was so very excited about the Stavendish collection. I felt quite guilty for my role in what happened.'

'Your role?' Dulcie asked. 'But—what did you do?'

'Nothing explicitly to harm him, of course. But I was part of what was to come. You have to understand what was going on with the entire library system at that time, Ms Schwartz.' He held her eye. 'It was a complete overhaul. A modernization, if you will. The beginning of the contemporary library system as we know it. There was a great push in those days to adopt best library practices, not only in terms of handling data but also in new forms of care and preservation, and that really was what was behind the university's decision to cull its collection. Not everything could be saved, you see. And with all the work that was being done, we were losing storage space—at least temporarily.'

He stopped there. They both knew what had happened.

'The work was good,' Griddlehaus said finally. 'Necessary. By the end of the summer, in addition to the digitizing, the university had also begun overhauling the climate control that is so crucial to the care and preservation of so many of our materials. The library had been part of the university's steam heat system for so long that to remove it—to disconnect from those antiquated steam tunnels—to give it its own circulatory system was a task as massive as—well, as a heart transplant. Or perhaps,' he paused to consider his own metaphor, 'a heart-lung transplant. At any rate, it was a monumental undertaking.

'The air-conditioning crew, as HVAC was called back then, had the more demanding work. Physically, that is. It was a prime job for the larger types, those more capable of difficult labor, but still students.' He stopped, clearly thinking back, but Dulcie could already see where this was headed.

'Stuart Truckworth was on the crew?' she asked.

'Not only on it, but leading it,' Griddlehaus confirmed. 'No, not at first, of course. At first, he was simply a hired hand. You see, the installation required the emptying out of a good deal of storage space for the creation of ducts, tearing out insulation, moving large boxes, and what not. And at first, Stuart was simply an able-bodied young man capable of lifting those boxes. But he was, by all accounts, a hard worker, and he seemed to have some luck. By August, he was leading a team. When September came around, he was hired on as special contractor—a concession, I gather, to his lack of formal engineering training. I don't believe he ever studied literature again.'

EIGHTEEN

DULCIE COULDN'T REMEMBER the last time she had heard Griddlehaus talk for so long or in such detail. Even after he fell silent, apparently stunned by his own garrulity, she found herself caught up in questions.

'Did you two fall out?' asked Dulcie, narrowing them down to one.

'What?' Griddlehaus looked up, and she realized she had interrupted him. 'Oh, well, not really. Stuart was really quite focused on learning the job back then. Whereas I...' He paused to push his glasses up on his nose, a move Dulcie recognized as a sign of the little man's shyness. 'I was much more of a bon vivant. And now, if you don't mind, Ms Schwartz, I really must focus on the work at hand.'

As much as Dulcie wanted to follow up on that intriguing lead, she caught herself. She had pushed a very private man out of his comfort zone.

Besides, she realized as she watched her companion huddle over a sheaf of papers, she had work to do too. Although she was in no way responsible for the hubbub that had gotten her kicked out of the library this morning, the reality was that she had now spent the greater part of the day unproductively.

'Well, unproductive in terms of my dissertation,

anyway,' she said softly. Griddlehaus did not look up, but Dulcie couldn't help thinking back to the cat she had seen—the cat she had found and which the experts might have overlooked were it not for her. That curve had done it—not a long snouty-type face, but the kind of pert feline profile that a Siamese might have. That, in fact, her dear Mr Grey had had. And those whiskers—slashes of silver—had the same long and graceful drape.

It was as if she had found Mr Grey—or some centuries-old depiction—hidden in the folds of an ancient manuscript.

'My author would have liked that,' Dulcie said to herself. In fact, she reminded herself, the passage she had been working on had referred to something hidden—a *'secret Store'* where a manuscript could be hidden *'safe from prying eyes.'*

There it was: the idea of safety again, of concealment. The concept wasn't unusual. Along with demons and ghosts, Gothic novels loved the motif of a hidden compartment. Some of that, Dulcie knew, was because so many English manors had such places— 'priest holes'—that had hidden if not actual priests then at least the sacraments that had to be concealed during the years of religious upheaval. Some of it, contemporary scholars had theorized, had deeper psychological roots. We all have a need for secrets, women authors and readers—the people who established the Gothic genre and kept it alive—perhaps more than most. More than a century later, Virginia Woolf would discuss the need for 'a room of one's own,' in order to write or even to think freely. For an author like the one Dulcie was studying, that room might just be a hidden compartment in the wall of a library.

It might even, she thought, be inside a book itself. That cat had cheered her, helping her recover from the conservator's bombshell—that the work she was studying—the very pages she was working so hard to decipher—had been used as filler. Paper stuffing to fill a back board and keep another, more important work safe. Yes, she knew that valuable works had been treated this way before. Only she couldn't help but take it personally. And knowing Griddlehaus had known—and that he had kept this knowledge from her—amplified the shame. She was, she thought, a literary trash picker.

'*But you found me...*' The voice came so clear that Dulcie looked up, expecting to see a stranger had entered the room. But no, her only companion was still Griddlehaus, and the little librarian remained hunched over his papers. He might even—Dulcie tried to peer around those big glasses—be asleep.

'*You found me in my hiding place.*' The voice was unmistakable, and Dulcie smiled.

'Yes, I did.' She kept her voice soft, barely enunciating the words. Not that it mattered. Clearly her spectral pet could understand her thoughts as well as her spoken words. 'I saw you on that page, or one of your forebears—forekittens?'

'*Forepaws.*' The voice had a bit of a rumble in it: the hint of a purr, or perhaps a laugh. '*As you've done before.*'

The memories came flooding back. Mr Grey had

been little more than a kitten. It had been a rainy
night. Pouring actually, and she and Suze had been
hurrying back to their dorm room, the pizza box
they were carrying growing increasingly sodden
with each block. Dulcie wasn't sure what it was that
had made her turn and look. They were passing an
old triple-decker, its wooden stairs rotted through,
when she saw him. Half under the stairs, taking shelter beneath a broken riser, he had looked more like
a scrawny rat than a feline.

'Come on,' Suze had said. Her room-mate hadn't
wanted to make the pizza run and had only come
out at Dulcie's urging. 'The pepperoni is going to
float off.'

'Wait,' said Dulcie. 'There's something under
there.'

'Don't!' Suze had been alarmed. 'It may bite!' But
as Dulcie had reached for the small, wet creature he
had come out to greet her.

'*Dulcie.*' She blinked. No, he hadn't spoken to
her. Not like that, but this was now, and she was
hearing him.

'What?' She asked the air.

'*You valued me then, small and discarded. You
knew...*' The voice was beginning to fade. Dulcie
told herself it didn't matter. She had gotten Mr Grey's
message: to uncover a treasure, even in the trash. To
find value hidden away in a dirty corner. These were
good things, traits to be prized. She would not think
less of the novel she was assembling just because
somebody else had used it as binding material. Instead, she would try to be grateful that these pages

had been saved for her to study and, some day, for other readers to share.

With new determination, she opened her laptop and started to read through what she had written. She had time and a quiet place to work, thanks to her friend. She would honor that by doing the work she was made for. And not by bothering Griddlehaus with more questions.

'*Thank you, Mr Grey,*' she said. But the air had changed. He had left, she could tell. She was alone in the reading room with the librarian, who was now working away, the sound of pen on paper reminiscent of the gentle scrabbling of claws.

NINETEEN

THAT TRAITOR TEAR, so quick to flee her uncertain Eye, was just as swiftly whisked away. Though it sprang forth with intent, slipping the bonds of lashes and of Will, that erring Drop could not betray, its passage fleeting as cloud before the moon, obstructing even in its ephemeral presence only the briefest shades of light, and yet its Mark remained, its passage recorded e'er so briefly upon the paper like her Footstep on a Virgin Shore. Albeit like those very Marks to fade, to wash away not in lapping Tides but in their Lack, drying to an Absence, a mere Echo of those waves. The Page before her Warped in Memory so slight, for though she could yet Perceive the imprint it would serve only for her Eyes, a Memory, like the great Bark that had carried her and her own Safe unto these Shores, so too her Secret store would prove the vessel of Deliverance, bringing to a Future port these very Words...

'THESE VERY WORDS...' Staring at the page, Dulcie tried to focus, conscious all the while of her companion, who still seemed to be quite absorbed in his own papers.

If only she could focus like that. Dulcie didn't like to think of the time she'd spent in the conser-

vators' workshop as wasted. Didn't want to think
about how the revelation about her pages had de-
railed her—or nearly so. If it hadn't been for that
mark—the silver cat…

Dulcie couldn't help but see it as a message,
maybe from her own Mr Grey. Maybe one that had
relevance to her own work.

Hidden in the old binding like that, the mark's
meaning had not at first been clear, despite its resemblance to her late, great cat. But as she reread
that passage in the manuscript, she could not help but
wonder—what if the hiding place referred to was not
a secret compartment within the walls of the library,
but within another book? That would explain why the
slight warping of a teardrop would cause such concern… Wasn't there a line about that? She began to
scroll back over her notes, looking for something…
a reference. A line. That blotted tear, for example.
Couldn't that mean…?

SHE SCROLLED THROUGH the text for several minutes,
as Griddlehaus softly hummed beside her. Maybe
it was that humming—the little man had no sense
of rhythm—that stopped her. She was being overly
literal. Almost structuralist, one might say, which
while it might please Thorpe, her adviser, was not
appropriate to the work in hand. The Gothic nov-
elists, her author included, tended to go overboard
with their imagery and mix and match their meta-
phors simply for the effect. The heroine blotting a
tear might be a clue—a semiotic signifier, if you

will—or simply a way to signal regret to the reader. Still, Dulcie wondered.

What if this novel had been hidden in the bindings of another book not by chance but by design?

She looked over at Griddlehaus, bent over his work and silent once again. What was the point of working with a colleague if she couldn't ask for a consult? But, no, she didn't dare disturb him. Not when he had opened his sanctuary up to her.

Besides, the idea was a silly one. Most of what Dulcie had uncovered of this new novel had come from a known collection. The Philadelphia bequest had contained references to a much-loved romantic adventure, as well as pages of the book itself from an edition printed in the early 1800s. This was not some kind of forbidden text, like the Islington Bible had been in its day. This was a novel. A fun work of fiction, designed to thrill and entertain.

Unless there was more to it. Dulcie sat back and closed her eyes, trying to think it through. There was a line she had read, she was sure of it. Something that referred to secrecy or to hiding manuscripts away.

She needed to consider this rationally, as an academic and not as some overheated fan. Odds were, the novel that meant so much to her had been used as scrap simply because it had not been highly valued. Most of the Gothic novels were not, even in their own day, and time had not been kind to the genre—or its reputation. Many had been lost to age and lack of concern, much like so much popular fiction of our own time was probably destined to be pulped. Just because one scholar or a collector had admired the work—and that letter Dulcie had found did prove her author had her fans—did not mean that this opinion was widely shared.

Besides, she thought, staring at the top of Griddle-haus's head, other factors could have come into play. Perhaps once the work was printed, the original man-uscript had been discarded intentionally, as so much rough copy or paper to be sold as scrap. From what Dulcie knew of the anonymous author, she was a self-supporting woman, a writer who lived by her novels and by the proceeds of a series of political essays—and perhaps by the sale of her unwanted or used materials. Everything she had written, under a variety of pseudonyms, shared certain distinctive phrases as well as a decidedly modern, egalitarian—and, yes, frugal—mindset.

Much like the heroine of this novel. The thought sprang into her head as if it had been whispered.

'Mr Grey?' She mouthed the words silently, re-sisting the urge to turn around, to search for the cat.

Silence. In truth, she wasn't sure she had heard anything. The scratching of her companion's pen. His gentle breathing. The voice—if voice it was—had merely followed her own train of thought. Dulcie had begun her thesis with the study of a different novel, *The Ravages of Umbria*. In that, Dulcie had discovered not only the author's unique voice but also a strong feminist sensibility, a moral sense turned into enthralling entertainment through the use of vivid characterization and hair-raising adventure. This new book, though, was something different. Yes, it still relied on many of the Gothic conventions:

its heroine was first seen fleeing from some kind
of demonic—or at least really nasty—suitor. And
that suitor—Dulcie was pretty sure it was him—
was then found bludgeoned in a library, possibly by
the heroine herself.

Yes, it was fantastic—in all senses of the word.
It was also, Dulcie had begun to suspect, based on
real-life experience. Although she had no hard proof,
Dulcie was becoming increasingly certain that the
author had fled England, fled an abusive relationship. Therefore, if she chose to write about her life,
she had reason to fear what reaction such a tale
might provoke. Even cloaked in the guise of fiction,
what she was saying was strong: speaking out for
the right of women, even married women, for self-
determination. Taking a stand against abuse, even
by '*the Lawful Mate to whom both Church and State
grant Power o'er our lesser Selves, e'en as his bodily
Might brooks no Challenge.*'

Yes, she might have feared the publication of this
book.

Dulcie opened her laptop, which sprang awake
with a swirl of light and color, and was about to start
typing, when another question stopped her hand. If,
she thought, fingers poised above the keyboard, writing such a work was so dangerous, why do it at all?

Dulcie sighed. This is where her argument fell
short. Sure, there were a dozen possibilities. Perhaps the author thought her story would prove more
palatable as fiction, its essential message of equal-
ity sugar-coated with the trappings of a wild adventure. Perhaps the author hoped to smuggle the book

to somewhere more permissive and the cover of fiction was to ease its passage. Perhaps she was waiting for someone—her abuser, perhaps, or his family—to die. Perhaps she was writing for her own posterity. Some of her pieces had hinted at a child, a daughter, who might one day seek to learn about her parentage and who would treasure the truth, even if she came of abuse and violence.

And perhaps Dulcie would never know. For now, however, she should concentrate on what she did know—or what she could determine. Shaking her head to clear it, she focused once more on the notes in front of her, the notes that she had compiled through long hours of serious study. At the very least, she had more information now about the source of some of those pages she had worked so hard to read. If the conservators could tell her any more about where those pages were found, well, that might give her more clues to follow. Real facts would trump idle speculation any day.

TWENTY

STOWED SO SAFELY in the Hold secure, a Passenger of faith within her Berth...

That was the line! It had taken her an hour at least, but once she found it, it was all Dulcie could do to not crow with glee. There it was—the phrase she had remembered, that had been tickling her consciousness. It wasn't proof—not in the sense that Chris would understand proof—but in her search for meaning, it was something upon which she could build a case.

These pages—the real, physical documents Dulcie had studied—were the stowaways to which the author was referring, Dulcie was sure of it. The author—*her* author—had wanted these pages to be read, even as she feared their reception.

It followed then that whether concealed with deliberate secrecy or hidden away by lucky fate, these pages had come down to her, Dulcinea Schwartz, for a reason. No, not a reason as Chris would understand it—he could be frighteningly literal—but in the sense that everything hidden deserved to be found. Or...

No, she would make that argument later. What mattered now was the text. *Stowed so safely...* She began a search for the metaphor of a ship, a passenger, or a passage. With furious fingers, she found

herself backspacing over sentences, erasing hours of
work about the author's use of symbolism as simple
social commentary. Well, she stopped herself, maybe
some of that was still true. The demon wolves, for
example, were probably stand-ins for a larger contemporary problem, rather than the author's own personal *bête noir* or, she shuddered to think of it, actual
possessed beasts. In fact, the two might intersect.
She paused. Had she erased too much?

'Bother,' she muttered, rereading what remained.
She had.

'What's that?' Griddlehaus sat up.

'Oh, sorry.' Dulcie said, looking up. She had become so involved in her own work that she had forgotten her friend trying to concentrate on his own
reading close by.

'No, not you.' Griddlehaus silenced her with a
raised hand, his head tilted as if on alert. 'I'm sorry,
Ms Schwartz, I thought I…yes, what is that?'

A muffled sound, like a bark. Or no, Dulcie
thought, a man's voice shouting.

'Could the burglars have broken in again?' She
rose from her seat before Griddlehaus could restrain
her.

'Ms Schwartz, perhaps we shouldn't—'

She was already out the door. Sure enough, the
source of the ruckus was right near by: a cluster of
people outside the back entrance of the library. From
the hall, she could see Ruby and two of the uniformed
police she had dealt with earlier. Stuart Truckworth
was there, too. He was the one who had been yelling,
apparently. His face red with effort, his fists clenched,

he was leaning in toward one of the young officers, who was staring wide-eyed at the older man.

'Sir!' he was saying. 'Sir, please!'

'No!' Truckworth yelled back, his voice hoarse but recognizable as the deep bark that had permeated Griddlehaus's sanctum. 'Please, you've got to understand. He's my son.'

'I kn-know he's your son,' the young cop managed to say, a slight stutter slowing his words. 'We know that, sir.'

Dulcie stepped forward toward the library exit, only to find herself stopped by the outstretched arm of another officer. 'Please, Miss.'

Still, from here she had a better view of the scene. Stuart Truckworth's body was heaving, his face red. And behind the young officer, the one charged with answering the angry man, was Truckworth's son: Kyle, his long, thin arms behind his back as another police officer read the skinny guard his rights.

'Kyle?' Surprise forced the question from Dulcie's mouth. The officer blocking her way turned slightly but said nothing. None of the small crowd that had gathered seemed to hear her, either, though she thought Ruby was looking in her direction.

'Excuse me, Officer?' If she was going to be restrained, Dulcie figured she should at least be told why. 'What's happening here? Why are they holding Kyle like that?'

'I'm sorry, Miss.' His eyes were straight ahead again, avoiding hers. 'I don't have any information for you.'

'Well, fine then.' There were advantages to being

short and so, without another word, Dulcie ducked
down under the officer's arm and darted out toward
her friend. Ruby would know what was going on.

'Miss!' The officer reached for her, but she
sprinted away. He stayed by the door, apparently
charged with keeping people out of the scene—but
not with seizing those who might evade him.

'Ruby!' She found her friend toward the back of
the small crowd. Truckworth was still arguing with
the officers. His lanky son, meanwhile, was being
placed in the back of a cruiser. 'What's going on?'

'It's crazy,' Ruby said, shaking her head in disbelief. 'They think Kyle was involved with the burglaries. That he was the inside source.'

'But why?' The crowd was growing, as the flashing light on the cop car drew curious bystanders from
the street. Even with the campus largely deserted,
it seemed, there were still enough people around
to make up a small, bloodthirsty pack. Now that
Kyle was out of sight, they were focusing on Stuart Truckworth. Still red-faced, his hands were no
longer clenched. He was pleading, his voice grown
hoarse with emotion.

'He's my son!' He was reaching out, grabbing
the arm of one of the cops, a big man in a knit cap.
'You can't think—' She turned and, although Dulcie
couldn't see the cop's look or what he said, she saw
Truckworth let go suddenly and step back.

'No idea. I mean, they'd started to search everyone's lockers, but then the big cop said something
to the uniforms.' Ruby's voice obscured the harried
man's pleas. 'And they went straight to Kyle's.'

'Did they get a tip?'

'Maybe.' Ruby shrugged. Truckworth, meanwhile, had gone from pleading to a more general wail.

'A thorn in my side!' He was crying out to anyone who would listen. 'All these years!'

'We were all hanging around, wondering if we could go back to work soon, and a cop trotted over from the direction of Holyoke Center,' Ruby was saying. 'That older guy—the big one with the hair—asked Kyle for permission to go into his locker, and he said, "Yeah, sure." The next thing I knew, they had asked Kyle to step aside and then they were putting cuffs on him.'

'Poor guy.' Dulcie didn't know the red-haired guard well, but she found it hard to believe that anybody who worked in the library would betray it like that.

'Yeah, really.' Ruby was looking past Dulcie. 'And after everything he's been through with his father, too.'

'His father didn't have anything to do with it. Did he?' Dulcie turned. The man had his face in his hands.

'You heard him.' Ruby nodded once toward the stricken man. 'Going on about Kyle that way.'

'Hang on,' said Dulcie. 'I just realized what's happened.'

Ruby looked at her, waiting.

'Someone must have told them to look in his locker.' Dulcie paused to work through the ramifications. 'Jeremy Mumbleigh must be awake.'

TWENTY-ONE

'WHAT ARE YOU talking about, Dulcie?' Ruby asked.

'The tip—the cop,' said Dulcie. 'You said one of them was coming from Holyoke, from the health services. The tip had to have come from Jeremy, from Mumbles. He must have identified his attacker. Hang on.'

Now that Kyle had been removed, the officer who had been standing guard on the library's back entrance had stepped aside, and Dulcie ducked back in to get her coat and bag.

'Ms Schwartz.' Griddlehaus was still seated, although his expression showed his concern. 'You ran off.'

'I did. I'm sorry.' She quickly pulled on her coat and threw her laptop and papers into her bag. 'Thank you so much for letting me work here this afternoon. It's a wonderful room,' she said. 'A real sanctuary.'

He looked down, a little abashed but obviously pleased by the compliment. 'I'm so glad you appreciate it,' he said. 'I've not invited many people here, you know.'

'I can understand that.' Dulcie did. Not only was the reading room small, it took some of its charm from its hidden nature. More than a private study, the room was a charming nook—like the private den of a small animal. 'And I'm very happy you did.'

'You may use it whenever you'd like, you know.' He was facing her now, though the pink in his cheeks was evidence of his earlier discomfort. 'I believe you saw where we leave the key. It isn't much of a secret, but we do like to keep the room locked, and as long as you promise to replace it when you are done, you should feel free to come and go. I myself find this room wonderfully conducive to research. In fact, I was also wondering if you might be interested in what I've uncovered.'

'Thank you, Mr Griddlehaus. That would be wonderful.' Dulcie was aware of the honor he was doing her. She was also aware of the passage of time. 'But I'm afraid I've got to run now.'

He blinked, and her heart sank. She had not wanted to insult the gentle man.

'I am interested, and I'd love to come here again, Mr Griddlehaus. Really,' she said, feeling a bit warm in her coat. 'But right now, well I'm not sure, but I think Jeremy Mumbleigh may have woken up.'

'Oh, my!' His reaction was not what she expected, as he jumped up and grabbed his own coat. 'We've got to go then!'

Griddlehaus was a small man, not much taller than she was, but he was striding forward with energy, head down into a wind that had grown much colder with the onset of dusk.

Some of his rush, Dulcie suspected, came from the time: visiting hours at the health services were roughly the same as with any hospital. But the fervor of the little man's drive seemed to come from a deeper source. Dulcie wondered how much her questions had awakened old memories, and as she worked to keep pace with him, what those remembrances were.

'Jeremy Mumbleigh.' He was asking at the front desk while she was still catching her breath.

'Third floor,' she managed to gasp out, even before the receptionist located the name. 'Thanks anyway.'

She led the way to the elevators. Just because Jeremy might have been able to talk to a cop didn't mean he would be considered up to receiving visitors—especially visitors who could not claim to be immediate family. 'Maybe we should come in below the radar,' she said softly to her colleague as the elevator pinged and rose.

'This way.' The doors had opened on to the third floor, and Dulcie stepped forward. She had meant to warn Griddlehaus about the restrictions on visiting, but nobody stopped them as they proceeded. Perhaps it was the hour, but Dulcie credited their approach. The key, she belatedly remembered, was to look like you knew where you were going. This was a lesson she had picked up from Esmé, although the little cat's occasional clumsiness often undermined her dignified—and seemingly entitled—mien.

The door to Jeremy's room was ajar as they approached. A chubby young man was taking notes on the numbers that glowed and beeped on a monitor. Dulcie paused, unsure about how to respond if questioned. But her concerns evaporated when he turned toward her and nodded. 'I'm almost done,' he said. 'You can come in.'

Dulcie wasn't sure what she had expected. For him to be sitting up and eating his dinner, perhaps. At least for him to be awake and talking. What she saw instead lying there, so still she was grateful for the glowing beeps and lines of the machines, was a shock. It was Jeremy—she knew that from the shaggy silver hair that had been brushed back from his forehead. But beyond that, he was nearly unrecognizable. The lines in his long, patrician face looked deeper, as if carved. Against the pallor of his winter-white skin, the red of his chapped cheeks appeared fake, as if someone had applied make-up to a wax mannequin. Even his hands, which lay on top of the faded blue coverlet, looked foreign. She had never seen those long, slim fingers so still.

'How is he?' She realized she was whispering, afraid to wake the man in the bed.

'He was awake earlier.' The nurse stepped back in a way that invited Dulcie to come close. 'I'm afraid his visitor agitated him.'

'Visitor?' Dulcie wondered for a moment. 'Oh, you mean the police.'

'I'm afraid so.' The young man looked down at his patient—and then up at Dulcie and her companion, his face thoughtful. 'But he seems peaceful now. Would either of you like a seat?'

'I'm fine,' said Dulcie. Griddlehaus, behind her, didn't seem so stable. The shock, she figured. 'Mr Griddlehaus, why don't you sit down?'

'I didn't think…' His voice was barely a whisper.

'He's better than he looks,' said the nurse. 'That officer kept peppering him with questions. But at least he seems to be coming back to himself.'

'I gather speaking with the cops tired him out?' Dulcie posited.

A sad shake of the head. '"Spoke" is maybe an exaggeration,' the nurse said. 'Of course, I was not *in* the room at the time, having been asked to leave.' He cleared his throat. 'The man is my patient.'

Dulcie looked at Griddlehaus. 'I thought he told them something. That they got something from him?'

The nurse shrugged. 'That one officer kept trying.'

'Scat,' the man on the bed said, quite clearly. 'Scat.'

'Oh!' Dulcie drew back. 'I'm sorry, Jeremy. Do you want us to go?'

'Tack.' Dry lips smacked shut. 'Tack,' he said again.

'At least he's talking to you,' said the nurse, heading toward the curtain. 'I'm going to get him some ice chips.'

'Do you think this is what the police heard?' Dulcie looked across the prone man to her friend. 'Do you think he said...' She paused, unwilling to incriminate the guard further. 'Kyle?' she said finally, her voice little more than a whisper.

'I don't know,' said Griddlehaus, his own voice soft. 'Jeremy?' He reached to take the other man's hand. 'Can you hear me? This is Thomas Griddlehaus, from the library. I was in the reading room today. Our private room.'

'Stack.' It could have been a word. It could have been an exhalation—the dry mouth opening in release.

Dulcie looked at her colleague, but his eyes were glued on Jeremy's lined face.

'Poor dear,' said the nurse. Dulcie started slightly. She hadn't heard the uniformed attendant return with the ice. 'He thinks he's back in the library. He used to be a student here, you know.'

'So he is talking about the library?' Dulcie wasn't sure if the nurse had heard Griddlehaus introduce himself. If he had heard what the little librarian had said.

'He keeps talking about the stacks. At least, I think that's what he's saying,' said the nurse. 'The officer would keep hounding him, and with injuries like this, thoughts can get jumbled.'

As she watched, those long fingers began to move, pushing the ice chips away. Dulcie wasn't sure, but she thought he was gesturing, motioning for her to come close.

'Jeremy, can you hear me?' she asked. His face looked so calm, but she was sure his eyelids fluttered.

'Attack in the stack.' His voice was barely more than breath.

'Could he be thinking that the accident was in the library?' Griddlehaus looked up at the nurse for confirmation. 'After all, I believe he was injured in one of the old steam tunnels, which led into the stacks and are also subterranean, so perhaps...' He broke off in an uncharacteristic display of uncertainty. 'Could it be?'

'Maybe.' The nurse shrugged. 'Or maybe he's just jumped back twenty, thirty years. Who knows?'

Dulcie leaned in to listen. Jeremy wasn't simply mumbling. He was trying to say something—to tell her something.

His lips moved, but no sound came out. A tongue darted out to lick dry lips. The white coverlet rose and fell as the prone man took deeper and deeper breaths.

'The cat.' A sound like the wind in dry leaves. 'The cat.'

She couldn't have heard that correctly, could she? She leaned in closer.

'Jeremy, what are you saying? What are you trying to tell me?'

'The cat,' he said again, his voice barely more than a whisper. 'The cat in the stacks.'

TWENTY-TWO

'WHAT DO YOU think it means?' Dulcie waited for Griddlehaus's response with bated breath. She had told the little clerk what she had heard after the nurse had shooed them away. Visiting hours had ended several minutes before, he had explained, and clearly the patient was tired. 'The cat in the stacks?'

Griddlehaus shook his head as the elevator whisked them back to the ground floor. 'I don't know,' he admitted. 'And I've been trying to think of other possibilities. Homonyms, perhaps, because, Ms Schwartz, I don't want to hurt your feelings, but in this case it is possible that you might be projecting, you know.'

'I know what I heard.' Dulcie couldn't get angry at the bespectacled librarian, but she did feel ever so slightly affronted. 'He said "cat"—something about a cat in the stacks.'

'I heard "stacks,"' said Griddlehaus as the doors slid open. 'I'll give you that. But what that means, if it means anything, is a mystery to me. You heard what the nurse said.' He held the door for Dulcie as the two left the warm lobby for the windswept plaza. 'He might not even have been talking to us, strictly speaking. He might have been reliving something from decades ago. My old friend does have some issues, you know.'

'Maybe.' Dulcie wasn't convinced. 'But he did seem to be gesturing to me, asking me to come closer so he could tell me something.'

'I saw those movements, Ms Schwartz.' His voice was sad. 'I've seen them before, when people are very ill or even dying.'

Dulcie shook her head. There was more going on here. More going on under that grey mop of hair, too, she was convinced. 'If Jeremy is that out of it, then what did he say that prompted the police to arrest Kyle?'

'I suspect our friend was slightly more alert when the police spoke to him.' Mr Griddlehaus was walking to the head of a line of cabs. 'I'm reasonably certain that if he had been in the same state we witnessed, no authorities would take him seriously—or at least would not take any action based on the few words he managed to produce.'

'Unless the police know more than they're letting on.' Already her mind was jumping ahead. Rogovoy. He might not be the cop in charge of this investigation, but he'd listen to her. She'd call him first thing in the morning. She was so busy formulating how she would phrase her question that she didn't notice Griddlehaus holding a cab door open.

'Ms Schwartz?' He dipped his head.

'Oh, I don't know.' She smiled in appreciation. The cab, the door—it was all more gallant than she ever would have expected from the librarian. 'I'm really not that far.'

'Please, Ms Schwartz.' Behind the glasses, the wide, pale face grew stern. 'It's dark out, and there have been too many unfortunate occurrences of late. In fact,' he paused, as if the thought had just hit him, 'if you and I both doubt that Kyle Truckworth is responsible for the recent crimes, then we have more reason for concern. There are unsavory types abroad, Ms Schwartz. You really shouldn't be too trusting.'

'Thanks.' Dulcie wasn't sure how else to respond. Thomas Griddlehaus might be making a friendly gesture—a gallant one—but she couldn't help notice how his words had echoed her mother's warning. Was he being mindful of her safety, or did he want to rid himself of her company for some reason? She couldn't be sure.

She got into the cab, and let him close the door behind her, noting how he used both hands, careful not to slam it. Another sign that he was a friend? Fastidious? Or that he wanted her to leave? It hit her, then, how much she missed Chris, and how she had grown used to him taking care of her. Not that she didn't do the same for him, of course, but that their daily rituals involved such nurturing.

Almost like that nurse. As Griddlehaus stepped back and the cab began to pull away from the curb, another possibility hit Dulcie. She leaned forward. 'Stop please.'

Without a comment, the cabby braked, and she rolled down the window. Griddlehaus had only begun to walk away and turned at the sound of her voice.

'Mr Griddlehaus,' she called, a new anxiety in

her voice. 'Why do you think the nurse kicked us
out when he did?'

Her friend looked at her but did not answer, puzzled by her query, she thought. Or caught up in his
own thoughts.

'Do you think, Mr Griddlehaus, that it's possible...'
Dulcie paused, unsure of how to phrase the question. 'That he wanted us to leave before Jeremy said
any more?'

TWENTY-THREE

'NO, CHRIS, IT wasn't like that.' As soon as she was home, Dulcie had dialed Chris. That might have been a tactical error, she realized, as she tried to balance the phone while also feed a rather insistent Esmé. 'It was all over before I even knew what was happening.'

'*A person could starve to death*,' Esmé was saying as she twined around Dulcie's ankles. '*And by a person, I mean, of course, a cat.*'

'But still, you went back in?' Chris's voice rose from the phone, which Dulcie had placed on the counter. 'And it was this new guy, Kyle, who was arrested? Dulcie, I know you think the best of everyone, but you don't know this guy—'

'Hang on!' Dulcie yelled. 'I'm trying to open a can.'

'*Why do I even bother?*' Esmé's thoughts accompanied her insistent mew as Dulcie was clearly taking too long. Meanwhile, Chris kept talking. '…pages…' She could hear his voice but not make out what she said.

'Sorry.' Dulcie figured her blanket apology would suffice for both her pet and her boyfriend as she picked up the phone once again. 'I missed that, Chris.

But if you were asking about my pages, you'll never believe what I found out.'

Esmé paused to look up at her, then once again sank her face into the dish.

'You've gotten some writing done?' The voice on the other end of the line came alive with joy.

'Not exactly.' At that moment, Dulcie thought her boyfriend sounded as single-minded as their cat. 'But I found out where some of the new pages came from, the ones in the Mildon?' She started to fill him in— to tell him about the conservation lab and about the printer's mark. There seemed to be static on the line, though. At least, she didn't think he was hearing her.

'Dulcie,' Chris cut in. 'Dulcie, stop. Please.'

'What?' Her breath caught in her throat. 'Are you all right? Is something wrong?'

'I'm fine.' The connection was loud and clear. 'But, Dulcie, are you hearing yourself? All this talk about new leads—new information about your pages. Dulcie, you're writing about the text. Not the physical book itself, right? So why does any of this matter?'

'Because…' She hesitated, unsure how to put her feelings into words. The truth was complicated. 'Because it might matter. It might be another clue about who this woman was. It might…' She struggled to find the right explanation.

'It might keep you from finishing.' Her boyfriend's voice sounded unaccountably sad. 'And maybe, Dulcie, that's really what you are afraid of.'

The rest of the conversation wasn't much better. Dulcie wanted to tell Chris about Jeremy and about her lunch with Griddlehaus, but he remained fix-

ated on how her writing was going—or not going,
as he put it. Even when she started asking about his
mother he didn't let up.

'You're starting to sound like Thorpe,' she grumbled. Her thesis adviser had been harping on about
her writing for months now. 'Like maybe you want
me to finish so you can get rid of me.'

'Dulcie, I'm just worried about you.' Chris was
hurt. She could hear it in his voice. But so was she. If
after all this time, he couldn't understand how exciting this was—how this revelation put her that much
closer to finally identifying the author she had studied all these years—well, then, maybe he just didn't
know her that well.

'Esmé, you understand why this is important.'
Dulcie turned to the black and white cat once the call
had ended. The little tuxedo had finished her dinner by then and was bathing, one white paw swiping
over a velvety black ear. 'Don't you?'

But the round little feline was silent, now that her
needs had been met. She didn't even mew as she went
on washing, making her black coat shine.

TWENTY-FOUR

CRADLED LIKE A Jewel beyond price, the Key shone out before her. Only now, in the darkness of the Storm would she dare to take it for herself, only under cover of such inky Dark would she dare to creep so softly, key in hand into the chamber to secrete that which she now concealed upon her Person. Step by step along the corridor, she made her silent Passage, mindful with each footfall of the dangers poised to betray her were she caught, were her Traitorous Words to be exposed.

DULCIE WOKE WITH a start, the dream vivid in her mind. The heroine—the one who had been busy writing—had come alive in her sleep. No longer a literary figure, a writer—perhaps the novelist—who spilled her thoughts out on the pages. Dulcie knew the convention; having a character reveal her deepest emotions in a letter or a diary was one way of showing these to the reader, simple enough. Dulcie had started to write about the convention yesterday—was it only yesterday?—in the morning before she had left her carrel in search of lunch and found the library in turmoil. That turmoil had to be what she was remembering in her dream. Only in her sleep,

she had the woman walking toward a silent passage,
perhaps in a library—silent and stealthy...

Unless...

Dulcie jumped out of bed, earning an annoyed
squawk from the cat by her side. 'Sorry, Esmé,' Dulcie
called as she fumbled in the dark for her laptop. Yes,
there it was: the first passage she had found from this
new novel. The scene she had recognized in the mess
of disorganized fragments that Thomas Griddlehaus
had shown her one day in the Mildon Collection. A
scene in which the heroine has come upon the body
of a man, his head caved in, in a library...

Could she have dreamed the intervening scene?

Dulcie skimmed through her notes, looking for
similarities. It was possible, certainly. But as the
dream faded into memory, she found herself slowing, her cursor flicking less and less frequently over
the unrelated bits of prose.

'I'm sorry, Esmé.' The little cat had come to lean
against her bare legs, as if to lure her back to bed.
'This is silly.'

Now that she was fully awake, she could see how
she had simply conflated the events of the day with
the pages she was writing about. Add in her desire,
conflicted as it may be, to finish her thesis and, less
conflicted but also less likely, to read the rest of the
story, and her unconscious had done the rest. There
was nothing in her dream, and so she followed the
restive cat into the kitchen to fix them both some
breakfast.

'Detective Rogovoy?' While the coffee brewed,
Dulcie decided to act on one of the few mysteries

she could solve. 'I was wondering if you would answer a question several of us had.'

She heard a deep sigh on the other end of the line. Fatigue, she figured, and plunged ahead. 'Several of us were wondering what evidence Jeremy Mumbleigh gave. You see, considering the state of his health, we're concerned that perhaps something was misinterpreted...'

'Ms Schwartz.' The detective had picked up his private line on the first ring and from the sound of his voice, he had been there a while already. As she poured her coffee, Dulcie found herself picturing the deep, dark rings around his tired eyes. 'What are you talking about?'

'Kyle Truckworth,' she said. The line was silent. Dulcie knew she should have called the head of the task force. Only Lieutenant Wardley hadn't seemed as open to discussion—or as intelligent—as Detective Rogovoy. The fact that he hadn't immediately directed her call elsewhere was proof that her instincts were correct.

Or that he'd drifted off to sleep. 'The library guard who was arrested yesterday?' Dulcie waited until she heard a grunt of confirmation. 'We heard he was arrested because of something that Jeremy Mumbleigh said, but when we went to visit Jeremy—'

'Wait, you heard what?' The big man was clearly waking up. 'Who told you that?'

Dulcie thought back. She couldn't exactly remember if someone had said the words. Ruby had said something about someone talking, and an officer had been seen hurrying from the direction of the health services.

'Someone said…' She stopped. 'Stuart Truckworth. He was going on about someone, calling someone "a thorn" in his side.' The memory was hazy. 'He had to have been talking about Jeremy. I'm sure of it.'

'Really?' Rogovoy wasn't. 'Ms Schwartz, you're a smart young lady, and I don't want to tell you what to do.'

Dulcie knew she shouldn't have tipped her hand. Except that the hints she'd gotten from Jeremy had been so intriguing. 'I know I shouldn't have gone to talk to Jeremy, Detective.' She rushed to cut him off. 'But you should have heard him. He was talking about—about *something* in the stacks.'

She was not going to mention the cat. The detective wouldn't believe that.

'Isn't it possible that he—and the book—were in the library when he was attacked?' Spoken aloud, the idea seemed a bit far-fetched. 'And that he was moved afterward? Dumped in that excavation?'

'And how would a homeless person with no current university credentials have gotten into the library?' There was a heaviness in Rogovoy's voice that she had never heard before. 'Even assuming he did—we know that some people tend to bend the rules for him—how would he have been taken out again? And why?

'Ms Schwartz, please.' The weight—the weariness—made her finally listen. 'I don't want to tell you what to do, and frankly I am glad you called me rather than bothering Lieutenant Wardley, and I promise I will let him know your concern. But I have something to say to you too, Ms Schwartz. This

is an ongoing investigation. A criminal matter. Not
something out of one of your books. You need to
leave this alone.'

'That's easy for him to say.' Several minutes later,
the effect of that deep rumbling had worn off and
Dulcie was regretting her silence. For relief, she
vented to the cat. 'He's not in jail or in the hospital.'

Esmé's silence, however, seemed as pointed a response as Rogovoy's, and so Dulcie tried to turn
her mind toward organizing her day. Usually, she'd
head into the Square, but with her office closed and
the situation with the library iffy, she wondered if
that made sense. If the main library were closed, she
could probably avail herself of Griddlehaus's reading room, she knew. The director of the Mildon had
invited her to use it, but she felt to do so would feel a
little funny. For starters, the little room was clearly a
private sanctuary. And while she knew that her nig-
gling concerns about Griddlehaus were just that—
bits of nightmare salted by her mother's half-digested
visions—she couldn't quite shake the feeling that the
librarian knew more than he was telling. Besides, a
peek out the window showed a heavy cloud cover
that threatened rain, if not sleet, which made a venture outside seem particularly unappealing.

What she ought to do, of course, was write, and
there was no reason that she couldn't do that in her
apartment. In fact, if Esmé was going to insist on ignoring her—and Dulcie found herself interpreting
the small cat's silence in the most pointed terms—
she might actually be able to get something done.

Assuming the persona of the protagonist, here an

*unnamed female whose limited point of view both de-
fines and extends the central mystery, to be a stand-
in for that authorial voice as well as for the intended
audience, would be in line with the standard post-
structuralist theory in that the text may be read at
times as contradictory and transgressive, a key signifier in the works previously identified as having been
written by the author of* The Ravages of Umbria,
or the Ravages *author, for ease of reference.*

Ease of reference indeed. Forty minutes of wres-
tling with that one sentence, and all Dulcie wanted
to do was hit 'erase.' Instead, she soldiered on.

*This commonality not only helps place this pre-
viously unidentified work in the* Ravages *canon, it
opens an intriguing door on the later career of the
author, which as has previously been posited, took
her from her native England to the shores of the
fledgling United States, where her political views,
though welcomed at first during a period of intellectual receptivity (ref: Franklin, 247) would soon have
found themselves as the increasingly anti-intellectual
foment of the war years brought in a new conservatism (see...).*

Pushing aside her laptop, she reached for her yellow legal pad. Surely, she had made a note there
of the citation she wanted, the nineteenth-century
legal scholar who had published a series of papers
about the intellectual backlash of the century prior.
She flipped through the pages. What was his name?
Crabitch? Cravish?

Never mind. She tossed the pad. Better to keep
writing. She'd find the reference later.

If, as the evidence suggests... That was weak. Thorpe was going to be all over that. *One reading of the retreat...* No, too negative...*of the return to fiction, specifically, the popular and often melodramatic stylings of the earlier work (see* Ravages*) is that such works served the dual purpose of camouflaging the author's more radical message, which may be strongly identified with the first-wave feminism of Mary Shelley, et al., and also of delivering it directly, one might almost say covertly, to its intended audience: the female reader, which is to say literate women with the means and independence to either buy or subscribe to a lending library and the leisure time as well as the not inconsiderable luxury of adequate lighting (cf. candles, oil lamps, etc., in an increasingly urban society) with which to enjoy such novels.*

Dulcie sat back, rather pleased. In an earlier chapter, she had already made the case for the importance of the author's female characters, stressing how even the villainous companion was important because she had an active role. Now, she felt, she was making the case for these novels as more than mere entertainment. Their very existence meant something—and the message they carried? Well, women were writers and readers, and maybe the heroines of their own tales.

'*Like me?*' A soft, warm weight pressed against Dulcie's legs. Esmé had evidently woken from her early-morning nap. '*What is my role?*'

'I don't know yet, kitty.' Dulcie reached down to pull the cat up into her lap and was rather surprised by how heavy she was. 'I would say it's considerable, though.'

'Hunh!' Esmé settled with a soft snort and began kneading.

'Esmé…' Dulcie waited a minute. It was very nice to have the warm, soft body on her lap. Even the sharp pinpricks of claws as her pet worked her paws rhythmically against her legs wasn't too bad. However, there was one inescapable fact. 'Esmé, darling, I think I have to put you down.' The black and white cat kept on kneading, refusing—Dulcie suspected—to meet her eyes. 'I don't think I can type with you on my lap. You're too large.'

From habit, she'd been stroking the cat's sleek black back, but now she removed her hands. In return, Esmé tipped her head up, pinning her with those green eyes.

'I'm sorry, kitty.' Dulcie shifted slightly, hoping the cat would leave of her own accord.

'Meh.' She did, finally, kicking off with what may have been a bit too much force in a move that dug her hind claws into Dulcie's legs. *'As if you ever notice the cat…'* Dulcie caught the tail end of the feline comment, as the tail end of the actual feline disappeared around the door. *'As if you paid any attention…'*

Maybe it was guilt, but Dulcie had a hard time concentrating after that. Without Chris, the apartment felt too big—too empty. And to top it off, the heat had come on with a hiss like a perturbed puss, and the clanking and banging of the old building's pipes were giving her a headache.

'I'm going to see if I can get back into the library, Esmé.' She called into the other room as she began to pack up her bag. 'I promise I won't stay so late tonight.'

The cat did not deign to answer.

TWENTY-FIVE

THE LIBRARY, TO Dulcie's surprise, was open. It was also buzzing, which while unusual was not an unexpected consequence of everything going on. As a result Dulcie made her way in almost without notice, swiping her ID card as a guard—one of the older men—waved her by without a glance, so absorbed was he in his conversation.

Dulcie paused in the main lobby, taking in the unaccustomed hubbub. With all the voices she must, she figured, be able to find someone to tell her what was going on.

'Ruby!' She called out to her friend, who looked up and waved her over to the circulation desk, where she was in a deep conversation with two other staffers.

'Dulcie, you've got to hear this,' said her friend.

'Erin, multimedia.' The redhead on the other side of the desk introduced herself. 'You know Kyle?'

'Kind of.' Dulcie shrugged, Chris's words of caution echoing in her ears. 'I hadn't known he was Stuart Truckworth's son until just this week.'

'Poor kid.' Erin shook her head. 'Yeah, he didn't like that to get around. You'd think his dad did all kinds of favors for him, but the truth was, he was really hard on Kyle.'

'He seemed upset that Kyle was arrested.' Dulcie tried to imagine how her father would have reacted in a similar situation, but there were too many impossible variables involved.

Erin and Ruby exchanged a glance that Dulcie couldn't read. 'Yeah, maybe,' the redhead said.

'What?' Dulcie waited.

'I think his dad thinks this all reflects badly on *him*.' The redhead made a point of emphasizing the last word.

'He can't be that bad.' Dulcie thought back. 'He seemed quite distraught.'

Erin shrugged. 'I guess. I think Kyle was an embarrassment to him—like Kyle could never be a buttoned-down professional, like he is.'

Somehow, this didn't jibe with the image in Dulcie's head. 'But he's facilities and maintenance, right?'

'He's still management.' Ruby leaned in. 'I heard that the cop who arrested Kyle is being called on the carpet.'

'I heard that he was gunning for Kyle because of his dad.' This latest came from Brian, the head of digital services. 'That it's a departmental rivalry thing.'

'Does anyone know anything concrete?' Dulcie's head was spinning from the gossip and speculation. 'Like, what evidence they have?'

'I thought old Mumbles said something.' Ruby looked at Dulcie for confirmation.

Dulcie felt the blush rise to her cheeks. 'I think I started that rumor by accident. Someone saw a cop coming from the direction of Holyoke Center…from the health services…' She paused. 'But, no, Jeremy is still not really conscious.'

'Poor guy.' Ruby shook her head. Erin, however, looked less convinced.

'I don't know,' she said. 'He creeps me out. He's always lurking, you know? Like he's hiding something.'

'He's just shy,' said Dulcie. 'Kind of like a cat.'

Erin raised her eyebrows at that, and Dulcie realized it was time for her to get to work. 'So, is the library back to normal?'

'No.' Erin had the latest. 'Level three is still considered a crime scene. I guess it's a mess. I heard one of the cops say something about seeing an animal down there.'

'Rats.' Ruby shuddered. 'I guess we've been lucky. Hey, Dulcie, maybe Mumbles is really a cat, and now that he's away…'

Dulcie forced a smile and made her farewell, heading toward the main reading room. She had no problem finding a good seat, with a working lamp and far enough away from the main entrance so that the unusual buzz wasn't audible. But she couldn't help but feel like an exile. Or, no, a small animal that had been driven from its lair. That, she realized, must have been what Jeremy had felt like, back in the day, when his very achievements had turned against him.

But even if everyone else made light of his plight, she wouldn't. Unsure where to go, Dulcie logged into the university search engine that Lala had used and entered the name *Jeremy Mumbleigh*. She saw the same headlines she had viewed before: *Wins*

Dorchester. Mumbleigh Identifies Islington Bible.
And finally, *Scholar Disputes University Decision,
Faces Disciplinary Action.* She couldn't tell for sure
if anything here had relevance. But the battle had
mattered so much to Jeremy. The least she could do
was search for individual titles to see if she could
discern their fate.

It wasn't easy. Perhaps because the disputed works
were considered of little value, very few of them
were mentioned. There were some novels from the
late nineteenth century described simply as 'sentimental.' A translation of lesser works by the Abbé
Constantin and some early mysteries by Mary Roberts
Rinehart. And while the Gothic found on Jeremy, *He
Could Not Tell Her,* was noted once for its length—
'belabored over two volumes'—it didn't merit a second mention. One article did make a vague reference
to 'early commercial fiction' that intrigued her, while
another noted that 'some of these works may be notable for their rarity today, if not their literary quality.' But that was it.

What all the journals focused on instead was the
battle waged by Jeremy Mumbleigh to save these
books—or, at least, to keep them in the original collection.

'How do you define "value"?' one piece began.
At least the argument hadn't been totally one-sided.
Dulcie found a point-counterpoint in an issue of a
now-defunct university quarterly. The writer, as far
as she could tell, took Jeremy's side, arguing that
no book was worthless, and that the gift should be
kept intact. 'Even if an individual title is not a prized

member of the literary canon,' she read, 'it may be useful for the insight it casts on the giver. That is, even a piece of trash fiction might tell us more about who saved such priceless works as the Islington Bible for posterity.'

Well, that probably would not have been Jeremy's argument, Dulcie decided. Although she couldn't be sure, she had a strong feeling that the wounded scholar would have valued the books for their own right, not simply because of their use as historical or biographical markers.

The counterpoint didn't even contest the first writer's argument, she saw as she moved on. Instead, it focused on practicalities, appealing to the reader's sense of reality.

'Clearly, a significant portion of the property was not original to the bequest,' began the opposing argument. 'If budgeting were not an issue, the university would happily maintain the gift as it was received. However, we must be practical about both money and storage limitations and harbor our resources for more deserving properties. Even were these pieces lost, the hunt to restore them would be more costly than their worth.'

'What a crock,' muttered Dulcie as she scrolled through the rest. But before she could close it, one more line held her transfixed. The piece, she now read, had been written by the then-assistant manager of facilities and maintenance. A bureaucrat named Stuart Truckworth.

TWENTY-SIX

WHY DID STUART TRUCKWORTH have it in for Jeremy?

As Dulcie sat looking at the news story, she found she could neither answer that question nor shake the idea that for nearly thirty years the two had been at odds. Maybe there was history she didn't know of. Maybe Truckworth had resented Mumbleigh back when both had been graduate students. After all, Jeremy had gone on to win the Dorchester, while Stuart had ended up leaving his studies behind for a far-from-unprofitable but certainly less glamorous career. But now, their roles had completely reversed. Truckworth was a success—a senior manager with a son with whom he was developing a relationship. What could such a man have against Mumbleigh, who had fallen so low?

'It's just not fair,' said Dulcie to the screen before her. 'It's not fair, and it's not very nice.' It was, however, curious, and Dulcie regretted that Griddlehaus wasn't around. Her friend might have been able to shed some light on his former colleagues. But, no… she looked around the reading room. The bespectacled librarian still had not surfaced. And as much as she was tempted to go look for him, she knew she shouldn't. Chris was right. The reason she had stayed on campus this week was to get work done. Yesterday was the exception. It would have been hard for anyone to concentrate after all the brouhaha. Besides, her side trip to the conservation lab had proved relevant to her work, sort of.

Today was a new day, and despite the slow start she had hours to get work done. She opened her document and thought about what to write next.

While the conflation of the author and the protagonist is a common mistake on the part of readers, the serious scholar should not assume...

She stopped herself. What she was writing might as well be dogma. Her thesis committee would know this—would know the dangers of reading the heroine as a stand-in for the author. Besides, wasn't she trying to make the opposite case? That one could use these books—the fragments of *The Ravages of Umbria* and this one, which Dulcie had privately dubbed *The Body in the Library*—as clues that would help her figure out the identity of the author?

She tried again. *While the conflation of the author and the protagonist is commonly viewed as a mistake, in the absence of other material, the fictionalized world may be examined for clues as to the author's identity.*

There, that was good. Only... Dulcie paused as the thought formed. She did have other clues: the pages she had pieced together. While she had first discovered this new novel from some surviving printed pages, what she was working from now were actual manuscript pages, written in the author's own hand. Surely, she could apply her own form of literary forensics to those primary sources.

She closed her eyes and conjured up those stained and tattered papers. If only she could get down to the Mildon again. Could once more view those actual pages. When she had first identified them, she had been focused on what they contained. Deciphering the faded words, picking out phrases that in some cases—thanks to corrosive ink—had eaten through the paper like moths in cashmere, had been her priority, and she had worked long hours to put together the bits and pieces. Now, however, she wished she had paid more attention to those pages themselves. They were a direct link to the woman she was seeking.

But Chris was right. This was a diversion. As a scholar, her goal was to trace the author through the text, not through some physical remnants. She looked over her notes again and started once more to write.

The author, whom we may presume to be the same person who... She paused again. Who or whom? 'Who' looked right. 'Who' was right, she was sure. She looked up. Working in the reading room had its distractions. For starters, the high ceilings and wide open space amplified every sound. She could hear Ruby's low chuckle all the way from circulation, and one of the guards had the squeakiest shoes. However, if she were downstairs, she wouldn't have such easy access to actual physical research materials, such as the OED or the various style books that were kept on hand here.

Even more important, she wouldn't have been able to ask Ruby for advice.

'Ruby?' Dulcie had tucked her laptop back into her messenger bag before leaving her seat. It wasn't that she didn't trust her colleagues. A few weeks ago, she would have left the machine as a place marker, a visible sign that, yes, this particular chair was indeed occupied. All the warnings had spooked her, however. The warnings and the thought that someone—or some group—had actually breached her beloved library. 'Ruby, may I ask your thoughts on a phrasing?'

Dulcie kept her voice low as she approached the circulation desk. The courtesy was a habit, but she had to raise her voice and ask again. Ruby and the two other staffers on duty were so caught up in their conversation, they didn't seem to hear her.

'I don't know why he doesn't get him removed,' another woman was saying. 'I think it's a gross dereliction of duty.'

'He's just doing his job,' said Ruby. She'd seen Dulcie by then and waved her over.

'Who's just doing his job?' Dulcie couldn't resist a little gossip.

'That cop.' Ruby shook her head. 'The one who arrested Kyle?'

'Have they let him go yet?' Dulcie looked around, hoping for an answer.

'No.' Ruby shook her head. 'I think he's being arraigned. Truckworth has been frantic.'

'That's what I'm talking about,' said the other clerk. 'This whole thing sounds like some kind of personal vendetta. That cop is like a mad dog.'

'Poor Kyle.' Dulcie didn't feel comfortable dissing the cops, even if they did make mistakes. 'But look what happened with Jeremy,' she said. 'They thought he was involved with the break-ins at first, but now they must know he can't be.'

'Yeah, and look what great shape he's in.' Ruby's voice sank. After a weighted moment, Ruby turned to her friend.

'You wanted to ask me something, Dulcie?'

Dulcie shrugged. The question of grammar seemed particularly irrelevant. 'Yeah, I guess.'

But before she could bring up the question of subjective or objective cases the relative peace of the library was broken by a loud noise—a series of loud noises, repeating like gunfire through the room.

'What the...?' Ruby looked around.

'It's coming from outside,' said Dulcie, and made for the door.

'Miss! Miss!' The guard, a substitute, came running behind her. 'Your purse!'

'Oh, sorry.' Dulcie turned. 'I just want to see what's happening.'

'That's not allowed...' The guard pointed to her bag. 'I have to search—'

'Of course.' Shrugging the strap off her shoulder, Dulcie deposited the denim holdall on the barrier. 'I'll be right back,' she promised as she raced after her friend.

'What are you doing?' Ruby was yelling down into a hole. Dulcie hurried over to her side, skirting around a barrier to do so. 'You! Put that down!'

Pulling her friend back from the edge, Dulcie joined her in peering down. The hole was deep—a good twenty feet—and seemed to have some kind of concrete floor. Even as they watched, a figure in

the hole—the hard hat and thick work gloves effectively obscured the person's gender—picked up a
T-shaped handle and flicked a switch. Once again,
the thunderous rat-a-tat-tat sounded, driving both
Dulcie and her friend back another few feet.

'Hey, you!' Ruby yelled at the next pause, leaning
perilously close. 'You!'

The person with the jackhammer didn't look up,
and as Ruby leaned farther, Dulcie saw the edge of
the hole begin to fracture. Clods of dirt fell, and
inside, behind the figure, a shadow—could it have
been something living?—seemed to race away.

'What's that?' Dulcie grabbed Ruby's arm as
the hammering stopped. The shadow had slipped
across the hole, but Dulcie could still see it—dark
and seemingly solid under the overhang of the far
wall. 'There!' Dulcie pointed.

'Where?' Ruby leaned forward to look. It was too
much. The earth, frozen for too long, had become
crumbly and dry. As Dulcie strained to see, she felt
it begin to give way, to fall. Her foot slipped.

'I've got you!' A strong hand clasped around her
upper arm, pulling Dulcie back.

'Wait—' She could just make out the shape below.
A triangular face. Two eyes.

'Mr Truckworth!'

Dulcie turned. Ruby was addressing the manager,
who now had one arm on each of the women and
was leaning back, pulling them away from the hole.

'You shouldn't be here, ladies,' he said, shaking
his head. 'It's a construction site and, as you can see,
not at all stable.'

'You shouldn't be working here.' Ruby put her hands on her hips. 'The noise carries right through the walls into the library.'

'I'm sorry.' Truckworth was shaking his head. 'None of this is ideal, I know. But we've got to get the repairs done as expeditiously as possible. The students will be back on Monday.'

'Where does this go?' Dulcie was still peering down into the hole. From this distance, she had lost sight of the shadow, but she could see that the side of the hole wasn't solid, as she had assumed. Instead, there seemed to be a tunnel or passage leading away from the opening.

'Storage. Steam tunnels.' Truckworth gestured. 'The entire substructure is falling apart.'

'I thought I saw something down there.' Dulcie craned to look. 'An animal.'

'Rats.' Truckworth's mouth was set in a grim line. 'We're going to have to put down traps everywhere.'

'Ew!' With a high-pitched squeal that seemed rather out of place for her size, Ruby recoiled, pulling her hands up as if she expected to get bitten.

'No, I don't think it was a rat…' Dulcie couldn't explain her feeling, but she had enough experience to trust it.

'Please, ladies.' Truckworth's hand was on her arm again. 'I am sorry for the disruption. As I said, we're trying to get the work done in as timely a manner as possible, despite everything else going on.'

Dulcie looked up. This was the opportunity she had been waiting for. 'Mr Truckworth, I'm sorry about your son.' This was true. It was also a way in.

'Thanks.' He rubbed a hand over his face, leaving a smear of dirt on his cheek. 'Kyle is…well, I'm doing what I can.'

'I'm sure you are, Mr Truckworth.' Dulcie pushed forward. 'And that's why I'm also sure you understand how important it is to be fair to people.'

He shook his head, his eyes tired.

'Why are you persecuting Jeremy Mumbleigh, Mr Truckworth?' Dulcie looked into those eyes. 'What did he ever do to you?'

'Dulcie!' Ruby's voice cut in. 'What are you… I'm sorry, Mr Truckworth. It's just been so crazy today, we're all out of sorts.'

She started to pull Dulcie away, but Dulcie resisted. 'No, hang on, Ruby. This is something I want to know about. Mr Truckworth has been down on Jeremy for years, and I want to know why. He had Jeremy arrested—'

'Jeremy Mumbleigh was arrested because he was found with unauthorized materials. That decision was out of my control.'

Before she could respond, another voice broke in on them.

'What's the trouble here?' They all turned to see a burly cop, a knit cap pulled down almost to his eyes. 'This area is off limits.'

'It is, Officer. It is indeed. Hard hats only.' Truckworth must have been grateful for the shift in concentration, Dulcie thought, considering the alacrity with which he jumped to answer the newcomer. 'In fact, I was about to escort these young women out of the area.'

He motioned as if to wave the two friends away, stepping between them and the excavation. Before she moved, though, Dulcie snuck another look down. The construction worker peered back up, no doubt intrigued by the conversation, but she could see no other signs of life. 'They wandered in,' Truckworth was saying.

The fat cop nodded, as if the facilities manager was in fact in charge of both Dulcie and her friend. It was too much.

'We're members of the university community.' Dulcie spoke up. It was hard enough being shorter than everyone, she wasn't going to accept being talked about as if she weren't here. 'We had a right to inquire as to what was going on.'

'We came to complain about the noise,' Ruby chimed in, in a tone that was a little conciliatory for Dulcie's taste.

'And about the persecution of Jeremy Mumbleigh,' Dulcie added, prompting a look of surprise from the officer.

'Well, Truckworth, it sounds like you've got a mutiny on your hands.' His comment—addressed to the administrator—was further proof to Dulcie that neither were taking her—or her complaint—seriously.

'Yes, Lieutenant Wardley.' Truckworth looked down at the ground, his voice tired. 'I'm sorry, Lieutenant. I'll take care of it.'

'See that you do.' The cop nodded as Truckworth glanced up and then turned and walked away.

TWENTY-SEVEN

'WHAT DO YOU think that was about?' Ruby asked as they made their way back up the stairs.

'What are you talking about?' Dulcie couldn't stop thinking about what she'd seen in the hole. It had been awfully large for a rat. And if it were any other animal, it might be trapped in the maze of tunnels and construction—too spooked by the noise to find its way back out.

'That was Wardley, the cop who arrested Kyle. I thought Truckworth would tear him a new one, but he seemed all diffident.' Ruby stopped to turn back toward the hole.

'His son's in trouble. Maybe he's hoping to get on the officer's good side?' Truckworth's reasoning didn't seem as pressing as the other issue the incident had raised. 'Ruby, did you see something down there?'

'Probably a rat.' Ruby shook off the residual horror and climbed the remaining stairs to return to work, hugging her arms around her. 'Whatever—it ran back down into the tunnel, and I've got to get back in too. It's freezing out here.'

It was, the wind hinting at more snow to come, but still Dulcie lingered on the stairs. She hadn't recognized Wardley in that knit cap, but knowing that he

was the task force leader made everything else make
a little more sense. The facilities manager struck
her as a bully, and a bully would be easily cowed by
someone with more power. What had struck her only
after they had started walking away was the manner
in which he had answered her question. Stuart Truckworth had immediately known whom Dulcie was
talking about. He might have had a point about the
poor man's offense, but Dulcie couldn't help thinking that there was something else going on between
the two, something more recent than a youthful acquaintance. What had Truckworth said? That Jeremy
had been a 'thorn in his side' for thirty years? There
was bad blood there, and it was current.

Griddlehaus would know, Dulcie decided. She
would have to ask him when he next surfaced, and
with that she walked back into the library.

'Miss.' The guard was glowering. Her bag was
nowhere in sight.

'I'm sorry,' she said. 'I really am. But I wanted to
see what all the ruckus was about. Do you…?' She
looked around. 'Where's my bag?'

'I thought about turning it over to the police.' He
looked down his nose at her. It wasn't difficult, seeing as how he was both tall and had an impressive
snout. 'For all I knew, it could have contained a bomb
or some kind of contraband.'

Dulcie had a flash of concern, imagining her laptop—all her work—in the hands of Lieutenant Wardley.
She thought back to their interaction. Had she been
rude? Chris was always telling her she needed to be
a bit more circumspect around authority. But, no,

the guard raised one finger and ducked under the counter. Then, with three giant strides he made his way over to the administrative office. Dulcie waited, wondering if she should follow him. But just as she had decided that, yes, she should, he emerged with her old familiar messenger bag. As he placed its worn canvas on the counter her gratitude—and remorse—were unfeigned.

'Thank you so much.' She reached for the denim strap. 'I'm really sorry to have just dumped it here. I just—'

'And I'm sorry to have kept you waiting, especially if I worried you. We don't have a protocol for storing student possessions and it took me a moment to locate it.' He was smiling. 'I don't think we've ever met, but I see you here all the time, and I didn't figure you for a terrorist.'

'Thank you.' She looked up. When he smiled, his nose didn't look quite so huge. 'I'm Dulcie, by the way. Dulcinea Schwartz.'

'Roger Thumbkin,' said the large guard, apparently unaware of any irony, as he held out his hand. 'Pleased to meet you.'

Dulcie smiled and nodded, not trusting herself to respond. If a giant could be named Thumbkin, she wasn't going to comment. The new guard wasn't through with her, however.

'One reason I brought it into the office,' he said, leaning over and dropping his voice, 'is I believe I heard a certain distinctive tone.' He pronounced the last word carefully. She met his eyes. They both knew what this meant: Dulcie had left her phone turned on in the library.

'I'm sorry,' she whispered back. 'I'll take care of it.'

Retreating to the portico, she saw a few fat flakes begin to fall. The damp gusts had indeed meant more wintry weather, and Dulcie shivered as she fished the device from the bag's depths. Sure enough, it was turned on. But in place of a message, she saw a text. Chris. The wind was whipping up—a snow squall— and Dulcie turned her back to it as she opened her phone.

Hope you're hard at work, it read. *Can't wait to read! Know Mr Grey would be proud of you.*

Dulcie swallowed. If only he knew. But it was too cold out here to explain—her teeth had begun to chatter. And since she couldn't lie, she merely typed in a smiley face and hit send. By the time they spoke tonight, she promised herself—and him—silently, she'd have some real progress to report.

Fifteen minutes later, she was back in the reading room, laptop open before her. The sudden storm had had one good effect—it seemed to have put the kibosh on any more excavation work outside. At any rate, the noise had ceased, and Dulcie should have been able to concentrate. The light was good, the seat more comfortable than in her carrel three levels down. In fact, if she were being completely honest, the reading room was probably more conducive to serious work. Although the cavernous space wasn't as private as her usual subterranean lair, the occasional footstep actually served to keep her focused. There were people here, other scholars, who just might notice if she were staring into space for too long. Or, worse, if she fell asleep.

Besides, all that talk of rats had disturbed her. Dulcie knew that she lived in a city—it was hard to ignore such things, especially with the frequent police updates. And rats were as much a part of the urban landscape as, well, rodents anywhere. Still, she couldn't help but be creeped out by the idea of such vermin in what was essentially her home. She told herself this was largely out of concern for the collection. The idea that some day she might pull a volume from the shelf and find that it had been gnawed on was simply horrible. But she couldn't help thinking of the movements she had seen—the shadowy shape darting around the edges of the stacks and, more recently, that hole. Had those been rodents, signs of a larger infestation? Even up here, in the well-lit confines of the reading room, Dulcie felt her toes curl at the idea.

Only, she realized now, staring at the screen which had—unlike its owner—drifted off to sleep, she hadn't felt that same queasiness outside. Unlike Ruby, who had recoiled at the idea of a rat, Dulcie had found herself leaning forward. Trying to get a glimpse of whatever it was that had scurried behind the worker with the jackhammer. It couldn't have been...

No. Mr Grey wouldn't have darted away like that. If anything, he would have stopped and looked up at her. Dulcie shook her head to clear it. Chris's message had made her think of Mr Grey. It was natural.

That didn't mean her spectral companion was haunt-
ing the grounds around the library.

But that didn't mean some other cat wasn't. After
all, cats and humans belonged together. Certainly
since the time of that printer's mark—the sign of
the 'printer's friend'—humans had been grateful for
their presence.

Dulcie could have laughed: it was all so obvious.
Feral cats were as much a part of the urban landscape as were rats. In fact, it only made sense that
if the rodents of the Yard were being displaced then
the felines of the area might be having a heyday.
Maybe there had been a rat down there, disturbed
by the jackhammering just like every other creature
in the vicinity had been. And maybe she had caught
a glimpse of a local cat in hot pursuit.

Poor thing. The thought came unbidden to Dulcie's
mind. Esmé, she realized immediately, would have a
field day with that: sympathy for a rat! Not that her
plump and pampered pet had ever been a mouser,
nor was likely to be. Esmé's prey tended toward the
inanimate: catnip mice and rolled-up balls of foil.
The few times last summer when Dulcie had seen
her stalk a moth, the result had clearly been so hu-
miliating for the erstwhile hunter that Dulcie had
refrained from ever mentioning it.

Poor Esmé. She missed Chris as much as Dulcie
did. More, maybe, because she didn't have the distraction of a dissertation to keep her busy. Though
certainly, if asked, the little tuxedo cat would have
declared that her days were quite full. Dulcie would
have to discuss this with Chris tonight, when they

talked. And now, she thought as she pulled her chair in, she really did have to get to work. If for no other reason than to be able to tell Chris—and Esmé—what she had gotten done.

With a poke, she woke her dozing laptop and began to type. *A closer examination of these pages*, she read, *sheds light on the author and her origins*.

Dulcie paused. This was where she had intended to talk about language, about repeated phrases that she had painstakingly traced back to both *The Ravages of Umbria* as well as to early feminist tracts of the time, writings that were more widely disseminated in England than in the young United States. In a previous chapter, Dulcie had already made the connection between this later, fragmented work and the earlier novel, tying in several pseudonymous essays that had appeared in Philadelphia about this time. Now she was going to take it even further, to look at how word usage and certain terms suggested the education and social class of the author.

The examination of these pages...

It was because of that cat—that or the mention of Mr Grey—but as she typed the final word, she thought of the mark she had seen in the conservator's lab. The profile of a cat, depicted so economically with just a few lines of silver—a touch of glitter reminiscent of another she had seen in the Mildon, right before it closed. The printer's friend, Griddlehaus had explained, because of his skill at keeping rats and mice at bay. The Mildon fragment had probably been something different. Those documents had already been thoroughly examined, Dulcie knew

now. Still, she had found that other mark—the one
in the binding of Jeremy's book—and she couldn't
help but think it couldn't have appeared without a
reason. Not with those long whiskers, so reminiscent
of someone else she knew.

Maybe, she thought, her hands pausing just above
the keyboard, she could make a little detour. Maybe
she could work in what she had just discovered and
not get too off track—and see if Margaret or her colleague wanted to look once more at that fragment.
Of course, if she were going to incorporate this new
information into her dissertation, she'd have to do
some more research.

The examination of these pages... She started typing, just to feel the idea out. *These pages, which
have only recently been revealed to have been found
within the binding of...*

The binding of what? The conservator—
Margaret—had been telling her about finding the
pages when they'd been interrupted by her colleague's discovery of the silver cat. She had never
found out what book had been holding these pages
all these years.

The documents themselves gave no clue. Dulcie
thought of the papers as she had first seen them—
tattered and dark—and found her mind wandering
back to that cat, the printer's mark, also secret—
also tucked away. Was it possible there was a connection? Or would it not—she could already hear
Chris's questions as well as Thorpe's—be a detour?

No, she reassured herself. Even if there were no
connection between her pages and the Felix, her av-

enue of inquiry was legitimate. If she could uncover anything concrete about where the pages had been hidden it might shed some light on the provenance of the fragmented manuscript, or maybe even on its author, and that would justify the time. If not, she would have done some background into one of her primary sources. Even a footnote would be worth it.

Once more, she slid her laptop into her bag. If she could chat with that conservator, she might be able to write up her findings tonight. The fact that the Mildon was closed was an impediment. She wouldn't be able to identify the fragments by number—or ask Margaret about that trace of glitter she had seen. Still, she thought, there was a lot she could learn. As she made her way to the exit, Dulcie began compiling questions. How many bindings in the collection had the conservators taken apart? How many sheets had they discovered, covered with writing? Were all the pages taken from one book, or had they been scattered? The idea of one printer pulling pages randomly from a manuscript made Dulcie shiver.

The chill in the main entrance didn't help. Outside, the weather had gotten worse, more true storm than a simple snow squall. Could she find her way through the tunnels without Griddlehaus to guide her? Dulcie hesitated, then decided to play it safe. Besides, she couldn't entirely dismiss the thought of rats. What was a little snow after the winter they had just had? Dulcie started buttoning her coat and headed toward the exit.

Which, she was surprised to see, wasn't staffed.

'Mr Thumbkin?' She put her bag up on the counter to be checked and looked around. The big man must not be aware of protocol, she thought. Surely one of the chief duties of a guard here was to make sure that nobody took anything from the library. 'Where are you?'

'He's gone back to his regular post,' said a familiar voice.

'Kyle!' Dulcie greeted the young guard in an unlibrary-like volume of voice. He was folding his coat over his arm as he came out of the staff office. 'They let you go,' she said, much more softly.

He shrugged as he positioned himself behind the counter and slid his coat beneath. 'For now,' he said. 'I've got to talk to a lawyer. It's crazy.'

'They can't really think you did anything.' She watched his face darken as he lifted the denim flap. 'I mean, they're wrong.'

'Thanks.' He looked inside, holding the flap open with his hand. 'I mean, for saying that. You'd be surprised at the fuss they made.' He paused and turned to her. 'The university police didn't even want me to come back to work.'

'That's awful.' Dulcie waited while he unzipped the outer pocket. Clearly, he was making a point of being careful. 'I'm sure this will all blow over. I mean, your father's on your side, right?'

Kyle laughed, a sort of gleeless snort, and handed her bag back. 'I don't know, Dulcie. My dad—man, it's like something from the last century with him. If it wasn't for him, I would never have been arrested.'

'I thought...' Dulcie wasn't sure how to phrase it. In truth, she could no longer remember exactly what she had heard. 'That they found something? In your locker?' It felt odd to even voice the words.

Kyle nodded, his mouth set in a grim line. 'Yeah, a book that had gone missing, and I have no idea how it got there. But because I was down by the old tunnels and they connect to the storage rooms, the cops seem to think they have a case. Like I'd even know what to do with a rare book anyway. I mean, they might as well be talking to him.' Kyle nodded over Dulcie's head and she turned.

'Mr Griddlehaus!' It was her friend, coming in the entrance and brushing snow from his shoulders as he did so. 'I was hoping to find you.'

Dulcie turned back toward Kyle. 'Thanks, anyway, Kyle. I think I'm not going to leave now.' She pulled her possessions toward her. 'And I'm glad you're out. I'm sure that this will work out all right. Really.'

'Ms Schwartz.' Before Kyle could respond, the diminutive librarian had come over and clasped one cold hand over Dulcie's. 'I have news for you. Do you have a moment?'

'Indeed, I do.' She turned to her friend.

'Please, follow me.' Griddlehaus wasn't a dramatic figure usually. In fact, with his quiet ways and short stature, he was more likely to be overlooked than noted. However, at this point, he seemed to be intentionally calling attention to himself, the way he looked from right to left and back again. 'This way.' His stage whisper wasn't helping, and Dulcie couldn't help wondering what was up as he led her, scurrying in a rather mouse-like fashion, through the library lobby and over to the elevators.

He pressed a button and the panel lit up and then, rather to her surprise, the doors opened once again.

'Mr Griddlehaus?' Dulcie stepped into the elevator and watched as the elevator sank two, then three floors. 'Are we going to…?'

'The Mildon,' said Griddlehaus, still using his stage whisper. 'They can't keep me out any longer.'

'Isn't this area off limits?' As the motion sensor lights went on along the blessedly quiet hallway, Dulcie followed her friend to the locked gates, and watched as he punched in a code and proceeded to turn off the various alarms that kept the priceless collection safe. 'I mean, if not for the water main repair then for the police investigation?'

'Ms Schwartz, if the elevator is working then I believe the power throughout this area is too. I suspect that Mr Truckworth simply neglected to inform me, which is perhaps understandable considering the pressure he is under,' he replied, as he switched on the lights. It was true, Dulcie noted, that there was neither any sign of water damage or crime scene tape. Even the fine layer of dust might, she acknowledged silently, be a figment of her imagination, if not the result of several days without the intensive air-filtration system at work.

'I do believe they've forgotten all about the Mildon.' Griddlehaus opened a closet and removed his coat, brushing the last drops of moisture from it as he did so. 'And even if not my first obligation is, of course, to the collection. Your coat and bag?'

She handed them over and looked around. Never before had the quiet preserve seemed so special. The Mildon Collection—this perfect library within a library—might appear sterile to an outsider. Its walls and furnishings were all matte white; its lighting the diffuse, colorless glow of energy-efficient halogen bulbs. Even the box of disposable gloves on the reading room table was white. But as Dulcie knew, behind all that white lay a rich and colorful history.

Out of habit, Dulcie reached for the gloves—and caught herself. 'I'm sorry,' she said. 'You had something to tell me?'

'Indeed.' Griddlehaus motioned for her to take a seat, and then sat beside her, catty corner at the reading table. This in itself was odd: Dulcie was accustomed to the librarian bustling about. If he wasn't fetching her another folder of documents—those pages that she had so carefully deciphered—he was looking over his own work at the front desk. Truly, ground was being broken today.

'You may have been aware that I've been conducting some research,' he said. His voice, though still soft, was back to its natural speaking tone. 'This has led me to…well, thus far it is inconclusive. But it has led me to some questions for our mutual friend, Jeremy. I have become convinced he knows more than he has been able to communicate.'

'You've seen him again?' Dulcie started to stand, but her friend held out a hand, as if to restrain her. 'Is he awake?'

'Yes and no.' Griddlehaus shook his head. 'Or, I should say, not entirely. He seemed to know that

I was there. He was, I'm afraid, conforming to his unfortunate nickname and mumbling.

'You see, Ms Schwartz, I didn't say anything yesterday. It all seemed too vague and inconclusive. But yesterday, after we left poor Jeremy, I carried with me a nagging impression. Something he had said seemed to hint at a certain incident, and I was hoping to find the paper trail.'

He paused, and Dulcie leaned forward. Could they both have picked up on the same clues?

'A certain phrase he insisted on repeating about the stacks,' Griddlehaus said, his voice low. 'Perhaps about being "attacked in the stacks?" At any rate, it stayed with me.'

'Oh.' Dulcie felt her excitement wane. 'I didn't hear him that way,' she said. 'I thought he said something about a cat in the stacks. In fact…' She broke off, remembering her own thoughts from not that long ago. 'I was wondering about that printer's mark we saw. The silver cat. I wanted to ask you if it were possible that that mark was on the books that held my pages.'

'Oh.' Griddlehaus blinked at her, his eyes huge behind his glasses. 'That may have some relevance. But, no, that was not what I had heard, nor was it what I was inquiring about, when I went to see the poor fellow today. You see, I was wondering if Jeremy was remembering an adventure—a misadventure, really—from our youth, and if it might pertain to his situation today.'

'An adventure?' Dulcie could not imagine Griddlehaus getting into trouble.

He nodded, the ghost of a smile playing around his lips. 'We were scamps. Or, I'm afraid, I was, Ms Schwartz, and our misbehavior nearly resulted in tragedy.' His face turned serious, as if clouded by memory. 'Are you familiar with the Cranston Tower?'

'In Cranston House? Sure.' The undergraduate residence, the university's equivalent of a dorm, was one of the older ones, distinguished by its cramped staircases and oddly shaped rooms as well as by its red and gold tower. 'I know it has that lovely clock. You can see it from the Yard.'

'But did you know about the room beneath the tower?'

Dulcie wracked her memory for any references to such a room. 'Isn't there a storage room up there?'

'Indeed there is—or was, at any rate.' Griddlehaus peered off into the distance. Dulcie wondered if he was seeing another time. 'I don't know if it has been used since.'

'The clock is still there.' Even here in the basement library, Dulcie could visualize its huge red face, the gold hands pointing out whether she would be late for class or not as she hurried from her own undergraduate house. Then the import of what Griddlehaus had said hit her. 'Why? What happened?'

The little man looked down at the table, and Dulcie thought for a moment that he was blushing. 'Even then, we were not supposed to have access, you understand.'

Dulcie waited.

'Jeremy was never the most social of our classmates, but back before—back when we first met, he did enjoy a good time.' Griddlehaus was again staring off into the distance, only now Dulcie had some idea of what he was seeing. 'I remember seeing him at the house parties, of course. And after a long day in the library, we'd both enjoy a beer. Perhaps more than one. And we'd heard the rumors, of course.'

'The rumors?' Dulcie spoke softly, unwilling to interrupt the flow.

'That there was something hidden up there. Some kind of treasure—or treasure map, at least. That added to the allure, of course, but what we were really looking for was the trap door that would lead us from the storage room into the clock itself.' Griddlehaus turned to her, and seemed to focus in. 'There had to be, of course. A way to maintain the clock working, to do repairs. Simply to clean and oil the workings. That clock was established long before our current digital age, after all. It made sense that the door into it would be from the storage room. At any rate, we never found it.'

Dulcie tried to imagine a younger Griddlehaus, perhaps a bit tipsy, poking about with his friends and finding only old steamer trunks and cleaning supplies. 'Did you spend a lot of time looking?'

'Enough.' Griddlehaus seemed to relish the memory. 'I confess, I was keen on gaining the tower for my own purposes. It was bandied about as the ultimate setting for, well, romantic liaisons. Not that I had much opportunity to try those out. But I had my chances…'

He smiled to himself, but Dulcie worked to maintain her own composure. Simply because she couldn't picture Griddlehaus as an amorous undergrad didn't mean he hadn't had his day. After a moment, the smile—and, she assumed, the memories—faded.

'At any rate,' he continued, 'we never found it. Only the storage room. Jeremy really loved that room. At least, I thought he did, which made what happened all the more horrible.' Griddlehaus stopped, lost in thought.

Dulcie waited, afraid to ask.

'There was an incident,' Griddlehaus said finally. 'A—well, there's no sense in denying it—Jeremy had what must have been his first breakdown. In retrospect, there may have been signs. His increasing isolation, his growing distrust of authority. All likely early manifestations of his—well, his illness for lack of a better term. In fact, looking back I am now no longer sure that what he was speaking of did happen. Perhaps it too was an indication of a certain detachment from reality…'

Seeing the sadness wash over his face, Dulcie sought to distract him. 'You were saying that Jeremy said something interesting?'

'Yes, yes.' He removed his glasses and began wiping them with a soft cloth. 'That bit about "attacked in the stacks". That's what he used to complain of, you see. That's why he would go to work in the tower room. Even before the brouhaha over the Dorchester bequest, he felt like someone or several someones had it in for him. I'm afraid Jeremy was often bullied. And then, afterward, he felt that the library had become a hostile environment.'

He put his glasses back on and blinked at Dulcie. 'Perhaps he was right. Tempers certainly ran high, and he did cast the libraries in a very unflattering light. But "attacked?" That seems a bit unlikely. Perhaps, when he wakes up, he will be able to explain everything.'

He had put a slight emphasis on that one word—when—and now the two sat thinking about it. 'When,' not 'if,' Dulcie said to herself. And then, after a moment's thoughtful silence, Dulcie remembered her own questions.

'Mr Griddlehaus,' she said. Her friend looked up, startled from his own memories. 'Was Stuart Truckworth part of that crowd?'

He blinked, uncomprehending, and so she went on. 'I feel like Mr Truckworth has it in for Jeremy in some way, and I was wondering if maybe he was the one who was picking on Jeremy, even back then.'

'No, no.' Griddlehaus smiled a little. 'Stuart and Jeremy might not have been close, but they were friendly back then. In fact, Stuart was part of our tower room crew. He was wilder back then. Perhaps we all were. He was often the instigator—the troublemaker, if you will—although I believe he acted out of a sense of fun.

'You have to understand, we were young then. In many ways, younger than today's students, Ms Schwartz, and we had fewer resources. Stuart Truckworth, in particular, was always broke, and so we had to make our own amusements. In fact, he was the one who got us access to the storage room. That's where much of the material that was being removed for the duct work was being kept, and as a young, reasonably strong student—not to mention the low person on the totem pole—he had carried much of it up there. But he was determined to find that trap door. He had a girlfriend, you see, and he was convinced that it would be the perfect place for a romantic rendezvous.'

'Did he ever get to bring her up there?'

'No.' He sighed, as he shook his head. 'That was when Jeremy had his episode—and the room was locked for good.'

Dulcie waited, as Griddlehaus fell silent. After a few moments, she dared a question. 'Mr Griddlehaus, what happened?'

'What happened?' He looked up, blinking, and she realized he had been lost in his memories. 'I'm afraid poor Jeremy found his way up to the tower. I never heard how, but I can remember it like it was yesterday. He was leaning out the window—hanging out, really—and yelling.'

'Hanging out the window?'

Griddlehaus nodded. 'He may have been delusional by then, I don't know. I do know that it was construed as a suicide attempt. He was hospitalized after that and although he was released after a few weeks, he was a changed man.'

'Poor guy.' Dulcie let the silence settle around them before asking, 'Do you think that's why Mr Truckworth resents him? Because Jeremy got the tower room locked up?'

'I don't know.' Griddlehaus shook his head. 'I do know Stuart—Mr Truckworth—certainly hewed to the straight and narrow after that, although once he dropped out and started working full time, we no longer spent as much time together.'

He paused, lost in thought. 'It is possible he blamed Jeremy for alerting the authorities to our hijinks, but what happened with Jeremy was so terrifying, I believe that simply served as a wake-up call. Perhaps for all of us. And, if anything, it was Jeremy who disconnected from his old friends after that. In truth, he became—I don't want to say paranoid. Perhaps I may say unduly concerned? Yes, he became unduly concerned about the authorities after that day, which I have always believed was based on an emotional sensitivity rather than anything concrete. It may be unfair, but our emotions aren't fair, are they?'

'No, I guess not,' Dulcie answered. Nothing about Jeremy Mumbleigh's life seemed particularly fair. It was interesting, however, to learn something about his history—and about that of her friend Griddlehaus. But while he stared off into space, apparently lost in thought, she had a more pressing question.

'Mr Griddlehaus, I was wondering if you could help me find out more about my pages?' She didn't have to elaborate. He would know which ones she meant. 'The book they were bound into may have some historical significance, and I was wondering if with your contacts in the conservation lab…' She left the thought open, hoping he would pick up on it.

'They won't have any records.' He rose from his seat and Dulcie's heart sank. 'They're much more likely to tear apart several more books looking for another of those cat marks as to take note of some stray filler material.'

'Oh!' Dulcie had been so hopeful. 'Are you sure?' Never before had she questioned any of Griddle-haus's pronouncements.

'Why, of course.' He walked over to one of the cabinets and tapped on a volume—a drawer popped out from the smooth white surface. He must have seen Dulcie's brows rise in surprise, but he only smiled as he pulled out what looked like a ledger. 'Why should they?'

'I was hoping to be able to trace it,' she said, her voice falling. 'At least I didn't waste their time.'

'You *can* trace it.' He turned toward her, the black bound volume in his hand. 'At least to some extent.' Returning to the table, he laid the ledger in front of her. 'The lab doesn't concern itself with details of provenance and history. They focus exclusively on the physical material. On preparation and restora-tion. But we here at the Mildon…well, Ms Schwartz, I thought you knew us better. We keep extensive re-cords on everything that comes into the collection. Even the origins of some scraps of paper that nobody else seems to want.'

TWENTY-EIGHT

'MR GRIDDLEHAUS!' DULCIE could have shouted for joy. As it was, she knew her exclamation was a tad loud for the small room.

'Ms Schwartz,' he responded with his usual quiet voice, but she could see that he was pleased. 'You've been so kind, listening to all of my reminiscences, and this is the least I could do.'

He began leafing through the ledger. Clearly, the notations—long strings of numbers and letters, which she could see over his shoulder—meant something to him. 'I seem to recall a designation of STV4.3.12. At least for the first box, from which I believe you have pulled three pages.'

'Yes, but what books were those from?' Dulcie kept her voice gentle. The librarian was being particularly obtuse today, but he had been a great help—and he was her friend.

'Oh, what book…' Griddlehaus sat back to consider. 'Well, it had to have been one of the better ones, of course. One of the volumes the board decided was worth restoring.'

Dulcie looked up, the question in her face.

'Why, from the collection, of course.' Now it was Griddlehaus's turn for consternation. 'It's in the designation: STV. Those pages were taken from books in the Stavendish bequest, of course.'

Dulcie considered this. 'Do you think Jeremy knew?' she asked. 'Could they have been from one of the books he was fighting to keep?'

'You'd have to ask Ms Constantine,' Griddlehaus answered. 'Now, if you'll excuse me…' He turned back to the ledger.

As she waited, another question came to her. 'Mr Griddlehaus, you said you had news for me,' she said. 'Something about Jeremy?'

'Oh, my, yes.' He looked up, his finger on one line. 'I'm so sorry. In my haste to explain my own unsuccessful quest, I forgot to tell you what he did say. Now, it may not be exactly relevant. You are aware I've been looking into the later period uses of the printer's mark we found? Specifically, its usage in America. It is quite rare, with its distinctive feline design, and I could see where it would appeal to you. I was wondering, however, if your discovery was more than mere coincidence.'

He blinked up at her. Dulcie had never actually explained about Mr Grey to Griddlehaus. However, he had known her long enough to know a bit about her history, and certainly to understand the importance of cats in her life.

'At any rate, I thought poor Jeremy might have some insight, seeing as how it was discovered in the book we found on him. And I believe, perhaps, there is a connection. It is possible I misheard him—that he did say "cat" rather than "stacks." What intrigued me was what he said afterward, when I was about to leave him. He grabbed my hand, Ms Schwartz, and as clear as day, he said to me, "It's a secret. You can't tell anyone."'

Dulcie was considering the ramifications of this as her companion turned back to his ledger. Before she could gather her thoughts about this latest revelation, he let out a muted cry. 'Oh, my!'

'Mr Griddlehaus?' Dulcie didn't think anything was wrong. Still, the little man was clearly surprised. 'Is everything all right?'

'What? Oh, yes.' He looked up from the ledger, but kept his finger on it. 'Let me check one thing.' Scribbling down a series of numbers on one of the pieces of scrap paper piled by the gloves, he jumped up and hurried over to the library's entrance alcove. Opening what Dulcie had previously thought was a cabinet, he revealed another surprise: a computer. A few moments of fast typing and a little more muttering—'oh, my!'—and he turned to her. Behind him, the screen glowed and pulsed.

'Well, this is an interesting coincidence.'

Dulcie waited.

'Those pages—the ones you've done so much work on—they were removed when the university conservators did that initial partial re-bind of *He Could Not Tell Her*, the first volume.'

Dulcie's voice registered her surprise. 'The volume that Jeremy had? The one that got him arrested? But—I don't understand.'

'I'm afraid I don't either.' Griddlehaus turned and went back to reading the screen. 'It does seem an odd choice for my old friend. Perhaps the poor man was more fond of the late Gothics than I knew, although I wouldn't have said that he was likely to favor such purple prose.'

'No, I'm sorry.' Dulcie didn't want to argue the merits of a Duxbury book. 'I meant, if older papers were found in part of the binding, why didn't they keep looking? They would have found the silver cat.'

'I'm afraid I have no answer for you,' Griddlehaus said, as he entered a few more keystrokes into the computer. 'All I can tell you is that once your pages were removed, the volume was partially re-bound and slated to be returned to the collection, and then it disappeared.'

He paused to read something on his screen. 'This was one of the books from the Stavendish bequest that was slated for deaccession. One of the books that Jeremy was defending.'

'Typical.' Dulcie had, of course, read modern editions of *He Could Not Tell Her* and found it middling prose at best. However, she didn't like the idea of considering any book disposable. 'Of course, if they knew those pages were part of another, infinitely better written Gothic…'

She was interrupted as Griddlehaus gave an excited peep and scurried off. 'What is it?' Dulcie called. He had disappeared down the back hallway, where even Dulcie was not permitted to enter.

'Hang on!' She heard a door and something sliding, and a few minutes later, he emerged, holding one of the document boxes she knew so well. He placed it on the table in front of her, opening it, as she reached for a pair of gloves. But before he could

remove the contents—a prerogative of the librarian—the respectful silence both had maintained was
broken by a ping.

'Oh, I'm sorry.' Griddlehaus jumped up. 'I need
to log off.'

'What were you searching?' Dulcie watched as
he began typing into the computer. 'Lexis Nexis?'

'No, no, it's an archivist's service. Rather—oh!
I'm sorry.' A moment of silence as he typed. 'I'm
afraid I need to concentrate to do this, Ms Schwartz.'
He turned and looked at her over his shoulder. 'Please
feel free to proceed without me.'

'Thank you.' Dulcie appreciated the trust this signified, and with the utmost care she lifted the first
document in its protective sheath. She smiled as she
looked down at the torn and yellowed document. Yes,
she remembered this page—the '*Helf*' that proved to
be a cry for 'Help' on closer examination. She placed
it gently to one side and removed another from its
polypropylene case. This was also from the manuscript. In the fragment she'd been able to make out
from this page, her heroine was still hoping to elude
the '*Night demons*' that howled outside.

'Bother.' Griddlehaus was still typing.

'Is there a problem?' Dulcie could see that the
librarian's shoulders were hunching over with the
stress.

'Yes, well, no, not really.' Griddlehaus didn't even
turn around. 'It seems that I've been locked out for
leaving in the middle of a session, and I am trying
to log back in, because I really do not want to have
to verify my identification again. Only the system

is being quite recalcitrant. Oh, wait!' He started typing furiously again.

Dulcie turned back to the box. The next page would be the one she had been looking at when they had been chased out of the library. The one with the faintest gleam of silver.

'Mr Griddlehaus?' She knew her voice was tentative. She was loath to disturb him. 'When you're done?'

'One moment, please.' More frantic typing. Dulcie thought he was murmuring under his breath as well. 'Hang on…'

'OK.' She would use this time. She closed her eyes and took a breath. Took another and then looked again.

Griddlehaus was staring at her. 'Ms Schwartz?'

'Mr Griddlehaus, I don't know what to say.' Her eyes went toward the box. The box where, by custom, there would be a third polypropylene folder, holding a third fragile and irreplaceable document. Where now—she looked and even put her hand in, running the gloved fingers along the archival board—there was nothing. 'I have these two.' She gestured to the two pages before her, lying on the table, in plain sight. 'But then…'

'I see,' said her colleague, perusing the works on the table. 'Or rather, I do not see. There should be a third piece in here. It was cataloged. It has been filed. And yet…'

He looked up, his eyes large behind the glasses. 'Ms Schwartz, what did you do with these pages?'

TWENTY-NINE

'MR GRIDDLEHAUS.' DULCIE didn't know if she was more hurt or angry. 'You can't think—I would never do anything against the protocol of the Mildon. Against any document. Surely you know that—'

'Yes, yes, of course.' Griddlehaus ran a hand over his forehead, and Dulcie saw it came away damp with sweat. 'I am sorry. It is simply that, through our long acquaintance, I have let our procedures slide, never thinking…and now…for a document to go missing…' He shook his head.

Dulcie was afraid he was going to be ill. 'Surely, it's been misfiled.' Even as she said the words, she knew it wasn't possible. Worse, it was insulting. 'Not that you would ever, but perhaps another scholar…' She let her words trail off.

'You're the only scholar in recent memory who has cared at all about Box 926-E,' he said, his voice growing sad. 'The only one with access.'

'Well then.' She reached for the two out on the table. Only his hands were quicker.

'I'll do that,' he said, his voice sharp. Although he didn't grab the propylene-sheathed pages—he was too careful for that—he did move swiftly to remove the two pieces to his side of the table. Dulcie simply watched as he did what she had planned to do: examine each page carefully to make sure that it was alone in its protective envelope. Not that such close scrutiny was necessary: neither page was complete. Although the missing page had seemed to be glued to another, both the remaining fragments were so torn and worn as to be more ragged scrap than complete sheet, capable of concealment.

Finally, after going back and forth between the two documents, Griddlehaus accepted the inevitable. 'It's not here,' he said, looking up at Dulcie, the loss visible on his face.

'It's got to be here somewhere,' she replied. Seeing his hurt, she forgot the sting she felt as he had taken over the examination of the pages. Instead, she wanted to find the pages—for him and for the collection. 'It has to be.'

He merely shook his head, lost. 'It's not possible.'

'Mr Griddlehaus.' Dulcie adopted a martial tone, the better to shake him from his torpor. 'Think! Who else has been in here?'

'Nobody!' His voice sounded high and tight, and Dulcie feared the onset of hysteria. 'We've been locked down. Closed.'

'What about maintenance or security?' Dulcie racked her brains. 'Who was repairing the pipes?'

'We never had any leakage in the Mildon.' It was doing Griddlehaus good to think back, Dulcie thought. His voice was becoming calmer and more thoughtful. 'Because we have our own alarm and ventilation system, we weren't affected by the frozen pipes or the flooding.'

'But they probably had to send someone in to check, right?' Dulcie was starting to feel better.

'You can't think… No!' Griddlehaus was not. 'I can't imagine that a university plumber would steal…' He stopped mid sentence, and when he leaned in to continue, he sounded like himself again. 'To be honest, Ms Schwartz, I doubt the majority of the university community would even consider these pages worth the effort. Not everyone appreciates the treasures that we have here.'

'I'm not saying anyone stole the page.' Dulcie felt her own breathing grow easier. 'Though I do wish they could be taught to value what we do. No, what I'm thinking, Mr Griddlehaus, is that a maintenance crew—or maybe just a single worker—was sent in while the Mildon was closed and tasked with checking things out. There have been so many problems elsewhere on this level that maybe he or she poked about a bit. Opened some drawers.'

Griddlehaus turned a little pale at the thought, but he nodded in agreement. 'It's plausible.'

'And maybe something got moved. Maybe something was dropped and put back by someone who didn't know, who didn't understand…'

'Oh, dear Lord.' Griddlehaus blinked rapidly, his face now a ghostly white. 'I fear you're right, Ms Schwartz. And I—I'm going to have to go through every drawer in every file. This will be the work of months.'

'I'll help you,' said Dulcie with a flood of relief. Seeing Griddlehaus drawn and panicked over a possible misfiling might be troubling, but it was also a lot better than the alternative. 'But first, would you like to get something to eat?'

'I don't know.' He looked around, eyes wide. Clearly the enormity of the task was getting to him. 'Yes, perhaps that would be best,' he said finally. 'Alexandria wasn't cataloged in a day.'

She smiled at his reference and removed her gloves, as Griddlehaus retrieved Dulcie's coat and bag.

'Shall we go to Lala's again?' he asked, donning his own coat.

'Why not?' She waited while he locked the gate behind them and then led the way to the elevator and out.

'I had been planning on visiting Jeremy again this afternoon.' Griddlehaus seemed to be thinking out loud as they approached the exit. 'I could be wrong, but I think that having company does him some good. Only now I feel I should start going through the catalog right away.'

'Let's grab a quick bite and then I can go visit him,' said Dulcie, as she put her bag on the counter. 'Maybe I can get him to talk some more.' She looked past him to the Yard outside. The storm seemed to have ended, and a pale blue sky was visible through the bare branches. Branches, she thought, that just might be showing the first beginnings of buds.

'Maybe you can get him to explain what he meant about the cat,' said Griddlehaus. 'You see, that's what had gotten me so excited. There was a notation—'

'Excuse me.' The guard at the desk—an older

man—was talking to her. 'Miss? Would you step over here, please?'

He motioned toward the administrative office. Puzzled, she reached for her bag—but he snatched it back. 'Please, Miss. Just wait here.'

He lifted a phone. 'Yes, I signaled. Immediately.'

'What?' She looked from the guard to Griddle-haus, but he only shook his head, as bewildered as she was. 'Excuse me?'

'Lieutenant?' The guard had put the phone down and was talking over her shoulder. Dulcie turned to see Lieutenant Wardley, a face like thunder.

'What is this about?' Wardley turned from the guard to Dulcie, who stood, mouth gaping.

'Here, sir.' Dulcie watched as the guard opened her bag and reached inside. When Wardley turned, holding up a clear folder, she felt her head spin. Wardley's large hand nearly obscured the scrap of paper inside the polypropylene sheath, but even so she recognized its ragged outline.

'That's not possible!' Griddlehaus rushed by her and, taking the sheet from Wardley, laid it flat on the counter. 'It's the missing page.'

'Miss, you're going to have to come with me.' The guard cleared his throat, clearly a little overwhelmed by the situation.

'I'll take over, guard,' said Wardley, his voice a low growl. 'Good work.' He then turned to Griddle-haus. 'I assume you can verify that this document belongs in the library?'

'Indeed, I can. We were just looking for it,' said

Griddlehaus. He turned from the burly officer to Dulcie. 'But how…'

'This is ridiculous.' The enormity of the situation was beginning to dawn on Dulcie. 'You can't think that I would steal something like this. It's too important. Too valuable…'

'Maybe too valuable to share?' Wardley's voice didn't invite an answer. In silence Dulcie just turned from the police officer to her friend Griddlehaus, who was staring at her, eyes wide.

THIRTY

'THIS IS RIDICULOUS.' DULCIE was talking to the young
guard, who seemed intent on leading her out of the
library in disgrace. 'You can't believe this,' she said
to Griddlehaus, who stood, staring at her. 'You can't.'

'Please, Miss.' The guard put his hand on her
upper arm. 'You'll have to come with me.'

'No, wait.' Dulcie reached for her bag, which still
lay on the counter. 'My phone.'

'There'll be plenty of time for calls once we have
this straightened out.' Wardley pulled the denim
holdall toward himself. 'I'm afraid I'll be taking this
down to the station.'

'What's going on here?' A familiar voice broke
in, and Dulcie turned to see Stuart Truckworth approaching. 'Is there a problem?'

'I'll say.' Wardley was scowling. 'It seems this
young lady had something in her purse that didn't
belong to her.'

Truckworth blanched. 'She what?'

'She was attempting to sneak a rare document out
of the library.' Wardley's voice was grim.

'I was not!' Dulcie was yelling now. Nobody
seemed to be listening to her. 'I have no idea how that
got into my bag. I never—I wouldn't have. Mr Griddlehaus?' She turned to her colleague. 'Tell them.'

For an awful moment, there was silence. Dulcie
stood there, waiting, while the librarian's mouth
opened and closed like a fish's. On every side of
her, people were waiting—Wardley, Truckworth, that
guard. She even caught a movement off by circulation: Ruby, come to see what all the fuss was about.
For a very long moment, nobody said anything.

Then, finally, Griddlehaus spoke. 'I'm sure
there's been a misunderstanding,' he said, pushing
his glasses up on his nose. 'In fact, I believe I can
explain everything. Ms Schwartz and I were looking for just this document, before she announced that
she had to leave. I wanted her to see it, of course, so
I put it right on top of her books. Clearly, she didn't
notice what I had done and packed it into her carryall
with her own materials. A perfectly ordinary, honest
mistake. That's all it was. An honest mistake, and
partly—' he paused and looked around—'my fault.'

Now it was Dulcie's turn to be dumbfounded. She
had expected—no, she had hoped for—a declaration
of support. Not an outright lie. 'Mr Griddlehaus…'
She stopped, unsure what to say.

'Well, there you go.' Truckworth barged in, before Dulcie could formulate a sentence. 'That explains everything.'

Stepping in front of Dulcie, he reached for her
bag. Lieutenant Wardley looked at him, eyes closing slightly, as if he didn't quite accept the explanation, but he released the worn denim holdall to the
facilities manager.

'You should be more careful,' Truckworth said,

handing it to her. 'You were lucky you had a member of the staff here to vouch for you.'

Turning to Griddlehaus, he pointed to the page in its clear cover. 'I assume there has been no harm done to the document? That you can put it back in its proper place?'

'Of course.' Griddlehaus didn't clasp the page to his chest. It was far too fragile for that. But Dulcie saw his hands tighten on it as he drew it closer. 'In fact, I'll go do that now.'

'Good.' Truckworth looked quite pleased with himself. 'All settled.'

'I'm not so sure.' Wardley's voice was a low growl. 'Truckworth, can I speak with you?'

'Of course,' said the facilities manager. 'Good day, all.'

Dulcie watched as Truckworth led the police lieutenant off to a private office and then turned to see Griddlehaus heading toward the elevators. More than anything, she wanted to follow him. To assure him that she had no idea how that page had come to be in her bag—and to thank him for his quick-witted response on her behalf. His lie, if she called it what it really was. But even though Wardley had disappeared in Truckworth's wake, the young guard who had been holding her arm remained. He had resumed his station behind the counter, but his glare did not make Dulcie feel welcome. No, she was innocent, and she knew it. But until this particular mystery was unraveled, she should give the library—or at least this particular guard—a wide berth.

Still, she wanted to speak to Griddlehaus, and

so even as she left the library, she lingered. He had been the one who had suggested lunch. Surely, he would still be hungry.

She certainly was. The entire episode couldn't have lasted more than ten minutes, and yet it had left her drained. Even standing, peering up the stairs at the library's main entrance, was an effort, and so Dulcie sat, first brushing off the lingering wet snow that had accumulated on the stone stairs and then tucking her coat underneath her.

What had happened made no sense. That document had been in the Mildon—Griddlehaus's filing system was beyond reproach. Then it hadn't been—not that either of them could see, at any rate. For it to show up—in her possession—meant that something was horribly amiss.

The library was not the safe place she had always assumed it was. Not if something like this could happen. Something that nearly got her…no, she didn't want to think about it. If the worst had happened, she would have called Suze. Her former room-mate might not have been supportive when it came to Jeremy's plight, but she would certainly rally in Dulcie's defense.

Yes, Dulcie decided, she ought to call Suze tonight, just in case that bully Wardley decided he didn't believe Griddlehaus's story. Besides, their last conversation had been so brief. It was her own fault, Dulcie knew. Between work and Chris and the ease of socializing with friends still on campus, she had let their friendship lapse. This week, with everyone else out of town, she was reminded of just how much she missed her one-time roomie. She would have to make the effort to keep up their relationship, and not just reach out when she needed help.

With that thought in mind, Dulcie wondered about talking to Detective Rogovoy. Dulcie wasn't sure what the hierarchy was in the university police department, but every interaction she had seen between the ogre-like detective and uniformed police officers had implied that he was, if not in charge, at least held in high esteem. He would believe in her innocence, if she needed another ally.

Of course, talking to Rogovoy was still talking to a cop. It would help if Dulcie had something to offer him. Some idea of how that precious scrap had gotten into her bag.

Now that she was out of danger—and getting cold—her mind began working again. Sadly, she realized that the possibilities were legion. First off was that big guard—Thumbkin. Dulcie didn't like to think he was behind slipping the document in among her belongings. She had thought him a gentle giant. A potential friend. Besides, he had done her a favor—taking her bag into the administrative office instead of turning it in. Anyone in there could have put the document inside, Dulcie realized. That meant anyone on the library staff. Or any number of university officials who might have reason to pass through.

Perhaps, she decided, she should start at the other end. Where had the document come from? Who had snuck it out of the Mildon and for what reason?

She could have laughed. For what reason? The scrap of paper with its nearly illegible writing was a rare thing, an artifact. Someone who coveted such things probably needed no other excuse. Why steal diamonds? Why steal books?

Unbidden, an image of Jeremy came to mind, skinny and shivering in his threadbare coat. The book he'd been found with hadn't been.the most valuable piece in the library, but it had been an antique and held some value. Why hadn't he sold it? Exchanged it at one of the Square's used and antiquarian booksellers for the means of purchasing food, shelter, and warmth? No, there was no questioning why. People either understood that books—that writing—had worth beyond their monetary value, or they didn't. So why did he have it at all?

That line of thought still led her back to her own situation. Could it all have been some awful form of practical joke? A mistake of some sort? Or had it been something more nefarious?

Had someone wanted to frame Dulcie? Someone who perhaps knew that the police lieutenant would be there, when she was caught? Someone who wanted to ruin her? This must have been what happened to Kyle, she found herself thinking. He had seemed unaware, too. Perhaps both of them had been set up.

Unless… The heavy sinking feeling that settled on Dulcie was due to more than cold and hunger. No, it came with the sudden realization that there was another person who had had access to her bag and, maybe, also to the Mildon. Kyle Truckworth. She had regarded him as a friend because he was part of her larger social circle. What did she know about him really? That he worked in the library. That he was at odds with his influential father—at odds, maybe, with the university his father represented. And that he, too, was under suspicion for theft.

Maybe Chris was right. And what had Lucy said, about her young companion? It saddened her to think this way, but she couldn't escape the idea that perhaps Kyle was behind her mishap. That he had secreted the purloined document in her bag as a way to deflect suspicion for the burglary on to her and, possibly, to clear himself.

There were too many loose ends, and Dulcie let her face sink into her hands as she sat there, her bottom growing cold from the stone. Too many mysteries about where the page had been and how it had been spirited out of the Mildon in the first place. And even though Griddlehaus had lied—there was no other word for it—to keep her from being taken away in shame, she knew he would never trust her again. She had been in the Mildon. He had turned his back, and a page had disappeared. He had to suspect her. She would suspect herself if the roles were reversed. Looked at objectively, she was the likeliest culprit. Besides, she had been sitting out here for a good fifteen minutes by then. Griddlehaus would have emerged by now if he still wanted to go to lunch with her. He would have come out to talk to her if he really believed in her innocence. If he really wanted to set things right. He couldn't trust her any more, she knew. That friendship, which had only started to blossom, was over.

Dulcie closed her eyes. It was all too much. But as she did, she saw a movement. Maybe an old, dried leaf caught up in the wind. Maybe something even less substantial—a shadow flitting, caught in the

corner of her eye—but it caught her attention, and
she jerked her head up.

'Mr Grey?' More likely a squirrel, she told herself.
A squirrel or one of those rats. Something scared out
of hiding by the jackhammer noise. But, no, she
saw it again—grey and too large to be either form
of rodent. 'Is that you?'

'*Courage, Dulcie.*' The voice seemed to sound
within her head, and yet as she looked the shadow
seemed to gather and form. Dulcie could make out
the sleek whiskers, the silver softness of the fur. '*You
must search for it—for me.*'

In response, Dulcie stood and stepped toward the
apparition. As she did, she brushed off the remnants
of the ice—and with it her most morbid thoughts—
and even as she did, the shape began to waver and
fade, till only the line of the whiskers was visible,
a silver flicker in the air. Then, even that was gone.
It didn't matter. Dulcie had been heartened by the
visit even as she puzzled over its enigmatic message.

Clearly, she decided, she had work to do. She had
to quit waiting for Griddlehaus. He was never going
to come out, but she—and this she felt firmly about—
was going to treat herself to a nice, albeit late lunch.

'Thank you, Mr Grey,' she whispered to the frosty
air. 'I needed that.'

What she needed to do was to figure out how to
proceed. What would Hermetria, the heroine of *The
Ravages of Umbria*, do? That intrepid character had
faced demon wolves and betrayal. Surely a library
mishap would not be beyond her. Surely Hermetria
would know how to decipher the various clues she
had been given.

Some steaming split pea soup would help, and she sped up as she turned the corner—and heard a strange hiss.

'Ms Schwartz!' The hiss was followed by a voice and she spun around, looking for its source. 'Ms Schwartz, over here!'

By the trees, where she had seen the shadow, a glint of light. The reflection of the weak sun on glasses. Griddlehaus was motioning for her to come closer.

'Mr Griddlehaus!' She raced over. 'But I thought you were inside—in the Mildon. That document...'

'I was.' He was crouched behind the tree, and now looked around nervously. 'I did. I filed it properly, and I made extra sure that the collection was secured when I left. I've been waiting here for you, Ms Schwartz. We have to talk.'

'I didn't do it.' Now that she had a chance to explain herself, the words poured forth. 'I don't know how that got into my bag or where it came from. I mean, I remember seeing it, but I would never—'

'No, no.' His voice, though hushed, carried a sense of urgency. 'I know that, Ms Schwartz. You can't believe for a minute that I would think you capable of—of showing such disrespect for the material.' He paused. 'Or for the Mildon.'

'Thank you.' She could have hugged the little man. 'I thought that when you didn't come out...'

'I left via the back entrance,' he said, his voice hushed. 'I've been trying to get your attention for some time now.'

She shook her head, confused.

'I don't think this is random, Ms Schwartz,' he said. 'I fear that you are being watched.'

THIRTY-ONE

'WHY?' DULCIE'S FIRST response was to spin around, as if she would spy a shadowy figure behind each tree. 'Mr Griddlehaus, what are you talking about?'

'Come with me.' He led the way out of the Yard, avoiding both the library's rear entrance and the excavation. Only once they were out on the street did he stop and turn to her again. 'I don't know if it was your questions or simply that you were convenient, but I do believe you were targeted, and I didn't want to take any chances. Lala's?'

The apparent non sequitur threw Dulcie for a few seconds, but her growling stomach understood. 'Yes, please.'

The combination of the hour—it was after three—and the break meant that the Mass Ave storefront was virtually empty when they walked inside. Still, Griddlehaus silently led them to a back table. Only once they had ordered did he begin to speak.

'Ms Schwartz, I know you didn't remove that fragment.' He leaned forward, his voice a conspiratorial hush. 'We both know that it went missing before I reopened the Mildon, before either of us was in there. The first question, therefore, is *when* did it go missing?'

'During the break-in?' Dulcie thought back to

what she knew. The Islington Bible had been the apparent target, but maybe the thieves were grabbing whatever they could.

Griddlehaus was shaking his head. 'I don't think so. We had the security gates down by then, and even if the thieves had managed to breach the Mildon, I doubt they would have had time to re-secure the gates. Not so that I wouldn't notice, at any rate.'

Dulcie nodded. 'How long has the Mildon been closed?'

'Since the first leak.' Griddlehaus's eyes sparkled behind his glasses. 'Exactly what I've been thinking.'

'So it was someone on the repair crew. I know what you said earlier, but really, who else had access?' Dulcie paused while their food was set down: soup for Griddlehaus and a hearty three-bean burger for her. Narrowly escaping arrest had given her an appetite.

'I supposed.' Griddlehaus looked doubtful. 'I still don't think it likely that some well-employed plumber would risk a union job, not to mention have the expertise…'

'Truckworth would.' She took a bite and chewed it, as she considered her words. 'He has the academic background and he would certainly have access. Plus, I knew he had it out for Jeremy. And I called him on it.'

She took another bite, rather proud of herself. Only, when she looked up, Griddlehaus was shaking his head.

'No, it doesn't make sense,' he said. 'He came to

your defense. He didn't have to. Your being implicated might have helped get his son off.'

'He didn't…' She stopped. Truckworth had not
defended her exactly. However, he had been the first
to accept Griddlehaus's explanation. He had been the
one to hand her bag over and to declare the matter
resolved. More telling, to her mind, was the look of
shock when Wardley had told him that Dulcie was
being held. 'Well, I guess he did, close enough.'

The two continued eating in silence, but even with
the hot sauce, Dulcie found she was barely tasting
her burger at all.

'I still think it must have been stolen during the
repairs,' she said at last. Griddlehaus nodded as he
sipped his soup. Dulcie took another bite and mulled
as she chewed.

'Was anything else taken?'

Griddlehaus stopped eating, spoon halfway to his
mouth, a look of horror on his face. 'I don't know,' he
said, his voice a whisper. 'I hadn't thought to check.'

'We'll go back as soon as we're done.' Dulcie
shifted into action mode. 'We should probably start
with the other fragments. They're easier to remove
than books. I'll read from the ledger and you can—'

'We can't.' Griddlehaus had put his spoon down
and was shaking his head. 'You can't, at any rate.
I'm sorry. I don't think it would be wise.'

She looked at him. Surely, he couldn't suspect
her…

'It's not you, Ms Schwartz.' He must have read
the fear on her face. 'I simply mean, if you are being
watched—or, well, being kept under surveillance

for any reason—then it won't do for you to be in the
Mildon. We have presented the fiction that you accidentally packed that document into your carryall.
If it becomes apparent that we are checking to see
that others have gone missing, that makes the fictive
nature of this story apparent.'

He hesitated for a moment, then continued. 'I believe I can manage an inventory, by myself. If I'm
questioned, I can explain my actions as a filing update or, perhaps, a logistical check.' Dulcie nodded,
even though she didn't exactly follow. What he said
next, however, made perfect sense. 'But you, Ms
Schwartz, can't come anywhere near the Mildon.
Not until we figure out exactly what is going on.
Because the second question—perhaps the bigger
one, if I dare be so bold—is why that fragment was
taken. And why, while we're on the subject, it was
returned.'

If Dulcie's burger tasted bland before, it turned
to sawdust now. Only concern that word might get
back to the motherly proprietor kept her from leaving the rest on the plate.

'Is it possible the thieves weren't sure what they
were after?' Out of habit, she dragged a french fry
through the pooled hot sauce. 'I mean, maybe they
grabbed the wrong item and then had to get rid of it?'

'It is possible.' Griddlehaus wiped his hands on
his napkin. 'Maybe the first question we should seek
to answer is why it was planted on you?'

THIRTY-TWO

THE TWO PARTED ways soon after, although Griddle-haus wrote Dulcie's cell number in a small notebook first. 'I will call if I discover anything,' he'd promised, tucking the notebook into his jacket pocket.

Somehow, Dulcie couldn't imagine the stately librarian using anything quite so modern as a telephone, but she trusted him. Besides, it wasn't as if she had any choice.

He had headed back toward the Mildon, doing his best to look nonchalant even as the March gusts buffeted him. She stood on the sidewalk, trying to figure out what to do next. The apartment made sense. She had promised Esmé that morning that she would not be out too late, and in truth she could easily spend the afternoon working on her chapter at the kitchen table. Even without Chris, the presence of the cat—as well as the late afternoon sun—would make the room a welcoming alternative to the library, if not quite as free from distraction.

Yes, she decided. She would head home. That way, when she and Chris spoke that evening, she'd have more to report than simply the morning's unpleasantness. Besides, she told herself, as she turned toward Central Square, this wind was not going to let up. Better to be indoors before the faint sun set.

Dulcie was walking by Holyoke Center when the next gust hit, whistling through the covered arcade like a demon. 'Ow,' she heard a passing pedestrian grunt, and in a moment Dulcie made a similar protest. All the salt and sand that had made the roads passable through the long winter now seemed airborne, scouring any exposed skin. She paused, waiting for the wind to die down, but it didn't, instead picking up speed and—it seemed—additional fuel.

As a particularly rough batch of grit hit her cheek and raked across it, rather like the claws of an aggrieved feline, Dulcie turned her head and winced. In any other circumstance, she would call out to Mr Grey, only he had always been much too gentle for this kind of punishment. *Find me*, he had said. But wasn't she more likely to find her old friend back in the apartment?

Another buffet of wind made her close her eyes. When she opened them again, she saw the entrance to the health services before her. Inside the glass doors, she could see the lobby, full of light and warmth, and she recalled her earlier plans. Jeremy had spent the winter out here, apparently. He had survived worse than this. At the very least, she could give him a little company.

'Hello, Jeremy.' Dulcie had made a point of striding purposefully, and nobody had tried to stop her as she made her way to his third-floor room. 'Oh, I'm sorry.'

Another nurse, or perhaps an orderly, was standing on the other side of the curtained bed. 'No worries,' he said, making a note on a chart. 'I just thought

I'd sneak in here while things were quiet and check in on our Mr Mumbleigh.'

'I can come back.' Dulcie motioned toward the door.

'No, please.' The orderly was already walking by her. 'I only needed a few minutes to check everything out, but I'm done now. Please, take a seat. He became agitated when the police came by earlier, but he seems to respond to his friends.'

'The police?' Dulcie felt her temper rise. 'They can't think of questioning the poor man while he's in this condition.'

'No, no.' The orderly's voice was calming. 'I'm sorry, I shouldn't have said anything if I wasn't clear. It wasn't that kind of visit. One of the top brass—a Lieutenant Wardley—came by, but he simply wanted to check on the patient.'

'Thanks.' Dulcie watched the orderly leave and then turned to the still, silent man on the bed. 'I guess you're Mr Popular.' Maybe the orderly had been exaggerating. Dulcie doubted anyone had been in since Griddlehaus's early-morning visit, but perhaps that had coincided with the white-coated professional's last set of rounds.

Jeremy lay still.

'Maybe your earlier visit tired you out,' said Dulcie, as much to fill the silence as to elicit an answer. 'Though you certainly gave Mr Griddlehaus something to think about.'

She paused. No, the name of the librarian hadn't done anything, and only the ticking of the radiator answered her back. She stood and removed her coat. 'I hope you don't mind, Jeremy,' she said, as she folded it over her lap and sat back down. 'It's so bitter out, maybe it's just as well you're back in here. It's not fit weather for man or beast.'

'Cat.'

She stopped. Had he said something?

'Jeremy?' She leaned in closer. 'Did you say "cat?"'

'Cat.' His face was so still, she would not have believed it, were it not that she had seen his pale, chapped lips form the one syllable. But although she waited for a full minute more, they did not move again.

'Do you like cats, Jeremy?' She would try to engage him. 'I have a cat, Esmé. She's a tuxedo cat, black and white. She's really talkative.'

The man in the bed didn't take the hint, so Dulcie kept on.

'Maybe you didn't mean a real cat,' she suggested. 'I was thinking I wanted to ask you about the printer's mark. You know, the silver cat that was found in the book binding?'

There—his lips were moving—though whether because of talk of the cat or books was anybody's guess.

'Jeremy, do you want to talk about books? About the printer's mark, the silver cat, maybe?' Dulcie leaned in, hoping to hear something, but although those dry lips were moving, she could make out no sound.

'Hang on.' Dulcie went to the door, which the orderly had left ajar, and peeked out. The floor seemed quiet. Off to her left, she could see the attendant she had greeted when she came in. Somewhere to her right, a machine beeped softly and then stopped. Neither the orderly nor anyone else was in sight.

'Jeremy, I'm back.' She didn't dare close the door, but she kept her eye on it as she resumed her seat. 'I wanted to ask you about something you said. Something about "a cat in the stacks."' His lips moved again, but still she could make out nothing. 'Mr Griddlehaus—your friend Thomas?—he thinks that you were referring to the printer's mark, but I wasn't sure. Jeremy, is there some secret you want to tell us? Something about the book that you were holding when you were injured, perhaps?'

'Cat.' There, she heard that quite clearly and held her breath hoping for more. 'Cat in the stacks.'

'It's not a real cat, is it, Jeremy?' Dulcie couldn't help but think of that shadow she had seen. 'I mean, if anything, that was a rat.' Unless, she thought to herself, it was a sign from Mr Grey...

'Rat...' Jeremy's tongue darted out but failed to dampen those lips.

'A rat?' Dulcie didn't know what he was trying to say.

'Not rat.' His voice was barely a whisper, and she put her ear up to his mouth. 'Secret,' he said. 'Can't tell. Secret.'

Another pause, and Dulcie racked her brain for what the prone man could be talking about. 'Are you talking about the Tower Room, Jeremy?' Dulcie thought back to what Griddlehaus had told her. 'The storage room beneath the clock?'

'Storage…' The tongue again, and a faint movement of the head. Was Jeremy nodding, or was he seeing something—maybe someone—a scene from long ago. 'Storage room.'

It was no use. The man on the bed was too out of it. He was merely parroting back everything she said, mixed with a few phrases he'd picked up along the way. Maybe Griddlehaus had gotten some sense out of him. Maybe Jeremy had been more awake earlier in the day. It was getting on now, and he had been seriously injured. He'd be better in the morning. Maybe he'd be fully conscious. Or maybe, Dulcie thought with a sinking feeling, the once-great scholar on the bed before her was never going to make sense again.

'Well, I should get going, Jeremy.' She grabbed her coat and started to stand. On a whim, she reached out to touch his pale face, brushing back the too-long bangs that had fallen over his pale brow. 'I hope you feel better in the morning.'

'Morning,' he said, as if to confirm her suspicions. 'Can't take the secret. Find the cat…the cat in the stacks.'

THIRTY-THREE

ESMÉ WAS WAITING when Dulcie got home and greeted her with a sharp 'mew.'

'What?' Dulcie asked, as she shed her coat. 'I'm early today. It's not even dark out yet.' As the cat rubbed against her ankles, Dulcie continued. 'And it's certainly not dinner time.'

Whether her pet understood or had simply completed her affectionate greeting, Dulcie would never know. The little jellicle chose that moment to dart off into the living room as if in pursuit of some small rodent that only she could see.

'Enjoy, Esmé.' Dulcie watched her pet go with regret. 'I've got to get to work.'

Settling into a kitchen chair, she opened her laptop and stared at the screen before her. *The question of authorship.* She managed that one sentence and wondered how to proceed.

What she wanted to do, of course, was talk about the pages—the ones that had been salvaged during the re-binding. Her return to the Mildon with Griddlehaus had been supposed to help with that, identifying the book from which they had been taken. That quest had been interrupted, but Dulcie thought she might still be able to make something out of Griddlehaus's discovery in the ledger.

The question of authorship might appear to be further obscured by the discovery of certain pages, she wrote. *However, a closer examination of these pages, and in particular, where they were found, allows us to home in on the date and location of their creation. Because they were used as binding material in a later Gothic novel,* He Could Not Tell Her, *dating roughly from the 1830s, we may safely assume that not only were the works first written before that date but that they or their author may have fallen out of favor by that time, which would have allowed the use of these original manuscript pages to be valued primarily for the quality of their paper.*

Dulcie stopped herself. This was a leap. For all she knew, the author herself could have disposed of these papers. They may have been a rough draft, or otherwise deemed unnecessary once the work was published. They may have been disposed of by accident, or…

No, this way madness lies. 'Here be dragons,' she muttered, and closed her eyes. If only her thesis had a map, even one in which the uncharted territories were marked in some way…

'*Dulcie…*' She started in her seat, opening her eyes to see that her laptop screen had gone dark. '*Don't you know how to navigate?*'

The voice, gently teasing, sounded like it was from behind her left ear. She knew better than to turn around, however, and sat staring, first at the screen and then up at the kitchen window, with its square of sky and tree tops.

'Mr Grey,' she addressed the dark branches, waving in the wind. 'It's not that I don't know how to research, but I keep getting shut out.' She paused, but heard no response. 'First, my office is closed. Then my carrel and the Mildon. I'm running out of resources,' she concluded.

'*Resources?*' The way he rolled the 'r' could have been a purr. It also, Dulcie thought, could have been a growl. A warning.

'Well, books.' Dulcie wasn't sure what she had done wrong. 'And documents. Source material. You know.'

The low rumble reminded Dulcie of the few times her late, great pet had gotten angry, the way his velvety ears would flatten against his skull and his snarl revealed his glistening fangs. This had only happened on two occasions, once when a guest, a rather oafish colleague of Suze's, had trod on his long grey plume of a tail. Once when an intruder had been trying to break in—Dulcie and Suze had found marks on their door lock in the morning. In each case, the growl had been defensive, Dulcie thought, and prompted by either a criminal or at least an unfortunate human action.

A human action. 'Mr Grey, what are you trying to tell me?'

The low rumble could have been the wind, rattling the window. Dulcie thought of those marks, of how scared she and Suze had been. Scratch marks, like some beast had tried to get into their home. Marks like…

'Is this about the printer's mark, Mr Grey?' She was growing more confused. 'But I don't have access to those papers any more. All I have are…'

She stopped herself. A human action. Her own work, for starters. For while she may be temporarily cut off from the primary source material, she still had years of her own research—and she had friends, human sources, on whom she could always rely.

'Chris? You wouldn't believe what happened.' Three hours later, and Dulcie was bursting with news. 'I think I've had a breakthrough. And, yes, I've been writing.'

'I miss you, too, sweetie.' Her boyfriend was laughing. 'And how was your day?'

'I'm sorry.' Dulcie had to chuckle, too. 'It's just—so much has happened today.'

'Then by all means.' Dulcie could visualize her boyfriend making a broad gesture, his long arms encouraging her to begin. 'Tell!'

'Well, to start with, my pages—the new ones?—they all came from the book that was found on Jeremy Mumbleigh. Yes, I know,' she cut Chris off before he could ask about the sequence of events. 'That book had been re-bound. My pages were part of the original binding. They were filler, and after the conservators found them, they were sent to the Mildon, where they ended up in the stray pages file.' That wasn't the formal name for the Mildon repository for unacknowledged and previously uncataloged materials, but Chris would know what she meant. 'At any rate, my pages—the new ones, that is…'

'ARE YOU STILL THERE?' She had been talking several minutes, without hearing a peep. 'I'm sorry,' she said, perhaps a bit belatedly. 'I can go on about this stuff, I know.'

'No, no,' Chris protested. 'I love it. You're so enthusiastic about your work, and that's just great to hear. I mean, I don't really understand it, I'll admit that. But it's so clear that you love your work. Or, no, I know.' He stopped her before she could protest—there were limits to work, even for her. 'You love me and you love Esmé, I know that. And you love your mom.' He paused, but she couldn't argue with that one. 'But you really value this writer. You're like a treasure hunter, uncovering golden nuggets in piles of paper.'

'Well, it *is* treasure,' she began. 'Not like…'

She broke off, the import of her own words hitting home. Everybody had assumed that the thieves had been after something rare and showy. The Islington Bible or, more accurately, its jewel-encrusted cover. When that had been recovered, everyone had assumed that the robbery had been interrupted. That the thieves had been thwarted.

But what if the Islington hadn't been the goal?

Could the thieves have been after the pages in the Mildon after all?

'Dulcie, are you there?' Chris's voice brought her back to the present. 'Did I say something?'

'No—or, well, yes.' Dulcie wasn't sure how to explain. 'You gave me an idea, saying that about buried treasure. Chris—I told you about the latest break-in, right? At the Mildon?'

'Uh huh.' He was with her. 'I read something online about how they think that the thieves were using the excavations to get into the library. About how they were probably counting on staffing being lower, what with the students being on break.'

Dulcie interrupted him, she was so excited. 'What if the thieves were really after my pages—the ones in the Mildon? I mean, they've been lost for years. First, they were hidden in the binding of a book. Then they were uncataloged and unknown. It wasn't until I started publishing about them that anyone—'

'Dulcie, wait.' Chris interrupted her. 'Please, sweetie, listen to yourself. I know you value these pages. I love that about you. But I didn't mean for you to take me literally. Why would someone who isn't a scholar, someone who doesn't know these works, want to steal them?'

'Because…' She started to answer, and then fell silent. The truth was that she had no answer to give.

THIRTY-FOUR

STEP BY STEP, each footfall placed with a care, she did hazard her way through the dark Shadows of the ill-illumined hall. No light, for e'en the softest Lamp might betray her stealthy passage. No faithless candle nor ill-betoken'd Lantern would dare disclose her progress. Silent as the Fog itself, which like the deep gloom shrouded the castle in its enveloping embrace, she made her way onward. Only this short Journey, made long by care and caution, did she venture, for at her sojourn's end would she find all Seclusion and Secrets still.

TRY AS SHE MIGHT, Dulcie could not burrow deep enough into the blankets. The insistent ringing of her phone seemed determined to wake her.

'Chris…' She woke, fully, to the realization that her boyfriend was not here to answer for her. And that, in fact, a call at this hour might presage something wrong.

'Hello?' By the time she found the phone, Dulcie was frantic. 'What's happening?'

'The moon! The moon is what's happening!' Several voices, chanting, and a sound like the wind through it all.

'Lucy?' It was a guess, but a good one. 'Is that you?'

'Of course it's me, Dulcinea.' One voice—her mother's—came in clear. Lucy had picked up the phone. 'Did you feel our energy?'

'No, I heard you though.' Dulcie slumped to the floor. Her mother hadn't called during a circle in a long time. 'Excuse me, Mom, but are you stoned?'

'Dulcinea!' Her mother's shock was a bit too exaggerated for innocence. 'What kind of question is that?'

'Sorry, Mom.' Dulcie leaned back against the wall. Usually, she managed to be more tolerant of her mother's unconventional ways. 'You woke me.'

'But it's the super moon.' Her mother sounded honestly perplexed. 'And it's not much past midnight.'

'It's three hours later here.' Dulcie didn't know why she even had to explain this one more time. 'I was in bed.'

'Go to the window, dear.' The chanting in the background grew louder. 'Come and sing with us.'

'I'll go look.' Dulcie pulled herself to her feet and made her way into the kitchen. There, through the bare branches, she could see an impressive moon, low in the sky. 'Very nice. Is that why you called?'

'I can't call to invite my only child to join our circle?' Dulcie didn't respond. Lucy tended to get rhetorical when embarrassed, and Dulcie suspected she had forgotten about the time difference. 'But I'm sorry, Dulcie. Really I am.'

'Thanks, Mom.' Dulcie leaned on the sill, looking at the glowing orb. Esmé's soft fur brushed against her ankles. 'It is gorgeous.'

'I'm so glad you have the cat with you.' Her mother sounded calmer now, even—dare she say it—maternal.

'Actually, she's right here.' Dulcie didn't want to look away, but she lifted one bare foot and felt the cool damp of a feline nose on her ankle. 'Do you want me to put her on?'

'Not Esmé.' Dulcie had been joking, but her mother's dismissal still surprised her. 'No, I meant the other cat.'

'The other cat?' Dulcie had never told her mother about Mr Grey's visits, though Lucy had picked up something about her daughter having a 'spirit animal,' as she put it. 'Lucy?'

'The cat of moonlight,' said Lucy. 'Of light and shadows—a creature of the hidden places. That's what I wanted to tell you. I had thought at first that he was simply a random beast. You understand, of course, a formless but fierce manifestation of the goddess Selene, a creature of light and shadow. And you have to trust the shadow. But now I know—he's a cat. It was hard for me to tell, Dulcie, because he's been so hidden, and he can be very dark, you know.'

'It's dark in your visions?' Dulcie closed her eyes. She couldn't concentrate on the moon and her mother. At least Esmé was comforting, leaning against her shin with a rumbling purr. 'Oh, wait, do you mean the dark of the moon?'

'Something like that, dear.' Her mother responded as if this were the most natural discussion in the world. 'What I'm getting is that he did not choose to manifest at first. Not in any corporeal plane. He did keep insisting, "It's a secret."'

That woke Dulcie up. 'He said what?'

'Oh, hang on!' The chanting was getting louder, and someone called Lucy's name.

'Mom?' The line went dead, and after a moment of silence, Dulcie put the phone down on the window sill. Outside, the moon had sunk further, and now looked as if it could be tangled in those trees. 'Just like your claws, Esmé,' she said, as the little cat scrambled on to the sill.

'*My claws are neater than that.*' As if to prove her point, Esmé started to groom, the moonlight picking up the silver in her guard hairs. '*And they never get caught in anything, unless I want them to.*'

'Point taken.' Dulcie stroked the silky black back as Esmé worked on her whiskers. The pressure on her ankles remained warm and constant, as together they watched the moon till it disappeared below the skyline.

THIRTY-FIVE

When Dulcie next awoke, the sun was shining through the window and Esmé was long gone. Her present-day pet had sat up with her until the spectral comfort had disappeared along with the moon, and then had accompanied her to bed, washing noisily on the pillow by her head as Dulcie slipped back into sleep.

That sleep had been dreamless, and she had woken refreshed. But her mother's comments had stayed with her.

'It's a secret,' she said out loud, as she started the coffee brewing. 'The moonlight cat.'

In general, Dulcie knew, it didn't make much sense to credit her mother's visions. Too often, these seemed to be the result of empty-nest syndrome, loneliness and perhaps regret. At times, as Dulcie had suspected the night before, they came directly out of her mother's propensity for psychotropic excursions. However, these words came awfully close to what Jeremy had said—and they were reminiscent of her own dreams of stealth and darkness.

'You don't think it was just the moonlight, do you, Mr Grey?' The spirit had not made an appearance this morning, but Dulcie could easily conjure up his wise green eyes. Besides, without Chris around—

and with Esmé being obstreperous, she wanted to talk to someone.

'*I'm here.*' A very solid head butt as the little jellicle made her morning debut. '*Breakfast?*'

'Of course.' Dulcie opened a can and, as her cat dug in, began to think about her day. The Mildon was probably still off limits, she thought with regret. Griddlehaus had said he would call her, but until then, she thought she should probably stay away. In fact, she realized, she should probably avoid the library entirely.

'It's not fair, Esmé,' Dulcie complained. 'I stayed in town to work.'

Esmé looked up, licking her chops. But now that she had received her morning due, she had lapsed back into a more usual catlike silence.

What she ought to be doing was writing. After Chris had shot down her latest theory about the break-in, she had gone on to tell him about her progress. Only she had exaggerated a bit, pretending that she had most of the new chapter drafted. It wasn't that she wanted to lie to Chris, only that she didn't want to disappoint him. Clearly, he didn't believe that unraveling what had happened to Jeremy—or why anyone had broken into the library—should be taking up so much of her time.

'You don't even know if they're all connected, Dulce,' he had said, putting it as gently as possible. 'Old Mumbles might have been mugged. Or maybe the cops have it wrong and he fell and hit his head.'

'But what about the book?' Dulcie had asked. 'Surely the fact that he had that book—from the

Stavendish bequest—means something.' She had
started to explain again about how her pages had
come from that volume, but Chris had interrupted.

'Sweetie, that book has been missing for years,' he
had said. 'Nobody ever sees him except in that big old
overcoat. You said that the book couldn't have been
stored in that hole, that it was in too good shape for
that. But Mumbles could have been carrying that book
around with him all along, and we just never knew.'

He was right, she knew it. Just as he was right
about how she should be applying herself to the chapter at hand—using what information she now had.

'If you wait until you know everything, you'll
never get your dissertation done,' he had said, his
voice soft. 'You might never even start. We call it
going down a wormhole in applied math. You start
chasing the source of something—the ultimate result—and you get lost.'

Dulcie opened her laptop and thought about that.
The imagery was great. A wormhole sounded dark
and deep. Kind of like how Lucy had described her
vision. Only that hadn't been a worm hole. That had
been some kind of cloudy scene with a cat in it. A
cat, like Dulcie had seen in the excavation by the
library. A cat like the printer's mark, intended as a
signal to readers—a sign to follow.

Could Jeremy have been hiding that book all these
years?

Dulcie's screen glowed to life. The previous day's
work opened before her, while another window
showed her latest notes with several lines highlighted.

It didn't matter. Closing the laptop, she tossed it

into her bag. Maybe she'd get a chance to use it later.
For now, she needed to get dressed and put on her
sturdiest shoes. Dulcie was going down a wormhole.

'I'M SORRY, MISS. I really am.' The guard at the back
entrance of the library looked honestly pained.

'You can't keep me out,' Dulcie protested. 'I'm a
member of the university in good standing.'

'No, I know that. I do.' His brow wrinkled with
the effort. 'It's only that I have your name on a list.
If you came in, I was told to call Mr Truckworth and
let him know, and well, I have to ask you to stay here
while I do that.'

Dulcie slumped against the wall. It was hopeless.
She had hoped to locate her colleague and enlist his
aid. If he had called, she would have explained it to
him—she felt sure the librarian would understand.
Except that he hadn't, not yet, and she realized she
had no way of reaching him. Unless…

'Look.' She reached out to the guard. He'd been
scrolling down a screen, clearly reluctant to make the
call. 'What if I don't go into the library proper? What
if I just poke my head into the staff reading room
over there?' She gestured past the guard's station,
to the door to Griddlehaus's book-lined sanctuary.
'Just a quick visit. I'm looking for Mr Griddlehaus
and either he'll be there or I can leave him a note. I
don't need to go into the stacks today.'

'Oh, well, if that's all you want.' Relief flooded
the guard's broad features. 'That's not really part of
the library.'

Dulcie smiled and nodded, giving her tacit agreement to the slight fiction. She was almost about to offer to leave her bag, as a surety, when she remembered what had happened the day before. Instead, with a smile and a nod, she tugged the strap up on her shoulder and—aware that his eyes were following her—she went up to the recessed door and knocked softly.

'Mr Griddlehaus?' She wasn't sure how well insulated the little room was. It had certainly seemed quite quiet when they had been there. 'Are you there?'

'I haven't seen him yet today.' The guard was standing right behind her. 'Maybe you should just leave him a note.'

'Maybe I'll do that then.' Retrieving the key from its niche, she unlocked the door. 'Mr Griddlehaus?'

The guard was right. There was nobody here. Even the motion-sensitive lights seemed to have been turned off, and the windowless room was pitch black. There had been a lamp, she recalled. A tall old-fashioned floor lamp, off to her left. She reached and felt cold metal. Working her hand up, she found the knob and turned it, closing her eyes against the sudden brightness.

'What the hey?' The guard's voice caused her to turn, so that her first sight was of his face, lit by the lamp, shocked and open.

'What do you mean?' she asked as she turned, and then gasped. The comfy chair she had relaxed in had been sliced open, its stuffing spilling out on to the floor. The lamp she had reached was the only one standing. And all the books—or what seemed like all of them—had been pulled from the shelves to lie in a heap on the floor.

THIRTY-SIX

'Oh, dear Goddess!' Dulcie wasn't sure how Lucy's expression got into her mouth, but the words seemed appropriate as she stared at the mess before her.

'What the hell?' The guard, who pushed by her, was a little more profane. 'I'm calling security.'

He turned and raced back to the booth, leaving Dulcie frozen to the spot.

'Hello? We've got a problem.' She heard his voice, as if from far away, but she couldn't stop staring. The neat little hideaway of the other day, Griddlehaus's sanctuary, was a mess. The chair…

'Yes, of course.' The guard was still speaking. 'Right away.'

Worst of all were the books. Dulcie saw one lying face down, splayed open, its leather spine already cracking. It had fallen—or been thrown—almost to the doorway. She couldn't stand it. She stepped in and picked it up.

Looking around for where to place the poor thing, she spotted another, its pages folded beneath it. And a third, the cover bent back by its odd angle against a fallen lamp. Before she knew what she was doing, Dulcie had her arms full of books and was reaching for another.

'Miss, Miss, you can't be in here.' She looked up

to see the guard standing in the doorway, a pained look on his face. 'Please, Miss.'

'But…' Dulcie paused, suddenly aware of the books she held against her body. 'They could have been damaged.' It was all she could think of to say. But as she was looking around, trying to find a flat surface where she could place the books, she heard a bustle in the hallway.

'What happened? Oh, no, not you.' Stuart Truckworth had stepped in front of the guard and was now coming forward. 'What have you done here? What did you pick up?'

'Just these.' Dulcie held out the books as evidence, but the facilities manager didn't seem interested in examining their cracked and twisted spines.

'Stupid.' With one long stride, he was by her side, grabbing the books out of her hands. 'Don't you have the sense—'

'What's going on here?' A gruff voice interrupted and Dulcie looked up to see that iron buzz cut backlit by the hall light. 'Truckworth?'

'It's nothing,' said the manager. 'I mean it's under control.'

'Doesn't look like it.' The bulky officer stepped in, nearly filling the doorway. 'Though it is interesting to find you in what is quite clearly a crime scene.'

'We were just leaving.' Truckworth looked around and—faced with the same problem Dulcie had—stooped to put the books on the floor. 'Come on, Ms Schwartz.'

'Wait, you shouldn't…' Dulcie reached for the books, but Truckworth was too fast for her. With one big hand on her back, he pushed her forward, and she stumbled toward the door.

'Watch it.' She turned as she righted herself. 'There's no need to be rude.'

'You should not have been in here.' Truckworth caught up with her and marched her toward the library exit, his voice strained. 'You shouldn't be in here at all.'

'I have a right.' As soon as she was out the door, Dulcie pulled away, whirling around to face the tall and balding manager. 'And you, sir, are totally out of bounds.'

'You are a stupid girl.' He was nearly spitting. 'Stay out of this, while you can.'

'Stay out of what? The library?' But he had already turned and stormed back in. Shaken, despite herself, Dulcie took a deep breath and then another, and straightened her coat collar where it had gotten rucked up. It was only when she reached up to brush her unruly curls off her face that she realized how close to tears she was. As she squeezed her eyes shut a few stray outliers made their escape down her cheeks.

'You OK?' She hadn't noticed the guard slipping out, but now he stood beside her, sheltering in the brick entranceway. 'That was a little rough.'

'Thanks.' A few blinks and her eyes cleared. 'I'll be fine. I was startled, that's all.' Embarrassed, she turned back toward the door. Inside, she could see Truckworth talking to Wardley. The facilities manager towered over the cop, but as skinny as he was tall, he appeared flimsy and insubstantial. 'What are they doing?'

The guard shook his head. 'Not much. The room's on lockdown until the cops can investigate. I don't know what they're going to find.'

'Maybe they can figure out who did it? I mean, the door wasn't forced, was it?'

'No.' Another shake, confirming what Dulcie had thought. 'I think most of the library staff knew about it. Knew where the key was, too.'

Dulcie didn't respond. There was something so depressing about it all: Griddlehaus's lovely reading room despoiled. 'Why would anyone do such a thing?'

'Some people don't like books,' said the guard. 'Or they don't like the university. Think we're privileged. You know.'

Dulcie nodded. She did. But as the guard turned and returned to his post, another thought occurred to her. Griddlehaus's private reading room was just that—private. Not obvious to the outside world, and certainly not ostentatious. Besides, the guard had said that its existence—and the whereabouts of its key—were known to the library staff. That was a large group—Ruby, Kyle, Griddlehaus himself—but a pretty cohesive one. At any rate, it wasn't made up of the kind of people who would be likely to trash a room just for having books.

Of course, there might be another reason to destroy library property. As Dulcie began to walk away, she recalled how upset she had been during that brief moment when she had been accused of stealing library property. Might Kyle be harboring enough resentment to take it out on some innocent books—or even on Griddlehaus himself?

As she wandered, collar up against the wind, she tried to think back to the diminutive librarian's involvement with Kyle's arrest. Had he given evidence? Had he been the one to identify the missing document? No. Dulcie kicked the ground. She was conflating events. Griddlehaus had identified the book that had been found on Jeremy. Kyle had been arrested by Wardley, though Dulcie still didn't know how the big cop had been led to the young guard. She would have to ask—

'Mr Griddlehaus!' Dulcie looked up in time to see him hurrying by, head down. 'It's me. I, I mean.'

'Ms Schwartz.' From the anguish on his face, Dulcie knew he had heard. 'I just received a call from Mr Truckworth. I'm afraid I have to hurry.'

'I know, Mr Griddlehaus.' She turned to accompany her friend. 'I was there.'

'You were…excuse me?' He stopped and turned toward her.

'Your reading room. I was looking for you. I hope you don't mind.' She realized how this could sound. 'I was hoping to find you.'

'I was visiting with Jeremy. I haven't found anything, you know.' His voice dropped to a conspiratorial whisper. 'In the Mildon. Nothing else missing, that is. I did say I would call.'

'I know.' Dulcie rushed to reassure him. 'It was just that I had this idea and I wanted to get started, and I felt funny about going into the library. But

I thought, your reading room…' In retrospect, it seemed a stupid idea. 'Anyway, I opened the door and saw what had happened.'

'Is it bad?' His voice fell to a whisper.

'It kind of is,' said Dulcie, hating to break the news. 'But maybe it's just a mess. You know, books tossed about, the chairs overturned…'

He started walking again, picking up the pace as he muttered. 'But why would anyone? It's simply a reading room. The equivalent of a staff lounge…'

'Were there any valuables?' Dulcie caught herself. 'I mean, something that someone who isn't a scholar might want to steal?'

He shook his head. 'I don't believe so.' They had arrived at the library, and Dulcie came to a halt.

'Why don't I wait here?' Griddlehaus stopped as well and turned toward her. 'I'll be fine,' she said. 'I just think it's better.'

With a nod, he visibly braced himself for what lay ahead, and entered the library.

'Poor guy,' Dulcie said to herself. His lovely little lair, all messed up. She couldn't find the heart to believe that Kyle had been behind this. Although if he were, it might help explain Stuart Truckworth's manner. Maybe he saw something in that room that implicated his son—or was afraid that Dulcie had. Closing her eyes, she tried to re-create the room as she had seen it. Books pulled off shelves. Lamps and chairs tipped over. It all seemed so random, and yet it could have been worse. For all the tossing and tipping, nothing appeared to have been intentionally harmed. It was almost as if someone had had a tantrum—had wanted to make a mess quickly. Or, she thought as she leaned against the brick, someone had wanted to make a point.

The library staff knew about the room—knew about the key. Could Kyle have done this to divert suspicion? Could his father? Or was this a random bit of lunacy, not unheard of—although more commonly encountered during finals?

None of it made sense. No more sense than the attack on poor Jeremy. It had been only five days since Dulcie had seen him here, in this sheltered alcove. Not that it provided much protection from the cold, she realized, shivering. How much worse it must have been for the skinny scholar in his threadbare tweed. She could still picture him, where she was standing now, scratching at the wall.

Thinking of that night, she turned. Yes, the scratches he had been making were still there, white incised in the dull red of the brick. A few letters—none of which made much sense: RT UP RT 6. Maybe they were part of some longer word, something that had been rubbed off by the wind or by one of the guards. Maybe they were a code, something that made sense only to Jeremy. Beside the letters, a few additional scratches seemed to outline a semi-circle—or, no, a pie chart, with slashes cutting off a hearty slice. On top, a triangle. Had Jeremy been hungry? Dulcie felt the stab of regret. If she had only invited him to dine, perhaps all of this would have been avoided. Or, wait—she squinted at the semi-circle, at the slashes and point. Could that be a cat?

No, a pie was more likely. A cat is something

she would draw. A reminder of Mr Grey and all he
meant to her. But before Dulcie could delve more
deeply into this idea, Griddlehaus emerged, pushing the heavy door open and almost falling out into
the cold air.

'Are you all right?' She hurried over. The little
man looked a bit stunned.

'Yes, yes.' He sighed heavily. 'They won't—they
won't let me in.'

'What?' Dulcie prepared to march back in. Her
being kept out of the library—or, to be fair, kept under
observation—was one thing. Thomas Griddlehaus,
however, was the director of the Mildon Collection.
A senior staffer and a very important part of the entire university library system.

'No, please.' Only his hand on her arm stopped
her, and for a moment, Dulcie wondered if he had
read her thoughts. 'I misrepresented.'

She exhaled, the steam going out of her.

'Neither Mr Truckworth nor Lieutenant Wardley
are there right now,' he explained. 'However, they
have stationed a young officer at the door, and he was
told not to allow entry. Clearly, there was a failure
in communication.'

'Sounds like Truckworth to me.' Dulcie wouldn't
soon forget her treatment at the manager's hands.

'Please, Dulcie,' Griddlehaus interrupted. 'It was
Mr Truckworth who called me and informed me of
the disruption, and this young officer is clearly doing
what he perceives as his job. Considering everything
that has been happening in the Yard, I suspect Lieu-

tenant Wardley is overemphasizing caution, but that isn't necessarily a bad thing.'

Dulcie nodded. He was right. 'I'm sorry,' she said.

'Thank you.' He took off his glasses and wiped them with a handkerchief. 'Well, Ms Schwartz, you had said you were looking for me?'

'Yes.' That seemed like hours ago. 'I was thinking about Jeremy.' She tried to piece her thoughts together and found herself remembering the animal she had seen in the excavation. That hadn't been merely a hole. It had been part of a tunnel, an interconnected system. 'Chris had said something about wormholes and it gave me an idea.'

'You're looking for a wormhole?' Griddlehaus blinked in confusion.

'Chris was talking about study habits. My study habits in particular.' Dulcie struggled to explain and realized she was staring at the scratches on the wall. At what might just be a cat…'It was just a concept, but it made me think of that tower room and, well, of all the—um—animals who have been displaced by the excavations.

'I thought that if we could find out where Jeremy had been living, we might be able to find some contact information for him. Maybe locate a family member. Maybe set him up with social services, so he could go home.' Dulcie shook her head. 'It was a silly idea. He probably bunks wherever he can find a dry, warm place.'

'That's a commendable idea, Ms Schwartz,' said Griddlehaus, once she was through. 'And very kind. I'm rather ashamed that I haven't thought of it.'

'Well, you've had your hands full.' Dulcie felt her cheeks color at the praise.

'No, it isn't that.' Griddlehaus stared off into space. 'I'm afraid it's that I simply haven't thought. You see, as long as I've known Jeremy, I've associated him with the library. I have, on occasion, asked him to join me for lunch, but beyond that, well, I've gone my own way and let my poor, old friend go his.'

He looked down at the ground, and Dulcie reached out and took his hand. 'You're being his friend now, Mr Griddlehaus. You've been visiting him, and trying to cheer him up. None of us have really paid much attention to Jeremy before now, but maybe now together we can help him.'

'He hasn't been exactly alone,' said Griddlehaus. 'After all, Lieutenant Wardley has been dropping in to see him.'

'Great.' Dulcie snorted. 'Just what he needs— more police harassment.'

'But Wardley's not—you can't think that.' Griddlehaus was shaking his head. 'They've known each other for years.'

'They have?' Dulcie thought of the big cop, of his gruff manner.

'Wardley was there the night that Jeremy tried to kill himself. Lieutenant Wardley—he was a patrolman back then—saved Jeremy's life.'

THIRTY-SEVEN

SITTING OVER A cup of hot cocoa in the Greenhouse Café, Dulcie struggled to get her mind around what Griddlehaus was telling her.

'Lieutenant Wardley saved Jeremy's life?' She tried to picture the big, bluff officer as a younger, friendlier man.

Griddlehaus nodded, repeating the basics one more time. 'Jeremy was half out the window, yelling. The next thing any of us knew, a young officer was hauling him back in, holding him in a bear hug.'

Not friendlier necessarily, Dulcie acknowledged. Just conscientious.

'Jeremy was going on about the books,' Griddlehaus continued. 'He called them *his* books—and about how he'd been betrayed. There really was no option but to have him taken to the hospital.'

'*His* books?' Maybe there was a reason Wardley had grown so gruff.

Another slow, sad nod. 'I'm afraid his obsession with the Stavendish bequest had put him over the edge. And now that one of the stolen books was found on him, I can't help but wonder if he *was* involved, all those years ago.'

'But he wouldn't have stolen from a library—not with the way he feels about books. What if,' she said now, leaning in to face Griddlehaus. 'What if Jeremy Mumbleigh didn't just find that book—and didn't steal it? What if he has been living with it all along?'

'I believe we considered that option initially,' said the librarian as he finished his grilled cheese. 'But the condition of the excavation, where he was found—'

She cut him off. 'No, I don't mean in some abandoned sub-basement. Certainly not in the hole where he was found. I mean, living with it *in the library*.' She fumbled, trying to put her thoughts into words. 'Everyone has been talking about the infrastructure of the Yard, of the rooms and tunnels under the library. And between the rats and when we were forced to leave—sorry.' She saw Griddlehaus wince at the unfortunate equivalence. 'I thought, maybe Jeremy had been forced out, too. Maybe he wasn't stealing that book. Maybe it was never stolen—only lost. And maybe he had been living where it was stored or misfiled or whatever, before the construction made him leave. And maybe he was saving that book.'

In the silence that followed, Dulcie could tell that Griddlehaus was thinking. 'It is possible,' he acknowledged after a few moments had passed. 'Not likely, but it would be in keeping with the character of the man.'

'Do you think that's why your reading room was broken into?' Dulcie sipped her cocoa, considering the possibilities. 'Do you think somebody was looking for a hidden cache?'

Griddlehaus shook his head. 'I doubt it. Our room might be private, but everything in it is from the general collection. Everything has been cataloged.'

'Maybe they didn't know that,' she said, as she and her friend gathered up their belongings. 'Whoever broke into your reading room and into the Mildon is looking for something. Something that maybe Jeremy has.'

Griddlehaus shook his head. 'I don't know, Ms Schwartz. I can't quite visualize that.'

'That's because you're not a larcenous thug,' said Dulcie as she buttoned her coat. 'Whoever did this is probably responsible for attacking Jeremy, too.'

'Wait.' Griddlehaus held up his hand. 'You were saying that he has been living with this book in some kind of hidden room. Now you're saying he was defending it?'

'I'm not clear on the details. But he might have been.' Dulcie mulled the possibility. 'Perhaps his hideaway had finally been breached. Perhaps he was busy moving his hidden cache to someplace safer when he ran into trouble. Perhaps the book had been stolen and he was injured trying to get it back. That's just it, Mr Griddlehaus, we don't know. So the best thing we can do,' she took a breath, 'is to find Jeremy's hideaway ourselves. That way, we can safeguard whatever it is, and maybe bring a scofflaw to justice.'

THIRTY-EIGHT

GRIDDLEHAUS WENT BACK to the Mildon after that, citing a pressing research question. Dulcie wasn't entirely sure he had bought her theory. He was still upset about the mess that had been made of his reading room though, and so she let him go without an argument.

Despite Griddlehaus's skepticism, Dulcie knew her theory was sound. Maybe there were no other missing books, but the idea that Jeremy had found this one in the library—and that he had been in the library—was growing on her. As to how he had gotten it—or himself—out of the library, well, that was obvious. The excavation where he had been found was not some simple hole. The more she thought about it, the more she was sure she had seen a cat down there. A cat who, after making eye contact, had run off. No, not run off—had shown her that there was more to the digging than was readily apparent. Had shown a connection to the old tunnels.

Only, how could she access them?

The early dusk was casting long shadows as she made her way back to the Yard, and her doubts grew with those shadows. When she had hoped to enlist Griddlehaus in her endeavors, she had envisioned him using his superior knowledge of the library system—and his staff ID—to give them access to all locked entrances to the underground storage and communication system. Without her bespectacled friend, Dulcie realized she faced a grimmer prospect: entering the warren of tunnels from one of the many holes in the Yard.

It was a daunting proposition, and Dulcie made her way over to the latest excavation slowly, trying to get her mind around the idea of climbing down in the cold and mud. If only, she thought, there was another way into the tunnels, besides going through the library. Another way to look for those books…

The conservation lab! With renewed vigor, Dulcie trotted across the Yard to the white building behind the Science Center. Without Griddlehaus's ID, she was forced to bang on the door, and for a few moments there, she was afraid that nobody would answer. A muted voice—'I'm coming!'—announced that the lab had not, in fact, closed for the day, and in a moment, the door swung open.

'Hello again.' The grey-haired woman who answered the door didn't seem surprised to see Dulcie there. 'Come to see more of the cat?'

'The cat?' Dulcie followed the conservator— Margaret Constantine—back into the pristine lab and toward a light table.

'The silver cat. The printer's mark you found. We've confirmed it.' She smiled at Dulcie. 'You have a good eye.'

'Thank you.' Dulcie recalled the sparkle of that feline. It seemed rude to say she only wanted an entrance to the tunnels. Besides, she was drawn to the curious mark. 'Yes, I guess I would like to see him—it—again.'

'"Him" is fine. He has that power over people, I know.' She turned with what looked suspiciously like a wink as she ushered Dulcie over to the table. 'I'm rather smitten with him myself.'

Margaret swung a magnifying lens over the table. Through it, Dulcie could clearly see the simple pen strokes—the profile, the ears, the whiskers—of the silver feline.

'We've been trying to stabilize it,' Margaret explained. 'We're lucky, you know. Being folded up in the binding helped preserve the page, although it is frustrating not to have a complete work.'

'Tell me about it,' murmured Dulcie. How someone could use something so beautiful as mere filler was beyond her. She looked up. 'I actually came by for a different reason, though.'

'Oh?' Margaret retrieved a tool that looked like something a dentist would use. 'Yes,' she caught Dulcie's glance. 'We improvise a lot of our tools here.'

'Cool,' said Dulcie. 'Actually, I was hoping you could let me into the tunnels.' She paused, unsure of how much more she should share. 'The situation at the library, with the water main break…'

'Not a problem.' Margaret replaced the dental pick on her tray. 'It's horrible what's happening over there. Particularly because situating so much of the library below ground was considered safer.'

'Safer?'

'For the materials, of course.' Margaret looked a little surprised. 'Before we had our current climate control systems, constant temperatures, not to mention light exposure, were easier to maintain in a subterranean setting.'

'Like that page, preserved in the binding.' Something was scratching at the edge of Dulcie's memory.

'Exactly. Like that cat hiding in his lair, until it was time for us to let him out.' After a last longing look at the tools laid out before her, the conservator stood, brushing an invisible speck of dust from her lab coat in a rather catlike gesture. 'The tunnel?'

'Thanks.' Dulcie followed, another question on the tip of her tongue. 'Margaret,' she asked the feline conservator finally. 'How valuable is the silver cat?' It wasn't what she was thinking exactly, but it was close.

'Depends on its condition,' she said as she led Dulcie through the back of the lab. 'And on the piece, of course. For us, the value lies in its rarity. Right now, there are fewer than a dozen "Felix" pages that are known to have survived. You know about the January auction, I gather? So you understand how the discovery of another, well, that could shift the entire market, couldn't it?'

The question was rhetorical, but it stayed with Dulcie as the conservator led her down the stairs and pushed open the doors. With a buzz and a hum, the lights turned on, illuminating the long, windowless passage.

'Don't worry.' Margaret must have seen something on her face. 'These are fire doors. You can always push them open and come out to the nearest exit. Good hunting, Dulcie.'

'Thanks,' said Dulcie. Only as the door swung shut behind her did she stop to consider. She had been too caught up in her own thoughts to ask where the other exits were—or if the path to the library was as straightforward as she remembered. Too busy thinking about the meaning of the hidden cat—and what role this latest discovery might have played in the strange events in the library. Too concerned with her own search to notice that the grey-haired conservator had not asked where she was going—or why—before wishing her luck on her search.

AT THE FIRST INTERSECTION, one of her immediate fears was allayed. A door with a small, wired window was clearly labeled 'Science Center,' while another sign—stenciled on the wall opposite—indicated 'Library' in one direction, 'Conservation Lab' back from where she'd come. She wasn't going to get lost, at any rate, as she made her way under the Yard.

That didn't make the walk any less unnerving. The buzzing of the lights and the cool click as they turned off behind her left Dulcie with the impression that she was being followed. Once she even stopped and turned, expecting to see a figure in the shadows behind her, her inability to make out anything in the darkness spooking her further still. Almost, she felt, someone was lurking back there, hanging back. But try as she might, she couldn't see anything in the recesses of the tunnel—and to return, in order to reactivate the lights, would simply have prolonged the trip.

Instead, she walked on, the sound of her footsteps

drowned in the hum of the fluorescents overhead. 'Utility A.' She didn't know where that was, but the reminder next to it—'Library,' with an arrow—was heartening. Behind her, a soft click as the lights went dark.

Like any unwitted Hare in a trap, she was caught, her limbs clasped tight about her heaving sides by the Treacherous Beast, as her Lungs gasped out for liberty as essential as the very Air. No matter her desperate struggle, 'twas too late.

No, she was not going to think of that passage. Nobody was coming up behind her. Nobody was about to grab her. Nobody—

'Dulcie!' A hand on her shoulder. Holding her.

She screamed.

THIRTY-NINE

'I'M SORRY!' KYLE stepped back, wide eyed, his hands raised. 'I didn't mean to startle you.'

'Kyle.' Dulcie could have collapsed with relief. As it was, she reached out for the wall, its white paint smooth beneath her hand. 'I didn't hear you.'

'I gather! I wasn't sure it was you, or I would've called your name.' He pointed back down the passage. 'I was just coming from the utility room and I saw you up ahead—at least, I was pretty sure it was you.'

The click. She'd thought it was the lights.

'I came down here through the conservation lab,' she explained. 'I didn't realize there were so many entrances.'

'There are a bunch.' He pointed to another, labeled 'Storage.' 'Some of them are blocked off now, but it used to be that you could get anywhere through these tunnels. Now we basically use them for maintenance work.'

She looked at him. The red-haired guard was dressed in his uniform coat and tie. 'Not that kind of maintenance,' he said. 'We got the OK to turn the ventilation on level three back on, but there was a question about whether the circuits needed to be reset. So they sent me, the errand boy.'

'At least you're back at work.'

'Yeah, I guess.' He didn't sound pleased. 'So, you're going up to the library?'

'That general direction.' She shrugged, unsure of how much to share. 'I was curious to see how much damage has been done. The leaks and the break-in.'

He nodded. 'It is something. You're on three, right? We've pretty much cleaned that up. It'll be a while before the smell goes away.'

She looked at him, waiting.

'Mold,' he said, his voice low. 'Not the books— don't worry—but they took down some walls and found rooms that have been there since the climate control system was added, at the very least.'

'Did you find anything there?'

'Tons of old plumbing. A coal shovel.' He shook his head. 'Some ancient insulation. You know what we didn't find, though?'

She waited.

'Rats.' He shivered. 'I was drafted to help haul away the trash, of course. My father says maybe we got lucky. He thought he saw a cat—must be a stray or something. At any rate, it seems that rat invasion we feared isn't going to happen.'

'Your father was there?' She stopped walking and turned to look at Kyle.

'Well, yeah.' He looked at her as if she had sprouted a second head. 'He is the head of facilities, why?'

'Nothing.' Dulcie kept walking. If she were right, then Stuart Truckworth might have already found Jeremy's hideaway. If only she knew what they were

looking for. 'Can you show me where you took the
walls down?'

'You sure?' He looked her up and down. 'It's
pretty filthy down there.'

She took in her coat and jeans. Nothing that
wasn't washable. 'Yeah, I'm sure.'

'OK, then.' He pushed open a door marked simply
'Utilities' and held it while Dulcie passed through.
Right away, she saw the difference. If these walls had
ever been painted white, that paint had long since
gone grey, while the roughness of the floor was ac-
centuated by shadows flung by the bare bulbs that
had replaced the cool fluorescents. Kyle didn't seem
deterred, however, and had grown almost chummy
as he led the way into the darkness.

'Hey, did you see the report on spring training?'
he asked, bobbing along ahead of her.

'No, how are the Sox looking?' Dulcie had lived
with Chris for long enough now that she knew the
right noises to make. And so as Kyle went on about
some pitcher—or perhaps it was a shortstop?—she
found herself watching her footing and mulling over
what he had told her. The newly exposed rooms were
filthy, Kyle had said, and the hall he was leading her
through was already noticeably dirtier. But Jeremy,
as far as she could recall, had always been clean.
Threadbare, yes, but presentable. Dulcie wasn't sure
his presence in the library would have been toler-
ated if his hygiene had been slack. Of course, that
didn't mean much. If a person were conscientious,
she supposed, he could clean up in any of the public
bathrooms in the Square.

'I'm thinking bleacher seats?' Kyle turned toward her like he expected an answer. Like he was trying to be friendly. They had just passed a turn-off, taking the left branch at a fork, the option that seemed to Dulcie to be even darker and danker than the right.

'I'll ask Chris,' she responded, trying not to look too closely at the walls around them—or to think about Kyle and his changeable moods. As her companion strode on, his long strides keeping her on the edge of breathlessness, Dulcie told herself that he knew where he was going. That he was, indeed, a friend.

The presence of Stuart Truckworth might have meant nothing, either. As Kyle had pointed out, his father was the director of facilities and maintenance. Perhaps it made sense for him to be on site for a project this big. Besides, she thought with a growing sense of relief, if Truckworth had found what he was looking for, then there would have been no reason to trash Griddlehaus's reading room only a few hours ago. No, she told herself, these storage rooms might reveal some interesting clues—but none of them were likely to be Jeremy Mumbleigh's secret home.

If, she reminded herself as Kyle rambled on, the scrawny scholar had a secret home at all. Dulcie had let her fancy run away with her before. She had done it just now, when she had thought that Kyle's hand was the grip of a demon or assassin. As much as she loved her novels, she had to remember that in the light of day—or under those bare bulbs—things were most likely just what they seemed.

FORTY

DULCIE FELT HER pulse begin to race as she followed Kyle through the tunnel. Her expectations grew as they climbed up into the library. When he picked up a flashlight and led her through a gap in the wall, her heart was in her mouth, along with a disturbing musty smell that had enveloped her as she followed him down another short passage. Then she remembered the excuse she had given the red-headed guard. He was, as she requested, showing her where the water main had burst open.

'This is it,' said Kyle, running his flashlight up and down the walls. Dirty brick made up the top half, the red-brown clay crumbling where moisture had seeped in. Dulcie could see where the trails of decay and mold had left a strange shimmer. Below the brick were huge, rough-cut stones. Foundation stones, she thought. This must be the lowest level of the library, maybe of any human involvement.

Although they were yards away from the tunnel, some ambient light had followed them into the enclosed space. Shadowy and dim, it illuminated enough so that Dulcie could see where she was stepping, although she needed the beam of Kyle's flashlight to make out the details of the space. 'At least what we've found so far.'

CLEA SIMON   295

'Oh.' Dulcie could hear the disappointment in her voice, but there wasn't really much she could do about it. She should have expected the dirt floor, uneven and a bit muddy in the corner where the old pipe had leaked. The pile of detritus—some broken bricks, bits of metal, and a plastic bag of chips—were disheartening, too.

'It's so…dank.' She couldn't think of another word. It was that—the combination of dampness and dust—that convinced her that nobody lived here. Nobody could. Certainly not Jeremy who, for all his issues, seemed as fastidious as a feline.

'Yeah, really.' The red-haired guard kicked at a brick. 'With all the leaks, the mold count must be through the roof. I don't know why my father doesn't just have these filled in.'

'Is that an option?' Dulcie looked at the guard with renewed interest. 'Do you know why?'

Kyle shrugged. 'He complains all the time about structural integrity, but then he insists on checking out each one of these we find. It's like he's a pack rat or something.'

Or a hound on a trail, Dulcie thought. Out loud, she posed another possibility. 'Maybe he's worried that if he closes one off, he'll cut off access to another that will cause trouble.'

'He worries, all right.' The guard shrugged, sending the flashlight beam skittering.

Dulcie felt a stab of sympathy, though whether for the anxious manager or his moody son, she couldn't tell.

'What happened with your father?' Dulcie asked, her voice soft. Something about the low lighting here made such a question possible. Maybe, she thought, because he would know that she couldn't see his face as he answered.

'You mean with my mom?' She heard a sigh. 'They split when I was so young. She always said he was haunted, but I don't know more than that. And then he was so weird when I got out here. I don't know.'

'But he still loves you.' She looked at him, barely able to make out his features in the gloom. 'Wasn't he trying to get the charges dropped?'

'I'm still being investigated,' he said. 'Any clout my father might once have had, he's not using it for me.' He shrugged, and as he did, his flashlight lit up a pile of bricks.

'What was that?' Dulcie hadn't been looking at the pile. Not directly, but she'd thought something had been reflected—or, no, sparkled when the flash-light hit it.

'What was what?' Kyle swung the light around. Another flash—silver in the dark.

'There!' Dulcie pointed. But as the lanky guard moved, the shadows shifted too.

'Oh, hell!' Kyle stepped back, bumping into Dul-cie. 'I thought they said there were no rats down here.'

'I don't think that was a rat.' Dulcie started for-ward, only to find the guard's arm in front of her, holding her.

'Don't, Dulcie.' Kyle was pulling her back. 'They bite.'

'But we don't know what that was.' Kyle trained the light on the corner where a large crack had opened up.

'It was probably only a shadow,' he said. 'Sorry if I spooked you.'

'But you didn't...' Dulcie sighed. Whatever it was had gone. 'Never mind.'

'I don't know what I was thinking.' Kyle's mood seemed to have shifted as well. 'If you had been bitten... I mean, we shouldn't be here.'

She had no heart to argue, and so she followed him out to where the repair crew had breached the library wall. She'd been planning on ditching him there so she could go back into the tunnels, but he put a stop to that.

'No way, Dulcie.' Back under the library lighting, he looked pale. 'The flooding is going to get worse before it gets better. My father—well, he's trying to control it, but there's going to be more drilling tomorrow. They're going to flush out the old steam tunnels so they can finally clean them up.'

She nodded and let him lead the way up the service stairs to the main floor. The only saving grace was that they came out in the hallway that led to the back entrance, and Kyle's ID got them out the door without anyone stopping to question why she was in the building after hours.

'Thanks, Kyle.' She turned to thank the red-haired guard as he held the door open. 'Are you heading home now?'

'No.' He shook his head. 'I've got too much work to do. Making up for lost time, you know.' Dulcie might have been imagining it, but in the seconds before he ducked back inside, letting the door close behind him, she thought she saw something pass over his face. Something like fear.

FORTY-ONE

'KYLE TRUCKWORTH KNOWS SOMETHING.' Dulcie had picked up Chris's call while walking home and was still relating the day's events as she drew near their building. 'He thinks his father is involved—he nearly said as much to me. I think his father is looking for Jeremy's hideaway, and he's got Kyle looking for it too.'

'Dulcie, wait.' Chris had been trying to cut in for several minutes now, Dulcie realized. Only she had had so much to tell him. 'Dulcie, do you hear yourself?'

'I do,' she was quick to reply. 'It's all so logical. I can't believe I didn't see it.'

'No. I mean what you're talking about,' he said. 'Look, I'm glad you picked up. I'm going out with some old high school friends later, and I was afraid we wouldn't connect.'

Dulcie swallowed. She trusted Chris, she really did. Only she was lonely. And the way he was talking was making her feel more alone.

'I understand that you're sympathetic to Mumbles,' he was saying. 'I get that. And, OK, this guy Kyle is someone you know—someone you see in the library. But you don't really know his whole story. He's facing charges. Maybe that's what's got him worried. Maybe there's a reason he's scared. It doesn't matter. None of it does, Dulcie. None of this has anything to do with you—with your work.'

'That's not true, Chris.' She couldn't believe he didn't see it. 'It has everything to do with my work— the thieves are after the same pages I am. I'm sure of it. And I think it may have something to do with the cat.'

As if on cue, Esmé mewed. Or, no—it was another call.

'Hang on.' She held the phone away from her face. 'Never mind. It's Lucy. I'll call her back.'

'Poor Lucy.' Chris sounded mournful. 'You have time for everybody but your mother. She misses you, you know.'

That mew again. Insistent.

'I know.' She knew her sigh would be audible in New Jersey. Still, talking to her mother just might be preferable to defending herself to her boyfriend when he was in this mood. 'Maybe I should take this.'

'You're a good daughter,' said Chris. That wasn't what she had wanted. 'We'll talk tomorrow.' Neither was that, but he was gone.

'Lucy? Are you still there?' Dulcie fished her keys out of her pocket and unlocked her door.

'Where else would I be?' When her daughter didn't respond, Lucy kept talking, leaving Dulcie free to shed her coat and boots—and to grab Esmé who had come to greet her. 'I'm worried about our last conversation. That I wasn't clear.'

'You don't have to explain.' Dulcie hefted the plump cat on to her shoulder and retreated to the living room. It would be easier to listen to Lucy's explanations if she were sitting down. 'I understand about the moon ceremony.'

'No, it's not that.' Lucy paused, leaving Dulcie to wonder if her mother's ramblings had made her unusually self-conscious. 'It's that I didn't make my point. The point about the cat.'

'The cat?' It had to be coincidence. Cats were everywhere, and Lucy certainly knew of the feline who had begun to knead Dulcie's lap.

'Yes, the cat of moonlight,' said Lucy. 'The cat you've bonded with. The cat you found. You should follow that cat, Dulcie. That cat will save you both.'

FORTY-TWO

'WHAT DO YOU want of me?' She turned, eyes flashing, on He who had taken her. Under duress, he had forced her halting steps further down the Shadow'd Passage, its very Darkness seeming to lend its cover to his nefarious purpose. Unable to protest, almost to even Breathe, she had proceeded as he brutally propelled her, through the umbra of that shade-bedecked Hall, along those familiar steps, and then into the room that once had been her Sanctuary, the home of her most secret Dreams and Aspirations. There, he had released his iron grip, permitting her first to partake of the cool, still air and then to turn upon him and to hazard that question on which all might depend. 'What do you want of me?' Willing herself not to allow her eyes to stray, not to with untrained gaze betray that very secret which she held most dear, she forced herself to hold his gaze. To stare into those deep green eyes, in which so much mystery remained...

'MEH.' DULCIE BLINKED awake to find herself confronted by green eyes. Round ones, with the distinctive feline iris of which she had grown so fond.

'Esmé! Good morning.' Dulcie sat up, discomfiting the cat on the pillow beside her. 'Did you need me for something?'

The cat remained silent and began kneading.

'Were you the reason I dreamed of those green eyes or…' Dulcie let the question drop. For quite a while now, she had wondered about the significance of her dreams. Specifically about what they might or might not reveal about the author's life—or her own connection to the novelist. While she hadn't inherited Lucy's green eyes, her mother often talked about how the mysterious color had been passed down the female line. Then again, she also talked about how her psychic abilities were matrilineal, too, so Dulcie wasn't entirely sure how far to credit her mother's sense of genetics.

Perhaps it was appropriate, then, that the little tuxedo ignored her query and concentrated on the pillow. If anything, Dulcie suspected, it was her way of saying that her human should emulate her industry.

'I know, Esmé.' Dulcie addressed the cat. 'I should focus. I should just stay home and work. I mean, it seems like the fates are conspiring against me doing anything with the library, don't they?'

Without acknowledging her, the cat shifted, moving on to more of the pillow and, with it, Dulcie's arm. It probably meant nothing, Dulcie knew. Most likely, the plump cat was done with the first part of her kneading. Probably, she wasn't aware that her distended claw, needle sharp, was piercing not fabric and down, but skin. But, possibly, she was sending a message.

Removing her arm from further damage, Dulcie looked down at her pet. 'You don't want me hanging around, do you?' The rhythmic motion continued without pause. 'Is that what this is about?'

At that, Esmé looked up, meeting Dulcie's gaze with those inscrutable green eyes. And as she did, her paws shifted again—and once more, Dulcie felt her claws.

'Ow, OK, I get it.' Dulcie stood up, removing herself from the cat's range. 'You know, you could have just said something. I know you can talk when you want to.'

On the bed, the cat simply turned to face the pillow again, and Dulcie was struck by her profile—the graceful curve of her nose, the poise of her ears. The simple lines of her whiskers, stark white against the black fur. It reminded her of the silver cat—the printer's mark—and made her realize that, yes, she wanted to unravel the mystery. To find out what that mark meant—and who was hunting it so diligently.

'All right, then, Esmé,' she said. 'You win.' She began to dress for her day, as the cat continued to knead, the silence warmed by her deep and rhythmic purr.

'MR GRIDDLEHAUS!' SEEING the diminutive librarian as she made her way across the Yard convinced Dulcie that she had made the right decision by coming in. She had found herself mulling over Lucy's words as she had walked—Lucy's words and her own disturbing dream—and was grateful for a reminder of her real purpose. And, realizing that Griddlehaus's determined stride was taking him toward the library, she trotted to catch up. 'Dare I ask?' Her voice was slightly breathless from the effort.

'I've been given the all-clear,' said the librarian, his cheer evident in his voice. 'I had been planning on starting my day with another visit to Jeremy, but I simply couldn't resist.'

'Of course not,' said Dulcie, matching her pace to his. Only as they approached the back door did she stop. This was where she had seen Jeremy less than a week before. There was his crude drawing—the profile of the cat that had seemed to weigh on his troubled mind. 'Only, I'm not sure that I should follow…'

'Stuff and nonsense.' Griddlehaus took her hand in a surprisingly firm grip. 'I need your assistance today, Ms Schwartz. I can't imagine who else would be qualified to help me.'

That was the explanation he gave the guard, who nodded them both in with barely a look. Perhaps, thought Dulcie, the mandate that she be watched had expired, and Stuart Truckworth had moved on to other pursuits. More likely, she realized as Griddlehaus fished out the key and made for the reading room door, her companion's senior standing stood as her bond.

Whatever authority he projected, however, crumbled as he opened the door.

'Oh my.' He blinked as the overhead lights came on, revealing the extent of the devastation. 'Oh, my.'

Dulcie looked around, surprised. She hadn't expected to be shocked, not this time. After all, she had already seen the mess that had been made of the neat little room. Perhaps it was witnessing her friend's dismay, but it looked worse today, the fallen books a little more careworn and the overturned furniture slightly more askew.

'I thought the police had been in here.' Dulcie stepped by Griddlehaus and reached to right a chair.

'I thought they might have done... I don't know, something.'

'I believe they did,' said Griddlehaus as he picked up a fallen volume. 'This seems to have been handled.' He showed her the book, which was in fact dusted with black powder, and then began to brush it off.

'They could have put it back on the shelf.' Dulcie picked up a lamp and checked it for a broken bulb. The small table where it had stood now held a pile of books, all fine editions. The stacked volumes, all edged in gold or silver, were piled so haphazardly that Dulcie set the lamp on the floor instead.

'At least they left it closed,' said Griddlehaus with a sigh. 'Besides, better to have them leave these books out then to mis-shelve them. Oh—oh, my.'

Dulcie looked over to where he was standing by a bookshelf. The volume he had retrieved was still in his hand, but he put it down carefully as he pulled another from the shelf. This book, Dulcie could see even from a distance, was in bad shape. Bound in worn leather, its corners were frayed and dented. The title, whatever it had been, may once have been inlaid in gilt. Now only the faintest impression of letters remained, and Griddlehaus adjusted his glasses as he struggled to read the words they had once formed.

'What is it?'

'I don't...' He opened the book carefully, supporting its cover with one hand, while turning the pages with another. 'I don't know how this got here,' he said, turning to look at Dulcie. 'This doesn't belong in the reading room.'

'Are you sure?' Dulcie came over to see. And as

she did, she felt a vibration beneath her feet. 'I guess all the systems are up and running again,' she said, reaching for the book.

'That's not the ventilation,' said Griddlehaus, looking around. 'We're on the surface level here, Ms Schwartz. That's underground.'

They're flooding the tunnels, Kyle had said. Flushing them out. She found her thoughts turning to the dark hallway of her dream. To Lucy's words—and Jeremy's. She was missing something.

'Mr Griddlehaus, you said that the cat's head—the printer's mark—meant something different in the later books, the American ones. What did you find out?'

'I'm not sure how this pertains.' A worry line had appeared on his high brow as he placed the battered book on the top of the nearest pile. 'In fact, I may have more pressing—'

'Mr Griddlehaus, please.'

One look at Dulcie, and he cleared his throat.

'If you insist,' Griddlehaus began, tenting his fingers as if to deliver a lecture. 'From its earliest appearance, around the time of John Wycliffe, the silver cat—the Felix—signified a hidden book—one that could be dangerous to the bearer. The earliest surviving examples date from approximately 1360, and we believe that the symbol was used, at least intermittently, throughout the following two hundred years.'

Dulcie nodded, unsure of what she was listening for.

'What intrigued me was seeing the mark in a much more recent work, the Stavendish edition of *He Could Not Tell Her*,' Griddlehaus continued. 'After all, the nineteenth century is comparatively modern, in the scheme of things. I had heard of this, of course, but I needed to do additional research to be sure. What I found was that in the New World the essential meaning of the symbol remained, but its usage changed, as such things will.'

Now fully engaged in lecture mode, he paused to consider her through those oversized glasses, ignoring the rumbling beneath them. 'To be honest, once I located the later reference, I was rather surprised that you had not recognized it from your American Studies coursework. The iconography lasted into the twentieth century. A whiskered cat, full face rather than in profile, became a valuable symbol in the so-called hobo iconography during the Great Depression.'

'The Depression?' Dulcie racked her brain. She did know something about this, only she couldn't remember exactly what—or why it might matter. 'Hobo iconography?'

'Definitions differ, of course, and usually it has been remembered as the symbol for a kind-hearted woman, one who would provide food or shelter. But at a more basic level, the whiskered cat signified "safe passage." It's the same meaning, really.'

'Safe passage?' Dulcie mulled it over. The tunnels—the symbol on the wall—Jeremy's semi-conscious words. Just then, the books piled so precariously fell, disturbed by the vibrations below. The flooding of the tunnels had begun.

'Mr Griddlehaus,' said Dulcie, jumping to her feet. 'I don't think this is about the printer's mark at all. And I'm afraid we're running out of time.'

FORTY-THREE

DULCIE LOST PRECIOUS seconds trying to explain and finally gave up, running down the fire stairs to the still-closed lower level. It took her several more minutes to find the opening Kyle had shown her, the gap where she had passed from the old storage space back into the library. Several more to backtrack to where the tunnel had branched out. Minutes that she hated to spare. But as she ran, pressing herself against the dirty walls at the hint of any other footfall, she tried to recall the letters that Jeremy had scratched into the wall. RT UP RT 6—and the cat. But what did it mean?

'Right up, right six?' Was there more that she couldn't remember? She had taken the right fork in the turning, so maybe that was part of it. But up? And right again? Or was she missing something?

'Turn right to stay right,' Jeremy had said to her that first day, sheltering in the entry. She kept going.

SHE WAS GETTING farther from the main library. Farther from the well-ordered tunnels that were still in use. The dirt floor was uneven here, and spotted with puddles, the light from the infrequent bulbs dim and shadowed, and despite her hurry, Dulcie moved carefully, her eyes open for unexpected dips or debris.

Or mud. She felt her shoes slip on a slick spot and caught herself, breathing hard. It had to be the leakage. She reminded herself of the damp of the walls, of the moist sheen she had seen on the stones. Still, she could feel her heart pounding as she started walking again. And something louder—a rumble, like water. The path seemed to be slanting upward, and Dulcie strained her eyes, looking for a door or a window. For a light. Could this be what Jeremy had meant—UP—or was she on a wild goose chase? She thought of the tons of earth above her. Felt its pressure. Felt her lungs contract.

No, that was nonsense. Every day for the last five years, she had gone underground. And every day that she wasn't in her carrel, she was in the Mildon, also three levels below the library. She wouldn't think of the earth on top of her. Wouldn't think of the rats.

'*Dulcie!*' A streak of grey ran by her. The warning came too late and she screamed—a quick startled yelp—as she slipped, scraping the heels of her hands as she fell.

'What was that?' Somewhere, not far behind her, a man's voice. And then a flashlight beam, sweeping the wall not two feet above where she was now kneeling.

Dulcie froze, listening.

'Damn rats.' Not one man: two. 'I tell you, as soon as we find it, I want you to flood this place for real.'

'We don't even know it exists.' A higher voice, anxious. Truckworth? 'And the substructure can't—'

'Shut up.' The other man—gruffer, deeper. 'You

know what they found on him. He had it down here, somewhere.'

They were talking about Jeremy—Jeremy and the book.

'Come on.' The gruff voice again, getting closer. Dulcie wiped her hands on her pants as she tried to think. Her palms smarted, and it hit her. She hadn't fallen in mud.

Still kneeling, she felt the floor. Stone. The rough stone of the foundation. Where was she?

'The original schematics show store rooms to the right.' Truckworth. Of course, he would have access to the blueprints, to decades of plans for reconstruction and rebuilding. 'But the way these were built, we may never find them.'

Another beam of light, and Dulcie scurried toward the wall, as if she were a rat. Or, no—a cat. It was a cat that had nearly tripped her. Had it been Mr Grey? Movement again, to the right—a flash of reflected light, green eyes—and then nothing. Working her way along the wall, she found herself turning. The blocks, each several feet high, protruded into the passageway, threatening to close it. She had reached a dead end. She was trapped.

Only, where had that cat gone?

Dulcie grabbed at the stone, feeling her way along the wall even as the flashlight beam grew brighter, scanning back and forth and throwing shadows that jumped like ghosts over the uneven surface.

Only, they shouldn't have. Dulcie didn't need Chris to tell her the laws of physics. The swing of the flashlight hadn't been that erratic. The shadows

signified something—something more than metaphor. As she crept a little farther—her hands raw
on the cold stone—she discovered what. The wall
was not complete, and by sidling against the huge
blocks, she was able to slide by…

And stepped up into a small room. Dulcie stood,
blinking, as her eyes adjusted to the dim light.
Cleaner and drier than anything she had yet seen,
the room—maybe ten by twelve—looked more akin
to Griddlehaus's private sanctuary than to any of the
basement tunnels she had yet encountered. Looking
around, she could see stained wainscoting, several
bookshelves, and—on a simple cot—a short-haired
grey cat, who sat watching her, and then began to
wash his face.

'Kitty!' With a whispered cry of joy, Dulcie ran
toward the cat. It was the cat that had tripped her—
and had shown her the entrance. 'Thank you.'

In response, the cat leaped into her arms and
began to purr. Dulcie held the lithe feline close—
under the soft fur she was skin and bones—and
waited, listening. With their bluster and their big
flashlights, it seemed likely the two men would miss
the narrow opening. If they did, she could take the
cat—it had to be Jeremy's cat—and retrace her steps.
Once they passed…assuming the passage back to
the library was still clear. Dulcie tried to recall what
Truckworth had said about the lower levels. About
structural integrity.

'You must be starving, little one,' she murmured
into the dusky fur, and looked around for a can—for

anything—to feed the hungry feline as they bided their time.

What she saw instead was a beam of light. 'Hey!' the gruff voice called out, as Dulcie—still holding the cat—ducked behind one of the bookshelves. If she could just stay quiet, maybe they'd leave.

'What's this?' The flashlight beam swept by and Dulcie shrank back, cowering behind it. 'Did you hear something?' The voice was masculine—someone she knew. In the dark, everything sounded strange, and yet that voice… It was tense and higher than she was used to but familiar, she was almost sure.

'Don't try to distract me.' A different voice. Gruffer, deeper. 'I heard about that page. About that book. It's worth millions, and you said there was nothing left.'

Leaning further, Dulcie realized there was space behind her, at least above the ankle level. She wasn't against the wall—she was at the base of a set of stairs. As quietly as she could, she stepped up. Stepped again and almost slipped. The edge of the stair was broken and rough.

'This is it.' The gruff voice, growing louder. They had found the room. 'They've got to be here.'

Moving with care, as silently as she could, Dulcie ascended another step. If only the two men kept talking, maybe they wouldn't notice her. Three more steps—and that was it. Wherever the stairway had led to was now blocked off. No matter, Dulcie balanced herself on that last crumbled fragment. She was hidden behind the bookcase. Here on step six. Six, Jeremy had written. Up and Six.

'I tell you, I heard something.' The voices were getting closer. They were in front of the bookshelf that shielded her. 'Someone's there!' The first man was panicking.

'Don't try to put me off.' The gruff voice. Up close, it too was familiar. Wardley! 'You've been holding out on me all these years.'

Dulcie started to breathe again. She didn't like the lieutenant—and she suspected the big cop didn't think much of her either—but if he were here, then this was probably part of his investigation. He was a gruff man, but it had only been the dark and her own fancy that had made him seem dangerous.

'I was a kid!' High and strained, but could it be Stuart Truckworth? 'If you'd busted me I'd have been out by now.'

'Too late for that; you're implicated in every theft since then.' Dulcie's head was spinning. Was this a bust? Was the manager the inside source? She had to be mishearing.

'They weren't worth it.' The panic had given way to glum resignation. 'They never were—the library was going to throw those books away anyway.'

'Your friend didn't think so.' Wardley's voice was low and guttural. 'And look what happened to him.'

'You don't have to remind me. Poor Jeremy.'

'Poor nothing. He was holding out on me, too. I'd have had them—all of them—only we were inter-rupted. But now I don't need you any more.' That gruff voice again. 'You or your son.'

'My son is innocent.' Truckworth, his voice rising again in anger—or fear. As much as she hated him,

Dulcie was glad the sleazy manager was taking the blame. Speaking out for his son. Now if only the big cop believed him.

'Your son's a killer.' The police lieutenant's voice was getting louder. He was getting closer. 'That's going to be clear tomorrow, when we find a blood-ied knife in his knapsack.'

'You can't say that.' Truckworth sounded fran-tic, his voice rising in volume and pitch. 'I've done everything—everything you've wanted. All these years!'

'I kept my end of the bargain, didn't I?' Wardley's voice had sunk to a low growl. Dulcie felt the cat in her arms stir, but she held on tight. 'I could have ru-ined you,' the big cop was saying. 'I could have had you expelled, but I didn't. And you held out on me.'

DULCIE PEEKED AROUND the edge of the bookshelf. In the dim light, she could make out the silhouettes of the speakers, both so different. Wardley, large and imposing, was shorter than Truckworth but his size gave him authority. Truckworth, tall but insubstan-tial, seemed to stumble as he drew away, stepping backward. But Wardley wasn't going to let him go. Wasn't going to let him escape. Dulcie took a step down. She saw Wardley as he reached for Truck-worth—and saw as well the wicked blade in his hand.

She gasped. She couldn't help it. She had been so sure she was about to witness an arrest. Justice being done. But the knife that Wardley held didn't look like evidence. Despite what the big cop had

said, the flashlight beam reflected off its smooth
and polished surface like a mirror. The knife wasn't
bloodied. Not yet.

'Wait, what—' Truckworth gasped, Wardley's intent suddenly clear. 'No!'

Dulcie shrank back, hoping that the gloom would
hide her. If she were a braver sort of person, she
would speak out. She should speak out. But how?

'Is someone there? Help!' Truckworth's voice
cracked.

'Shut up,' Wardley snarled. 'You can't scare me.
Nobody comes down here any more. Not since we
got rid of your crazy friend. And don't worry, he's
not going to last long once the infirmary releases
him. These homeless guys have a nasty mortality
rate. Besides, he's got a history. You remember—'

'No—wait.' Truckworth pointed, aiming his
beam, one long finger extending to a shadow right
by Dulcie's feet.

Dulcie held her breath.

'Help me,' Truckworth called. 'Please!'

'Wait a minute…' Wardley, coming toward her.

Dulcie was trapped and clutched the cat close, as
if to comfort herself with the soft fur. Only it was too
much. The skinny animal squirmed and pushed—
and jumped out of her arms. Clearly as terrified of
the two men as Dulcie herself was, the cat bounded
back up the stairs and reached up, desperate, claw-
ing at the wall.

'It's no use,' Dulcie whispered in despair. But then
she saw it—a sliver of light. Light that had been

seeping in through cracks in the walls around her all along.

'Come here, you.' Wardley's hand reached for her as she threw herself at the barrier at the top of the stairs.

It gave way, and she stumbled forward. The cat jumped ahead and she scrambled to follow through what she now realized was a door. Falling, she reached back to slam it—slam it shut—only collapsing when she heard it latch with a satisfying click.

'Ms Schwartz!' Thomas Griddlehaus was staring at her, eyes wide. Dulcie was on her knees, on the floor in the private reading room of the library.

FORTY-FOUR

'CALL THE COPS!' Dulcie yelled, pulling herself to her feet. 'Only not—'

'We're already on it,' said a voice as familiar as the large hand that reached forward to help Dulcie to her feet.

'Detective Rogovoy.' Dulcie blinked up at him, the sudden brightness bringing tears to her eyes. 'Lieutenant Wardley is down there. He's got a knife! He's been blackmailing Mr Truckworth…' She stopped. *A thorn in my side all these years.* Truckworth had been talking about Wardley. The lieutenant had been making the manager do his dirty work. Had framed his son for additional leverage…

Dulcie looked up. The big detective was waiting for her to finish.

'Don't worry. My guys were just waiting to move in. Believe it or not, we weren't that far behind you.' The lumpy face broke into a grin. 'We had to turn off the water before we could move in. But why am I not surprised to find you here—with a cat, no less? Now, if you'll excuse me.' Reaching out with one massive finger, the detective touched the edge of a shelf—and the door sprang open again. 'You might want to clean up,' he said, as he closed the door behind him.

Already, she could hear new voices—Rogovoy's

people—behind the hidden door. Then sounds of a struggle, mercifully brief, and then that big head popped up again.

'All clear, folks,' he said. 'But we will be marking these tunnels off as a crime scene, so no more exploring. That OK by you, Ms Schwartz?' Without waiting for an answer, he withdrew.

'I called as soon as you ran off,' said Griddlehaus, after the door had closed once more. 'The detective was already in the building. Oh, my!' The librarian stepped back, and Dulcie saw the cat from the basement looking up at him. In the light, Dulcie could see that she wasn't grey, not at all. Instead, her coat was a soft, tawny brown, only very, very dirty. And very— if her knowledge of cats told her anything—hungry.

'Is there anything we could feed her?' asked Dulcie.

'I do have a turkey sandwich I'd planned for lunch,' said the librarian. He rummaged in his desk and emerged with a paper bag. Within seconds of opening it, the brown cat was on the desk top, rumbling with an anticipatory purr that filled the room.

'I bet she hasn't eaten much these last few days,' said Dulcie, looking down at her own muddy disarray. 'It's a wonder she survived at all.'

'Well, she had water and I dare say there are some rodents down in the workings, albeit not the infestation we had once feared. Speaking of which...' Griddlehaus excused himself, returning a few moments later with a damp washcloth from the employee's washroom.

'Thanks.' The pair watched the little cat eat, as Dulcie did her best to wipe her scraped hands clean.

'Poor Jeremy,' she said as the cat finished her meal and began to bathe. 'He wasn't talking about the printer's mark at all. He meant his pet. He must have been so frightened when he woke up in the hospital, not knowing what had happened to this little girl. Do you think he had a premonition, leaving that note?'

'He would have been quite aware of the symbol,' said Griddlehaus. 'After all, he was a scholar.'

'But—it's latest meaning. Do you really think Jeremy would use hobo iconography?'

'You never let me finish, you know.' Now that order had been restored, Griddlehaus had regained his usual poise. 'There was a transitional period, you see. In the New World, before the Felix was picked up by our more recent unfortunates, the mark of the cat came to symbolize safe passage of another sort. Perhaps Jeremy knew this, and applied it to his situation—or his cat's.'

'It could be...' Dulcie was skeptical.

Griddlehaus handed her a book. 'It took a bit of searching,' he said. 'But I knew I had seen a reference to another usage, one that might have relevance to your work, Ms Schwartz.'

Wiping her hands once more, Dulcie took the book and began to read: *'The cat being associated with the female ever since the Egyptian age, the Felix mark served as code for a kind of underground railroad. Its appearance in a book, often of the sentimental or sensational kind passed hand to hand among female readers and largely ignored by men, indicated safe passage for women who were forced*

*to flee from abusive marriages for example, or who
wanted to protect their daughters.'*

Or both, thought Dulcie. Out loud, she said, 'Perhaps that's the connection with my pages. With the
author of *The Ravages of Umbria.'*

She continued reading, this time out loud. *'With
the rise of female literacy—and the preponderance
of certain genres that catered primarily to these new
female readers, coded books, imprinted with a certain mark, could have served as passports, or as
signs that a bearer could be trusted. Little concrete
proof of this exists, but if one reads Clavistock...'*

'Thank you, Mr Griddlehaus.' This was a priceless find.

'You're most welcome,' he replied, his pale cheeks
coloring ever so slightly. 'As a library sciences professional, I'm always glad to help. You will, of
course, need proof of your theories.'

He stopped, and she nodded. She didn't, not really. She would get proof, of course. She would find
the citations, the history, and more. But even before, she knew.

FORTY-FIVE

DULCIE HAD MANAGED to wash up more thoroughly by the time Rogovoy resurfaced to tell them that both Wardley and Truckworth were in custody. 'I think Truckworth is relieved,' he'd said, his voice a quiet rumble. 'He was worried about his kid. About you, too, Ms Schwartz.'

'Well, then why did he put that page in my bag?' Now that the fear had worn off, Dulcie was angry. But Rogovoy was shaking his head.

'That was Wardley. He's been behind these thefts all along. That's why he's had such a good record with stolen property—he'd have Truckworth bring him things, and then "recover" what he couldn't turn into ready cash.

'Truckworth's talking now. Telling us everything. He stole that page—the one from the Mildon—for Wardley when the collection was closed. Took quite a risk, since he was the only one with access, but he was desperate to get his kid off, by that point, and Wardley was putting the pressure on. Truckworth had a sense of its value. He was hoping to buy his kid's freedom, but Wardley didn't think it looked like much.'

'He couldn't know that,' said Dulcie. Very aware of how filthy her clothes were, she was sitting care-

fully on the edge of one of Griddlehaus's upholstered
chairs. 'It was a fragment. It could have been a Felix
page. A partial.' She thought of the glitter—the slight
curving line she had spotted. 'In fact, I have reason
to believe it might be.'

'Whatever.' Rogovoy didn't sound impressed.
'He's not a book guy. Not much of a cop, either.
And he was looking for a way to get rid of you,
Ms Schwartz. Maybe he was sick of your questions.
You have been poking about a bit much. But don't
sweat it. His days of making trouble are over. I fig-
ured what with your help and all.' He paused, and
Dulcie thought she saw the hint of a dimple in his
granite face. 'I wanted to fill you in.'

WITH THAT HE was gone, the two were left in silence,
and Dulcie realized that she was not only dirty but
exhausted. As she sat there, willing herself to rise,
her gaze fell on the battered book once again piled
on the table.

'Mr Griddlehaus,' said Dulcie, staring at the nondescript cover. 'Don't you want to return this to the
general collection?'

'I can't,' Griddlehaus replied. 'After the detective
went looking for you, I did a bit of my own detecting.
As I suspected, that's not where it belongs.'

'It's not in the catalog?' Dulcie was too tired to
understand.

'It had been removed,' said her friend. 'It was
listed as missing.' He held it out to her. 'You never
got a chance to make out its title.'

She took the battered book. The gilt lettering had

worn away, but opening it to the title page, she read
He Could Not Tell Her, Vol. 2.

'Missing or stolen,' Griddlehaus continued. 'Like
so many others from the Stavendish bequest. Yet
someone saved it from Truckworth—and from
Wardley. Someone hid it away.'

'Jeremy,' said Dulcie. 'He didn't want it to be
sold or, worse, destroyed. And when the excavations
began, he must have started trying to save his collection, like a cat with her kittens. He was probably
on his way with the other volume.'

'It's a wonder that it wasn't found when the reading room was tossed.' Griddlehaus shook his head.

'That must have been Wardley.' Dulcie thought of
what Rogovoy had said. Of what she had witnessed.
'He must have realized pretty quickly that this wasn't
Jeremy's cache. He was looking for rarities. For treasure, and to him, these were just plain old books.'

She looked at her friend again, her voice growing
soft. 'Jeremy hid it in plain sight. He knew you, Mr
Griddlehaus. He trusted you. That's why he brought
this book up here.'

'Why this one volume?' Griddlehaus looked down
at the damaged cover to hide his blush. 'It isn't in
particularly good shape, is it?'

'That's it.' Dulcie looked around for something—
anything—to use as a tool, and her eyes lit on
Griddlehaus's letter opener.

'What? Ms Schwartz!' The librarian jumped up
as she inserted the tip of the blade into the inside of
the book's front cover. 'Please, stop!'

'Just this one sheet.' As carefully as she could,

Dulcie emulated what she had seen in the lab, work-ing the opener around, separating the paper from its backing. The paper was old, but sturdy, and the glue had long since dried. Once the seal was broken, it came away easily, and Dulcie was able to ease the blade's thin edge further along. It was painstaking work, but before long she had the entire bottom de-tached and began on the corner.

'What are you doing?' Griddlehaus was no longer trying to stop her and instead stood at her shoulder, peering down.

'Looking for something,' she said. The vertical went more quickly, and soon the loosened page was curling back on itself. Behind it, she could see folds of paper. Waste paper that had been used to thicken the board, to strengthen the cover, perhaps. Or per-haps the book had been the cover all along—a sec-ond-rate novel, one likely to be overlooked, served to disguise some of the most valuable documents of a very special collection.

'We should go to the conservation lab,' said Griddlehaus. His voice had fallen to a hush as Dulcie put down her improvised tool. She had done enough. With the oversheet curling back, they could both see what had been hidden, protected, for so long. Spar-kling in the light: the silver cat.

FORTY-SIX

DULCIE SCROLLED THROUGH her pages. '*The increasingly anti-intellectual foment of the war years brought in a new conservatism...*' She had never gotten that reference. With a sigh, Dulcie went back to her notes. *(see Kravitz.)* There, that was done.

Despite—or perhaps because of—the excitement of the morning, Dulcie had found herself quite productive the rest of the day. Even the prolonged break, when Suze had called, had added to Dulcie's general sense of closure.

For starters, the friends had agreed that too much time had passed.

'I'm sorry I was so terse,' Suze had said. 'It's work. It's been crazy. Really makes me miss the academic year.'

Dulcie had bit her tongue on that and been rewarded.

'I've been thinking about your friend,' her old room-mate had continued. 'Jeremy? I've made some calls, and I am sure he won't serve any time.'

'Diminished capacity?' Dulcie had been Suze's room-mate all through law school, after all.

'Well, certainly.' Suze chuckled. 'We could fall back on that, but we won't have to. You know where the books were found, right? My boss has already presented the argument that the books could not be considered stolen if all Jeremy did was take them from an illegal off-site location and bring them back into the library.

'By the way,' Suze had continued, once her revelation had sunk in. 'I think I'll have some housing options for him once he gets out of the infirmary. And, yes, at least one allows cats...'

Once Dulcie had washed up, there had been the sweet, if brief, reunion of Jeremy and his pet. Griddlehaus had given the feline a thorough brushing while Dulcie had gone home to change, and together they had smuggled her into the health services, where Jeremy was sitting up and eating his lunch. He'd dropped the fork of what looked like pot roast as soon as she saw the triangular brown head peeking out from Griddlehaus's jacket and reached his arms out for his pet.

'Secret!' he'd said, as he held the brown cat close.

'She'll be safe with me until you're out of here, my old friend,' said Griddlehaus. With that, he motioned for Dulcie to step back, to give the reunited friends time alone, but Dulcie hesitated.

'Jeremy?' The man on the bed looked up, his eyes newly clear. 'Where did you find the books, the two volumes of *He Could Not Tell Her*?'

'Dulcie, please.' Griddlehaus reached for her arm. 'That was so long ago.'

'Jeremy?' Dulcie feared for a moment that she had pushed too hard. The man was ill. He was fragile. 'You trusted me with Secret,' she said now.

With a barely perceptible nod, Jeremy started

talking again. 'Box,' he said, his voice cracking. 'Box,' he repeated, more clearly. 'Tower Room. Never tell.'

'It's OK, Jeremy,' said Dulcie. 'I think I know the rest.' With a glance at Griddlehaus, she began to explain. 'I think you found Truckworth's cache, the stolen books. I bet he thought it wouldn't be a big deal—that the university was going to pulp half of them anyway. Maybe it even started as a safety measure. Those books were badly stored, and they were at risk of getting wet, of being damaged, as the construction work went on, and so he moved them to the tower room for safe keeping. Maybe he was waiting to see if anyone noticed they were missing. Maybe he would have returned them, but he didn't get the chance. Did he?'

The man in the bed didn't answer, and so Dulcie kept talking. 'I think Wardley got there first. He figured out what Truckworth had done and made him his patsy—threatening him with expulsion or arrest—unless he dropped out. Dropped out and got a job where he could give Wardley access whenever he wanted.' Dulcie paused, working it out.

'Wardley "recovered" some of the books—enough to secure his career—and arranged for a fence to sell the others, starting with the most obviously valuable ones, I guess. Maybe he was going to "recover" the rest. Maybe he was hoping the market would heat up and he could get a good price for some of the lesser works. Maybe he was going to dump them. After all, nobody was ever prosecuted and if Wardley "found" too many of the stolen books, people might have started asking questions.'

She paused. Jeremy was staring at her, eyes wide.

'You knew those books had value,' she said, her voice gentle. 'Scholarly value. Maybe you could have reasoned with Truckworth. I gather he wasn't a bad soul, just broke and reckless. But not Wardley. He didn't care.'

Jeremy gave a wordless cry. His face had gone white, and he was clutching the cat to his breast.

'Ms Schwartz...' Griddlehaus leaned forward, but Dulcie was already responding.

'Oh, Jeremy,' she said, placing one hand on his arm. 'I'm so sorry. Wardley caught you, didn't he? The incident in the tower room...' She paused. 'He didn't rescue you, did he? Any more than he "rescued" you from the pit outside the library.'

Jeremy buried his face in the cat's fur.

'Well, you don't have to worry any more. Not now.' Dulcie didn't need any more confirmation. 'You and Secret are safe.'

Her words seemed to calm the bedridden man. Her words and the presence of his purring cat. She and Griddlehaus watched as Jeremy relaxed, years of fear finally beginning to fade. They waited until Jeremy was nearly asleep again before—with her owner's consent—Griddlehaus bundled the purring feline back into his jacket and left a renewed Jeremy to complete his convalescence.

'All he cared about were the books,' said Dulcie, as the elevator took them back down. 'The books and Secret, of course. I bet Wardley has been harassing him for years. Jeremy's breakdown was a stroke of luck for Wardley. Who would believe anything a crazy person would say about a hero cop?'

Griddlehaus shook his head. 'I never knew.'

'Nobody would have,' said Dulcie. 'Only Wardley overreached. I wonder why?'

'The Bethesda sale,' responded her friend. 'The Felix psalter that went to auction in January. If what you surmise is true, and it rings true to me, I would not be surprised if the news of a multimillion dollar sale made the lieutenant re-evaluate those lost "worthless" books.'

'And he's been hunting for them since. Tearing books apart, looking for a similar prize.' Dulcie thought about the break-ins. About the task force, and about a poor scholar, terrorized and thrown in a pit, when he wouldn't give up his secrets. 'And pressuring Truckworth for help.'

'Poor Stuart.' Griddlehaus sighed. 'I hear he's making a deal to testify against Wardley and to help track down the stolen items, but I fear he is still going to have to serve some time. Whatever bargain he made, it cost him dearly. I wonder if Kyle will ever forgive him?'

AND NOW DULCIE was—finally—writing. The books from the Stavendish were safe now. They had survived the purge, if not the academic trend that devalued them so, and their recovery had given them a certain luster. But Dulcie's self-imposed deadline still loomed. She'd finish this chapter tonight, if the cat would let her.

Perhaps it was the moonlight. The super moon may have passed, but even the waning gibbous was bright, casting silver shadows across the kitchen table. Whatever the reason, Esmé was acting odd, darting about and howling. 'Is it the moon, kitty?' Dulcie asked. 'Are you my new moon cat?'

Esmé stared at her, as if she were mad.

'Well, if you're not going to tell me what's going on, kitty—'

Dulcie stopped. She'd heard—what? A noise. The sound of scraping, of metal, outside. By her door. She had been feeling good. Too good, maybe. A woman alone shouldn't take chances. She thought of her heroine—and then of Jeremy and even Stuart Truckworth. Men, too, could be victimized, and she needed to be alert.

Another scrape. This wasn't theoretical. Someone was at the door. She looked around. The can opener. It wasn't much but if she hit someone hard with it…

'Esmé, no!' The little cat had jumped off the table and was charging at the door, clearly determined to tackle the intruder before Dulcie could. But Esmé was only a cat—a small cat. Dulcie dived, reaching for her, and heard the startled 'Mew!' as the round feline slipped through her hands and dove for the feet that had appeared in the doorway.

'Esmé!' Hands reached for her. 'Dulcie, are you OK? Why are you on the floor?'

She looked up, blinking. Chris was standing in the doorway, while their pet pushed up against him, purring.

'You're home!' She stood, aware once more of the toll of the day.

'I came home one day early,' he said, hugging her as he reached to pull her to her feet.

'You were worried about me?' Dulcie stepped back to look at him. So much had happened in one week. Did he look the same to her? Did she to him?

'Not really. I know you can take care of yourself,' he said. 'But I missed you.'

'I missed you, too,' said Dulcie, and reached to hold him close again. Esmé twined around both their ankles now, but it wasn't merely her purr that rose to envelope them with warmth.

We are all creatures of moonlight and dreams, Dulcie. The voice in the purr might be for her alone. Its meaning, she would share. *'Moonlight and dreams, little one. Only together, we may be more.'*

* * * * *